FRAGMENTARY BLUE

by
Erica Abbott

Bella
BOOKS

2012

Bella Books, Inc.
P.O. Box 10543
Tallahassee, FL 32302

Printed in the United States of America on acid-free paper
First published 2012

Editor: Katherine V. Forrest
Cover Designer: Judy Fellows

ISBN 13: 978-1-59493-274-8

PUBLISHER'S NOTE

To love, always and forever.

Acknowledgments

The desire to write is born out of a love for reading. I will forever be grateful to my parents for giving me a passion for books and the tales they tell. By reading to me, and encouraging my early efforts at telling stories, they gave me a most precious gift.

My brother and his wonderful family have been a source of joy for me for many years, and I would like to thank them for their support.

To everyone at Bella Publishing, including Linda Hill, Judith, Jessica, and the other professionals who participated in the publishing process, my deepest gratitude. You made this experience for a first time author easy, and I can't imagine a better team.

My thanks especially to Karin Kallmaker at Bella for making this book a reality. Aside from the inspiration I received from her own delightful writing, her gentle encouragement of a new author made this book possible.

To the legendary Katherine V. Forrest, who edited the manuscript, I can only say how grateful I am for her care, attention, and occasional well-placed rap on the knuckles. Editing is quite a different skill from writing, and she does both brilliantly. This book is much better for having passed through her hands.

Finally, to Kathryn, who has been cheerleader, critic, reader, and above all my friend: thank you for making my work, and my life, better.

About The Author

Erica Abbott was born and raised in the Midwest, and is a graduate of the University of Denver. She has been a government lawyer and prosecutor, a college professor, sung mezzo-soprano on stage, and played first base on the diamond. She likes dogs, cats, music of all kinds, and playing bridge. She also has a love/hate relationship with golf. She lives near Denver, Colorado.

CHAPTER ONE

CJ took off her high heels so she could run up the stairs to the second floor of the Colfax Police Department building. She was seven minutes late for her meeting with the Deputy Chief, and she had heard, more than once, that he was not a man flexible about time. She trotted to his office, shoes in hand, greeting the clerk seated at a computer outside the closed door.

"Hi," CJ said breathlessly. "I have an eight thirty appointment with Chief Duncan."

The clerk eyed her, missing the identification badge that had nestled inside the neckline of CJ's silk blouse.

"And you are...?" the clerk asked suspiciously.

"CJ St. Clair," she replied, still getting her breath, and thinking she was going to have to find a new gym soon. Or perhaps she should cut out the croissant with her morning latte.

"I'm the new Internal Affairs Inspector." She offered her free hand and said, "I'm pleased to meet ya'll."

The clerk reflexively shook the offered hand, looking surprised, as if no one ever bothered to be nice to her. She said, "I'm, um, Sharon. He's expecting you, so you can go on in."

"Thanks so much," CJ said warmly, and started for the door.

"Er, Inspector?"

CJ turned back. "Yes, Sharon?"

"You might want to put your shoes back on first."

CJ looked down at her stocking-clad feet and laughed. "Great idea," she said, slipping on her heels again.

Deputy Police Chief Paul Duncan, in full navy blue uniform, sat behind his desk, punching at the keys on his computer keyboard one at a time. CJ stood in the doorway, doing penance for her tardiness by waiting silently.

The deputy chief's office overlooked the parking lot of the police building in the south suburb of Denver. Across the street was a pocket park lined with the ubiquitous aspen trees of Colorado, their bark starkly white against the grass, still yellow-brown from the winter. Spring was finally coming, and the leaves were beginning to unfurl from bare branches, a hopeful bright green.

CJ loved having four seasons of weather to enjoy, a far cry from the consistent humidity of Georgia. She'd been here eight springtimes, and loved it more every year.

Duncan finally looked up and said, "Inspector."

"Sir. I'm sorry I'm late."

He made a grunting sound, halfway between a reprimand and absolution. "Sit," he said tersely.

CJ towered over him, six feet tall with her heels on, and she quickly took his visitor's chair.

"I have a nine o'clock with the chief, so let's make it brief," Duncan said, running a hand over his shaved head, reflecting an ebony gleam in the overhead fluorescent lights. "How's the orientation going?"

"It's going well." CJ ran through the department organizational chart in her head. The chief of police had set up a simple structure: three divisions, plus a separate office for Internal Affairs. The Patrol division and the Investigations division, which handled all investigations from homicide to criminal mischief, were each headed by a captain who reported to Deputy Chief Duncan. Duncan also supervised the third division, Administration, which handled operations such as their emergency call center, crime scene, and evidence room, which was in the charge of a lieutenant.

Internal Affairs, however, reported directly to the police chief, so that I.A. could act independently. The office supervisor held the rank of lieutenant, but the title of inspector. CJ had one sergeant assigned to her full-time, and the two of them would be expected to handle any allegations of professional wrongdoing within the department. As the Internal Affairs Inspector, she didn't report to Duncan, but she understood that he was the chief's liaison, and she would be meeting with him regularly.

She answered, "I've met Captain Robards and all three of his patrol watch lieutenants, Lieutenant Maggio in Administration, and a number of the civilian employees in Crime Scene. I also made it over to the county jail, met with the sheriff's staff over there."

She tried to sound conscientious, for she knew Duncan hadn't been thrilled at the chief of police's decision to hire her, a cop from another jurisdiction, to fill the inspector's position at Colfax. She wondered if it was because she was a woman, or because of her age, or perhaps her looks.

Not gender, surely. Colfax had women in command positions. Thirty-three was a little young to be a lieutenant already, CJ knew, but she'd had the advantage of a master's degree and eight years of solid work at the Roosevelt Sheriff's Office before making the move to Colfax.

CJ had always tried to make her appearance work in her favor. Her soft Southern drawl helped, too. People usually liked her, and she knew she could be a good Internal Affairs officer. She was hoping to win the deputy chief over soon. But showing up late for meetings won't help, she thought wryly.

He leaned heavily onto his desktop, his navy blue tie looping over the edge. "Have you met with Captain Ryan yet?" he asked.

She cleared her throat, smoothing the creases in her linen

slacks. "She and I keep missing each other," she answered, her voice carefully neutral.

He grunted again, and she knew she had to be cautious. She had discovered that Ryan was a special favorite of Duncan's, and CJ didn't want to criticize the head of the Investigations Unit to his face. Still, she'd been trying for the two weeks she'd been here to set a meeting with the elusive captain, and she was beginning to think the woman didn't want to meet with her.

"I'll call her," he said. "She's been up to her ears with a series of burglaries around the Hartman Park area, but she still needs to make time to see you. How's McCarthy?"

"Sergeant McCarthy is fine," she said. "He's very organized, which helps me out a lot." She cocked an eyebrow and said, "May I ask ya'll a question about him?"

At Duncan's nod, she asked, "Did he apply for the position as Inspector? I know he's been here a long time. He told me he's been in I.A. almost three years."

Duncan cleared his throat and laced thick fingers together on the desktop. "He did apply, actually," he answered. "McCarthy is a good officer, but he's probably reached the height of his career. He may be organized, but he lacks...imagination, I would say."

She nodded. Nothing Duncan had just said surprised her. No wonder they had looked outside the department for a new I.A. inspector.

"Is that it?" He glanced at his watch. "I'll call you when I get a hold of Alex...ah, Captain Ryan."

"Yes, thank you." She stood.

As the Internal Affairs Inspector, she had a private office, tucked between a tiny space for her sergeant and an interview room on the first floor of the building. The office was very small, just about big enough for her desk, visitor's chair and three filing cabinets. CJ did have a single window that looked out over the parking lot, and across the way she could see some of the small park that gave her a view of the aspen trees and grass between the cars and trucks.

Before she could sit down, her office phone rang.

"I just talked to Alex," Duncan explained abruptly. "She's at a scene. Couple of her people were serving a search warrant and there were shots fired."

"Officers hurt?" she asked sharply.

"No, but the suspect is still at large. Why don't you go out and see the unit in action?" He rattled off the address, and she repeated it.

"I'm on my way," she told him.

CJ pulled her shiny black Lexus sedan onto the street as close to the staging area as she could get. There was a pair of Colfax navy blue patrol cars, light bars flashing, blocking the entrance to the block where the shooting had happened. Beyond them, a three-story apartment building, squat and painted an ugly gray-green, sat in the middle of a parking lot half-full of cars. There were more emergency vehicles scattered in the lot, including a couple of ambulances.

She took her shoes off again, this time replacing them with a butter-soft pair of leather driving flats. She knew there was often a lot of standing around at crime scenes, so she might as well be comfortable. She locked her purse in the trunk, made sure her Sig-Sauer .357 was secure on her left hip, and draped her badge around her neck on the department-issued lanyard.

The nearest uniformed officer had drawn the boring task of securing the perimeter and he was happy to have something to do when CJ approached.

"This area is restricted, ma'am," he announced in his best command voice. The effect was somewhat ruined by a tiny smear of egg yolk on his chin.

She lifted the badge and said, "Lieutenant St. Clair. I'm looking for Captain Ryan."

He eyed her up and down, and CJ waited, idly wondering whether he was admiring her linen suit, speculating on why she was here, or considering what she'd be like in bed. After a moment, she said, more firmly, "Captain Ryan?"

He jerked himself to attention. "Uh, command center is over there."

"Thank you, Officer," she said sweetly. She walked away, not looking back.

Under the sounds of traffic from Broadway a couple of blocks away, she could hear a few birds happily chirping from the trees around the parking lot. The air was beginning to warm a little, but it was still cool and crisp. The Rocky Mountains to the west looked sharp and bright, the sun dancing on the snow that still remained. She imagined a few spring skiers were up in Arapahoe Basin or Copper Mountain, enjoying the last of the snow for the season.

One man was sitting in the back of an ambulance, getting a penlight in the eyes from a paramedic. Another man was standing with a group of plainclothes and uniformed officers, gesturing. Describing what happened, she thought.

Next to the trunk of a patrol vehicle that served as a makeshift table, another group of three people stood, looking at some kind of map. One man, in uniform, wore sergeant's stripes. The second man, wearing a slightly rumpled gray suit, was staring at the map. Neither man was saying anything that she could hear.

In between the two men was a woman, pointing and, from her tone of voice, crisply issuing commands. CJ stood a moment, a few feet away, to look at her.

CJ could see her profile as she bent slightly over the map. Medium height, very trim, with medium length, almost-black hair pulled back into a loose ponytail, she was dressed in black slacks, a pink oxford-cloth shirt and a gray wool blazer. As she leaned forward, CJ could see a flash of color: earrings with some bright blue stones.

She looked too young to be a captain, but there was no mistaking that she was in charge at the scene. The men were watching her and listening respectfully, and beyond that, she simply had an intense air about her that exemplified command.

As if the captain could sense the new arrival, she straightened, turned, and looked directly at CJ. She stepped away from the patrol car and approached her.

"Who are you?" she asked, challenge in her tone.

She was a little older than CJ might have guessed from her body. There were a few laugh lines around her eyes, a little gray just at her temples. Perhaps forty but not much past that, indeed very young to be in command of a detective squad. Her first impression of the fit-looking body was accurate, though: small, high breasts, flat stomach, gentle curve to her hips. CJ swept her eyes down appreciatively, then realized with a jolt that she was doing exactly what the patrol officer had been doing to her a few moments before. She brought her eyes back up to meet the captain's gaze.

Lovely eyes. Somewhere between blue and gray, a bright contrast to the dark hair and pale skin. Not a beautiful face, but still attractive, all high cheekbones and interesting angles. It would be interesting to sketch her.

CJ felt a flutter in her stomach as Ryan leaned into her and lifted the badge away from CJ's chest to look at it. CJ realized that she hadn't answered the question and said, belatedly, "CJ St. Clair, Captain Ryan. I'm the new I.A. inspector."

She stepped away from Ryan, ostensibly to offer her hand, but mostly to get a little distance away from her. She was wearing some subtle perfume—sandalwood?—and CJ found herself distracted by it.

Ryan took the hand and grasped it firmly. CJ was surprised at how warm the touch was, how strong her hand seemed.

"Inspector," she said. "Is there a problem?"

"What? No, I'm not here on an investigation. It's just that we haven't had a chance to meet, and Chief Duncan thought it would be a good idea for me to come out here and—"

Ryan dropped the hand and shook her head angrily. "Inspector, I'm sorry I haven't been able to see you, but we're just a little busy here. The suspect who took a half-dozen shots at my officers is wandering around the neighborhood somewhere with a gun, so if you'll excuse me, we're going to try to find him before he hurts a civilian or gets away completely."

She turned away, but CJ asked, "May I help?"

Ryan looked back at her. "I don't know. Can you?"

The frank response startled her for a second. Captain Ryan was a very focused officer, it would seem. CJ wished the flicker in her stomach would go away. More briskly than she intended, she answered, "I was in patrol for five years and a detective for three before I got here. I think I can ask a few questions competently."

Ryan didn't react to her tone except by looking her in the eyes again for a moment. Then she nodded and said, "Come with me."

CJ followed her back to the patrol car, trying to regain her composure. Ryan introduced her briefly: the patrol sergeant was Thompson, the guy in the suit was one of the detectives, Sergeant Frank Morelli.

Ryan said, "Okay, Thompson, your people will do the door-to-door in the apartment house, get everybody out to make sure he's not hiding or threatening anybody. And have some uniforms check the parking lot here, too, make sure he's not hiding in a vehicle. If you don't find him, start on the single-family houses. Frank, what's the guy's description?"

Morelli looked at his notebook. "Bobby Milton, male, Caucasian, five nine, three twenty, brown and brown, goatee. Wearing blue jeans and a black T-shirt. They're getting a driver's license photo through."

Ryan nodded. "Good. Distribute it to everybody as soon as you can. Everybody keeps in radio contact, clear? No heroics. This guy has already tried to kill some cops today, so let's make sure he doesn't get another chance."

Thompson said, "Got it, Captain," and peeled off toward his officers.

CJ said thoughtfully, "If this guy's three hundred and twenty pounds, I bet he's not running very far on foot. What's the nearest commercial establishment?"

Ryan looked at her, in appraisal, and CJ felt the pull of the blue-gray eyes once more. She and Ryan leaned over the map together. CJ caught the sandalwood scent again, more strongly.

Ryan spread the map out with her left hand and CJ carefully noted the absence of a wedding ring, or any rings at all.

Stop it, she told herself firmly.

Alex said, "K-Mart three blocks away, on Broadway, looks like."

"How about I go over there and see if there's any sign of him?" CJ suggested. "He might shop there and maybe he's gone to hide out. Let me have a radio and I'll see what I can find."

Ryan eyed her and said, "Frank, go with Lieutenant St. Clair. I don't want anybody on their own until we get this guy."

Morelli had an unmarked car, so they drove the three blocks to the department store. She was just as happy not to reveal her Lexus. Morelli asked CJ, "You just got hired, right?"

"Yes. Not quite two weeks ago. I was just making the rounds, trying to meet everyone."

He had kind brown eyes, and a shy smile. "Didn't expect to actually be in the field today, huh?"

She glanced down at her outfit and laughed. "You're right. These are my office clothes. But don't worry, Detective. I've made a few arrests in my time, if it comes to that."

He parked the car and asked, "Anything really fun?"

As they got out of the car in a far corner of the lot, they checked out the nearby RTD bus stop on Broadway. Two women and a skinny teenaged boy, no one who looked like their suspect.

She wondered if Morelli was just making conversation, or if he really wanted to know. He seemed like a nice guy, so she answered, "I worked with the Feds once, on an undercover operation. The bad guys decided to shoot it out when we showed up with the warrants. I could not believe how many shots you can exchange in just a couple of minutes." She shook her head.

Frank cleared his throat and said, "Sounds hairy. You get them?"

CJ wondered again how much he really wanted to know. "Yes," she said quietly. "One of our guys went to the hospital. Two of theirs went to the morgue."

She heard it sometimes, lying awake in the cold gray minutes before dawn, the sound of gunfire.

"Jesus!" he said, and she liked him because he didn't try to sound cool about it. She considered whether it made him feel better or worse to be with her, knowing about the shooting, whether he thought she was bad luck.

They walked up and down the aisles in the parking lot, trying to look like they were a couple out for a little morning shopping while seeing everyone and everything. A young, harried-looking woman was trying to pry a stroller out of the back of her SUV while corralling a fussy toddler; a man with wisps of gray hair was pushing a shopping cart from the parking lot toward the store; a couple of girls who looked like they were skipping high school algebra were walking next to each other, each busy texting on a cell phone to someone else.

CJ caught a flicker of movement a couple of rows away. At first she thought it was someone wrestling shopping bags into a car, but a moment later she saw it for what it was.

"Frank," she said softly.

He answered, "Yeah, I see him."

A huge man was concentrating on maneuvering a wire coat hanger—*where on earth had he found one of those?*—into an ancient-looking hatchback.

Swiftly she said, "Call it in. I'm going to go over there and engage him in a little distracting conversation. Get behind him and let's arrest his sorry ass."

"You sure?" He looked at her in surprise.

"Absolutely." She flashed him a reassuring smile.

She made sure Frank was out of earshot to radio their position, then she strolled casually over to their suspect, unbuttoning the top two buttons of her silk shirt, just enough to let the lace on the top of her bra show.

When she got close enough, she saw him look up. His face was running with sweat, soaking into his goatee. There were stains under his arms and across his chest, visible even on the black T-shirt.

"Hey!" she greeted him. "Bobby, right? You remember me, don't you, honey?"

"Fuck off, bitch," was his response.

"Now, honey, don't be like that," CJ purred. "You remember that bar over on...where was it?"

"I said, fuck off!" he growled. "I don't know you."

"Sure ya'll do." She subtly shifted her position so that he would turn a little away from the side of the car to face her, exposing his back to Frank. She could see Frank moving up as carefully as he could. "I mean," she cooed, looking at the faded Harley logo on his shirt, "the motorcycle and all…you were so hot."

She leaned forward, just a little, to give him a glance at her cleavage. Fleetingly she thought: *Hope he's straight, or this is so not going to work.*

He dropped his eyes and licked his lips.

Frank had his handcuff on one wrist before the guy even knew he was there.

"Colfax P.D. You're under…"

He never finished the sentence. Milton swung his free arm back and Frank bounced off the hood of the hatchback.

Milton took off across the parking lot, running like an offensive tackle, not fast, but with determination. CJ, dodging people and parked cars, sprinted after him, alert to any movement he might make toward a weapon.

He just kept running, but he was already exhausted, and she brought him down with a dive that took out his legs.

He rolled, trying to kick her off, but she had a good grip on his belt and hung on. He tried punching her. She ducked the first one, but the second blow caught her in the mouth, stunning her for a moment.

He pulled her off, tried to scramble to his feet. CJ reached out with one arm and wrapped it around one of his legs, thick as a tree stump. He grabbed at her blouse, yanking it to try to get her off him. She felt it rip, but she held on.

He tried punching her again, battering her shoulders and chest as she moved, trying to protect her head.

She winced as one giant fist connected solidly with her ribs. *I hope that one hurt his hand, at least. Come on, Frank!*

She tugged at his leg, got him off balance, and he went down heavily.

She grabbed one of his arms, tried to get it behind him, but it was like wrestling a steer. He was still trying to punch her, and she was ducking and twisting as he tried to throw her off.

Then suddenly help was there, another set of arms grabbing the man and helping CJ get him onto his stomach. It took both of them to bring his arms close enough together for CJ to fasten the handcuff onto his other wrist.

Finally he gave up, sagging into the pavement.

CJ sat back heavily down on the ground, breathing hard. She looked up into Captain Ryan's face.

"I don't know where you came from," she gasped, "but I'm really glad to see ya'll, Captain."

"Glad I could drop in," Ryan said, breathing hard herself.

CJ could see her face was flushed. "What did you do, Captain," she joked, "run all the way?"

As soon as she said it, she realized that was exactly what had happened. The sirens came screaming into the parking lot behind them a few seconds later.

The first uniformed officer to reach them got an earful of instructions.

"Get the ambulances here, now," Ryan snapped. "They need to check Frank right away. And search the suspect and the immediate area for the gun." She looked down at CJ. "Did you see a weapon?"

CJ shook her head and then wished she hadn't. Everything from the elbows up hurt.

Ryan knelt down and touched her shoulder lightly. "You're hurt," she said, a statement rather than a question.

Carefully CJ answered, "Not too much."

She realized her chest was cold and she looked down. Her blouse was torn open to the waist, and the circle of officers around her had a nice view of her ivory lace bra.

She looked at the nearest uniformed officer staring at her, apparently transfixed by her breasts. He looked to be all of twenty-two, and she said, lightly, "Bali. Thirty-eight C. You can put it in the report."

Ryan snapped her head around and said, "Get a blanket from your unit for the *inspector*, Officer. *Now*."

Every man suddenly had something else to do, three of them picking up the suspect and putting him to a very thorough search.

"Got the gun, Captain," one of them called. "Looks like it's empty."

"That explains why he didn't take a shot at me," CJ said. "How's Frank?"

"Bleeding," Ryan answered, looking over CJ's shoulder. "Paramedics are with him. Broken nose, I'm guessing. What happened?"

"Our suspect put an elbow in his face. Definitely a personal foul. Frank should get the two free throws."

Ryan sat back on her heels and said in faint amusement, "Do you always make jokes when you've been assaulted by a suspect?"

CJ lifted an eyebrow and answered, "I'm not sure. It's only happened a couple of times before. Hard to establish a pattern from that."

A dark blue blanket stenciled with Colfax P.D. appeared. Ryan shook it out and draped it over CJ's shoulders, closing it over her chest with surprising gentleness.

CJ closed her fingers over the blanket, brushing against the captain's wrist. It felt surprisingly good, comforting to be wrapped up by her. CJ shivered. *I'm just coming down from the adrenaline rush*, she told herself.

"I want you to go to the hospital, get checked out," Ryan said briskly.

"I don't think I need to do that," CJ answered. "I'm just a little bruised."

"Hospital, Lieutenant," Ryan repeated, in a voice that did not invite argument. "Think of it as gathering evidence. I'm going to charge this son-of-a-bitch with ten or twelve counts of assault. *Nobody* tries to hurt my officers."

It occurred to CJ that, technically, she wasn't one of Ryan's officers, but she decided she liked being treated as if she were.

CHAPTER TWO

Alex Ryan dropped wearily into the visitor's chair in Paul Duncan's office.

"I have no idea," she sighed, "why I even bother to plan my days, Paul. Nothing ever seems to go the way I think it will."

Paul barked a laugh. "Welcome to the wonderful world of police work, Alex," he said and smiled at her.

"You would really think I'd have gotten the hang of it by now," Alex continued, closing her eyes and leaning her head back. "Jesus, twenty years this summer. I can hardly believe it."

"*You* can hardly believe it? I remember when you were born like it was yesterday. Okay, maybe last week."

Alex laughed. "Very funny."

"Charlie was so proud to have a kid," he mused. "You'd have thought he was the first man in the history of the planet to successfully produce offspring. We had to look at new pictures every week."

Eyes still closed, Alex said, "I guess I always wondered if he'd really wished for a boy."

"Alex!" he barked at her. She sat up and looked at him.

"Your father couldn't have been prouder of you if you'd been triplets. He used to bring your tennis trophies into the office, did you know that? Showed them off. I think I saw your report cards before you did."

She smiled at the thought. "I miss him," she said simply. "Sometimes I'll go for weeks without really thinking about him, then something happens, and I miss him as if it were yesterday."

They were silent, letting the weight of the memories settle over them.

"So," Paul said after a minute, "how are your people?"

"Everybody's fine. Kelly got a minor bump banging into the railing, when the suspect started shooting and he was trying to get his ass under cover. Roger wasn't hurt."

Paul grunted. "What a surprise."

"Yes, he does have a great talent for self-preservation. Frank got the worst of it: broken nose, couple of black eyes. He'll be all right, too."

Paul drummed his stubby fingers on his desktop. "You got our brand-new Internal Affairs inspector banged up, too, I hear."

"She's a little worse for wear. Some abrasions, one slightly bruised rib. In all fairness," she added acerbically, "*I* didn't get her banged up. *She* decided to make the arrest."

"You sound angry. Should they have waited for backup?"

Alex had already thought this through, as he'd known she would. She shook her head and said, "It was a good call. The guy had already popped the door lock on the car. He would have been gone in less than a minute if they'd waited. Actually, her approach was a good one, the guy was just a little faster than Frank thought. But she didn't flinch, stayed on the suspect until we got there."

"So why are you mad about it?"

She hadn't quite figured that out yet. She shrugged and said,

"I think I'm just pissed off that she got hurt. I don't want I.A. mad at me, do I?"

He stopped drumming his fingers and said, "Did I tell you why the chief hired her?"

"Not exactly," she answered carefully. She was always cautious about not taking advantage of the fact that Paul was her godfather. She'd made it to her rank based on her own accomplishments, and didn't want to presume on their relationship.

Paul sat back. "Nathan wanted somebody who'd been in a serious incident in the past. He thought it would make for the right blend of toughness and compassion. You know he takes I.A. seriously, and there was no one here at the correct rank he wanted to lose from their current position."

Alex frowned. What Paul wasn't saying was that nobody really wanted to be with Internal Affairs. No cop liked the Internal Affairs officers.

"So what's the story on St. Clair?" she asked.

"She killed a suspect during an arrest."

"What?" Alex was shocked. When she'd first seen CJ St. Clair at the parking lot, she couldn't imagine she was cop. Alex had assumed she was press, a reporter who had gotten through the perimeter for one of the local television stations. She looked like an anchor for one of the morning shows: perfectly cut red hair that fell to her shoulders, flawless pale skin, features movie-star pretty but for a straight nose that added a little character. She'd been wearing a beautiful cream linen suit, professional-looking French manicure, and understated makeup that enhanced her bright green eyes.

To discover that she was the new Internal Affairs inspector had been a bit of a surprise.

"Yeah," Paul continued. "She was with the Roosevelt Sheriff's Office. Just after she got promoted to investigator, ATF borrowed her for an undercover operation they were running, some guys stealing water gel explosives and selling them. They wanted her to play a girlfriend or something, make the agent look more credible. Anyway, she went out on the arrests with them and the suspects started shooting. One of the ATF agents was wounded, and two of the suspects were killed. She shot one of them, saved the wounded guy's life, apparently. She's got a medal."

Alex looked at him narrowly. "You didn't get all of that from her file."

"No," he admitted. "After Nathan told me he was going to hire her, I called Rod Chavez, an old friend over at Roosevelt. He knows St. Clair real well, filled me in on her."

The woman Alex had met that morning seemed kind and funny and thoughtful. It was hard to picture her killing somebody.

Unbidden, the memory of the sight of CJ on the ground, her blouse ripped open, came to Alex's mind. Maybe she was a lot tougher than she looked. Alex blinked to clear the picture and said, "Interesting. She's not what I would have expected."

Paul looked at the big stainless steel watch on his wrist and rumbled, "I gotta go. Betty is making tuna casserole for the Bible study tonight." He looked at Alex slyly. "Want to come?"

Alex laughed, pushing herself out of the chair. "To church? No, thanks. Though the offer of Betty's tuna casserole is tempting."

"You could consider going to church, you know," he said mildly. "The Baptists would be happy to have you, lapsed Catholic and all."

She shook her head. "I'm not a lapsed Catholic. I'm just resting."

He grunted out a laugh, then added, "Betty asked me last night to remind you that you haven't been over to the house in a while."

"Those burglaries had us running," she explained feebly. She didn't want to tell him that she really had no good excuse for not visiting more often.

"Well, you've got the guys, so find a time, okay? Dinner, soon. I've gotta go. Go home yourself, will you, Alex? You look beat."

"Soon," she hedged. "I've got some more paperwork to do on the Milton arrest. Report for the Use of Excessive Force Review Team. We can't have our new I.A. inspector tied up in an investigation, can we?"

She left him, feeling his concerned stare on her back.

Vivian Wong demanded, "What the hell happened to you?"

CJ, moving carefully, unfolded the linen napkin into her lap, and said, "How about I had a disagreement with the valet and he slugged me."

"You are a laugh a minute. Seriously, either you had a really bad collagen injection since I last saw you or somebody smacked you in the mouth. And you're moving like you really overdid the bedroom gymnastics last night."

CJ chuckled, then flinched. "The x-rays were negative. Just a tiny little ole bruise on a rib," she answered. "But do *not* make me laugh."

"Christ on a unicycle, seriously," Vivian uttered. "Car accident?"

"I was assisting with an arrest and things got a little rough." CJ's voice was dismissive.

Vivian knew asking for details would get her nothing more, so she opened her menu and said, "You could have canceled."

"What, and miss shoe shopping night? Be serious. Besides, it's your turn to buy dinner."

Vivian snorted, then said, "The maple-cured salmon is supposed to be fabulous here."

CJ, perusing the menu, said, "For some reason, I have trouble ordering seafood in Denver. It's too far from the ocean. We actually had the real thing back home."

"When in Rome. Perhaps you'd prefer the Rocky Mountain oysters?"

"You are so very amusing. So, how's the mortgage business?"

Vivian sighed, glancing around the dark wood and railway-themed design of the Great Northern Tavern, one of the many restaurants in the Denver Tech Center. It was impossible to get in during the day, the place crowded with real estate agents and managers who descended for lunch from the nearby forest of high-rise office buildings, but it was after seven o'clock, so the place was half-full.

"Do not even attempt to discuss my job with me, CJ. It's a mess, and interest rates are ridiculous, and we're all going to be out of a job by this time next year. This quarter has been a disaster, and the next one looks worse. I hate my job."

"Yes, so you keep saying. Yet it keeps you in Jimmy Choos, so you keep at it."

"True, true. It's not like being a police officer could support my habit."

"It's not being a cop that supports mine, and you know it."

"Yeah, I should have chosen a richer family to be born into."

As soon as she said the words, Vivian regretted them, for she saw the shadow that crossed her friend's face. "Sorry, CJ," she apologized quickly. "That whole thing with your family…it really sucks."

CJ said, "Yes, darlin', it does really suck."

"Their loss," Vivian said loyally. "So, tell me all about the new job. The one that was supposed to keep you from being beaten up or shot at during arrests, if I recall."

CJ smiled. "I love it. Almost everyone has been nice, even though I'm the big, bad Internal Affairs inspector. It's a much bigger department than the Roosevelt Sheriff's Office, more than two hundred officers. They deal with a lot more serious crime."

The waitress appeared and they ordered: salmon for the banker, Caesar salad with chicken for the detective. As the waitress left, Vivian eyed her appraisingly and said, "She's cute."

"Oh, for heaven's sake, Viv, don't tell me you and Lisa have broken up again."

"No, we're good. I'm just keeping in practice."

CJ shook her head in disapproval of infidelity in any form.

"Oh, please," Vivian said, "I have to take this from a woman who has a date once a decade."

"I go out," CJ said, defensively.

"Please," Vivian said again, "I know nuns who date more than you do."

"You know nuns who date?" CJ exclaimed in mock horror.

"Figure of speech." Vivian continued, "The most important question: how are the prospects? Anybody hit on you yet?"

CJ gave her the full dazzling smile. "Nope, not even the hint of a pass. Everybody has been very professional, for a nice change."

"Well, that's disappointing." Vivian put her chin on her hand, her smooth black hair swinging easily on either side of her heart-shaped face. "Not even one cute girl in uniform?"

CJ said, "Viv, it's my job, not a dating service."

But she had dropped her eyes and Vivian pounced.

"You're holding out," she said shrewdly. "Who is she?"

Swallowing before she answered, CJ said, "I met the captain in charge of the detective squad today, finally."

"Yes?"

"She was…interesting."

"Interesting is good. Say more. Is she cute?"

"Viv, I just met the woman. I don't know her, all right? She's probably straight."

"Well, there's an easy way to find out. What are you getting all protective for? And you didn't answer the question."

"Which question was that?"

Vivian tapped her iced tea glass with a red lacquered fingernail. "Is she cute?"

"I wouldn't say cute, exactly," CJ answered slowly. "I would say Captain Ryan is…focused. Smart. Protective of her fellow officers. Very dry sense of humor, I think."

Vivian laughed. "None of that tells me what she looks like, sweetie."

"Oh. Ah, around forty, I'd say, shoulder-length dark hair, five six or so, seems very fit. It looks like she bikes or runs or something." CJ reflected a moment, and then added, "She does have nice eyes."

"Really?" Vivian was interested.

"Yes, sort of a gray-blue. Like faded denim."

"Really?" Viv said again. "Sounds very nice indeed. I love older women. Sure she's straight?"

CJ answered, smiling, "She's not that much older. And she's not your type, Viv."

"What do you mean, not my type? The only type I have is female."

"I'll introduce ya'll. With your track record, I'm sure you'll find out in about thirty seconds flat."

Vivian eyed her. "So when will you be asking her?"

"What?"

"If she likes girls, of course."

Exasperated, CJ said again, "Viv, I don't know her. For heaven's sake."

"Yes, right. So when will that conversation be happening?"

"Don't push me, Viv," CJ's voice was soft but held warning. "I'm not like you."

"Well, that's for damn sure. If you were like me, we'd already have had a torrid affair, broken up, and no longer be speaking. Maybe you could break the ice by telling her what 'CJ' stands for."

CJ smiled. "You just can't stand that I haven't told ya'll, can you?"

"No," Vivian pouted. "And I've known you, what? Four or five years? You told me about your family, why won't you tell me your damn name?"

CJ sat back in her chair and said, "It's all tied together, what happened with me and my family. I left Savannah, I reinvented myself, and I like myself as CJ St. Clair. Let's leave it, okay?"

Vivian picked up her fork as their entrees arrived. "Tell me again why we're friends?" she asked petulantly. "You won't tell me your full name, you won't scope out interesting girls for me, and you don't date, so you don't have any hot, steamy stories to tell. Why the hell do I hang out with you?"

"I'm the only one who will shop for shoes with you. You're impossible to please."

Vivian, chewing her salmon, muttered, "Good point."

When Alex got home to her small mid-century house, she changed into sweats and a T-shirt. It was after nine o'clock, and she realized she didn't remember eating lunch. Her choices for dinner seemed limited to cereal, canned soup or a peanut butter sandwich.

After turning on Tony Bennett, Alex chose the cereal, and sat at her kitchen table. She took out the morning paper, since she hadn't had time to look at it after her run that morning. She tried to read, but instead she thought again about CJ St. Clair.

There were a few moments that kept coming back to her. The dazzling smile, the soft voice with the slight drawl. The way she strolled to the car behind Frank, just a little sway in her walk as if she loved having curves. How she looked, battered and vulnerable, sitting on the ground in the parking lot, but with an air of calm strength too.

And those beautiful green eyes, looking up at Alex with gratitude.

She finished eating and wandered into the living room where her book lay on the coffee table. When she awoke on the couch a couple of hours later, Tony was still crooning at her from the CD player.

After Alex washed her face and brushed her teeth, she looked into her mirror.

Almost forty. It's probably way past time for a moisturizer. Something with a sunscreen.

She sighed. First moisturizer, then the slippery slope of actually wearing more makeup than her usual quick mascara and lip gloss routine.

She studied her face for a moment. She had always thought of herself as almost completely ordinary. Every woman she knew, including her sister, was prettier than she was, but it rarely bothered her. How she looked wasn't really important—what mattered was how hard she could work, how well she could solve the puzzles and how quickly she could get the bad guys.

Still, one encounter with CJ St. Clair, and she was thinking about moisturizer, and trying to decide if it was time to cut her hair.

"Idiot," she chided herself aloud. "Like you're going to compete with somebody who looks like that."

But it wasn't about competition, and she knew it.

CHAPTER THREE

Alex waited until lunchtime two days later before she phoned CJ.

"Captain, how nice of you to call," CJ said brightly.

"How are you feeling?" Alex asked.

"Like a slacker," CJ laughed. "Ten days on the job, and I'm already limited to just sitting here."

"You shouldn't be here at all, not with an injured rib," Alex said seriously.

"It's not broken, just a little bruise. And I can certainly sit at my desk and work."

"What did the doctor say?"

She heard the sigh over the phone line. "No running, twisting, or getting whomped on by bad guys for a couple of weeks."

Alex leaned back, found herself grinning into the receiver. "Whomped on? Is that a technical phrase?"

CJ laughed again. "Absolutely. Although it usually refers to the beating the University of Georgia football team puts on its hapless opponents."

The pile of work waiting on her desk, the blinking message light on her phone suddenly seemed relatively unimportant. Alex swiveled her chair slightly so that she could see the steel gray rain clouds building over the mountains in the far distance.

"You're a sports fan, I guess?" she asked, wondering why she cared.

"I am a native of the state of Georgia, and so I am therefore required to be fluent in football and baseball, able to speak conversational basketball, and to be completely uninterested in hockey," CJ replied.

Alex smiled again. "I feel a little guilty about you getting hurt on my watch," she said. "How about I buy you a drink tonight? I know we haven't had a chance to sit down and talk about the job yet. It would probably be easier, for me at least, to find time off-site."

Alex found herself waiting, a little breathlessly, for the answer.

"I'd like that," came the warm response. "I'm going a little stir-crazy sitting here in my little closet office today. Where would you like to go?"

They settled on a grill not far from Alex's house, and Alex hung up, feeling cheerful.

"Hey, Captain," Detective Kelly Porter stuck his head into her office. "We just got a…"

He stopped, momentarily startled by a sight he didn't remember seeing before: his boss sitting in her office, smiling.

"Captain?" he asked, uncertainly.

Alex rearranged her expression and waved him in. "What's up?" she asked, frowning in concentration.

Kelly sighed in relief. Order had been restored to the universe.

"They have a hundred and two kinds of beer?" CJ asked incredulously. "Why do you come here? Do you like making yourself crazy with choices, or are you trying them all, one by one?"

Alex replied, "No, I come here because it's close to my house, and it's quieter than most bars." She smiled and added, "And because they have a hundred and two choices."

CJ stared helplessly at the beer list. "I have no idea what to order. Just pick something and get two of them."

Alex said to their waiter, "We'll try two of the Mighty Arrow Pale Ales, please."

"Well, that sounds good," CJ said when the waiter left. "I don't drink much beer, myself, but ale always sounds classier."

Alex looked across the table at her. CJ was casually dressed, khakis and a light camel-colored sweater, but everything about her said money: her bearing, the tasteful but expensive gold wristwatch, the tiny diamond studs in her ears, her perfect grooming, marred only by the still swollen lip and some light bruising over one cheekbone her makeup couldn't quite hide.

"How's Frank doing?" CJ asked, carefully selecting a pretzel.

"He's fine, back at work today. He does look like a raccoon, poor guy. How are you?"

"Fine," CJ said easily.

Alex said carefully, "I think you're lying."

"Only a little." CJ smiled at her.

"You know it could have been a lot worse."

"Good thing he'd spent all his bullets missing your two detectives," CJ answered lightly. "What was the warrant for, anyway?"

"He was fencing some stuff. From the guys we thought were the burglars we've been looking for. His sheet didn't have any prior weapons charges, so Roger and Kelly weren't prepared for him to start blasting at them. Not that that's any excuse."

"That kind of thing could happen to anybody," CJ said

mildly, and Alex remembered that CJ had already lived through a shooting.

The beers arrived and CJ sipped tentatively at hers. "This is good, Alex," she said, in surprise. "A kind of a bitter honey flavor. Ah, may I call you Alex?" she added hurriedly.

"Sure, CJ. Glad you like it."

"So what happened? Did you get your suspects?"

"Oh, yes," Alex said, with satisfaction. "Milton served them up on a silver platter. They're both in custody, and we cleared about twenty cases as a result. They were very busy burglars."

"Good for you." CJ took another drink and said, "So tell me about your squad."

Alex glanced at her sharply. CJ's bright green eyes were almost dark in the yellow lights of the bar.

"Gathering intelligence, Inspector?" She heard the harshness in her own voice, but she didn't know this woman, and she was, after all, Internal Affairs.

CJ leaned forward a little, meeting Alex's gaze. "I'm not on duty, Alex," she said softly. "And just so ya'll know, my job here is to protect good cops from unfair accusations and false charges. If I find a bad cop or two, I'm going to do my best to get rid of them so that we can all do a better job for the public. I'm not on a mission and I don't have an agenda other than that. All right?"

After a long, tense moment, Alex said, "Look, if I offended you, I'm sorry. You have to admit some I.A. officers do seem like they're on a vendetta."

CJ ran a finger along her beer glass. "I have known some who were like that," she admitted. "It's one reason I took the job. I suppose I thought I could do better." She looked over and gave Alex a sudden, dazzling smile. "Maybe I do have an agenda, after all."

"Trying to do a good job isn't an agenda," Alex answered, leaning back and taking a long drink. "It's a way of life."

"Perhaps," CJ agreed thoughtfully. "But it's not all there is to life."

Isn't it? Alex thought.

"Come on now, Captain," CJ asked, her voice light, "tell me about your detectives."

They chatted, finishing the first beer and talking through the second. When the waiter returned a third time, Alex glanced at her watch and saw with surprise that almost two hours had passed. When was the last time she'd spent two hours in conversation with someone and not felt the minutes drag? They'd discussed everyone and everything in the department she could think of, but for some reason she didn't want to leave yet.

She looked at CJ as she said to the waiter, "I'm thinking coffee for this round. Decaf for me."

"Yes, I'll have coffee as well," CJ said. "Full octane. With cream, please."

Alex watched, amused, as CJ took a long drink of the black coffee to make room, then added a very generous amount of cream until the coffee was almost the color of her camel sweater.

"You actually like coffee spoiling all that cream?" Alex kidded her.

CJ said loftily, "I don't discuss real coffee with people who drink decaffeinated. What is the point of that?"

"The point is that this won't keep me up half the night," Alex said, still amused. "Wait another decade or so and see how you manage it then."

"Oh, come on, ya'll aren't that much older."

"Oh, I think I'm at least that," Alex said.

CJ drank coffee and asked carefully, "Tell me why you became a cop."

Alex looked at her and wondered why she wanted to know.

"Runs in the family," she answered at length. "My dad was in the department."

"Retired?"

Alex took a deep breath and said, "He was killed on duty when I was nineteen. He was a sergeant in Patrol, working an accident on County Line Road. Hit and run. We never found who hit him." A little to her surprise, she read deep sympathy in CJ's eyes.

"That must have been terrible for you. Do ya'll have brothers and sisters?"

"One sister, five years younger. When Dad died, I decided to quit college so she could live with me and finish school. That's when I joined the department. Deputy Chief Duncan used to be my Dad's partner, he helped me get a job there."

CJ was frowning. "Your mother wasn't around?" she asked.

Alex looked away for a second before answering. "She died when I was ten. Breast cancer."

Why did it still hurt? Alex wondered. It was so long ago.

"Oh, Alex," CJ said gently.

Alex took another deep breath and released it. CJ was throwing her off-balance, the soft blend of humor and compassion mixed with a sharp mind. A very attractive combination.

"It all worked out," Alex said, forcing cheerfulness. "I've been with the department almost twenty years, and I love police work. My sister got through college and law school. She's with one of the downtown firms. She's married to a professor at Metro, and my handsome nephew is going to be five in May."

"No children of your own?" CJ asked.

"No. Just a bad marriage in my distant past."

She saw something flicker across CJ's face, but the expression was gone before she could identify it.

"No one?" CJ asked. It seemed to Alex as if she was trying very hard to sound casual.

Alex thought of the empty house waiting for her a few blocks away. "No," she answered. "I'm not even home enough to have a dog. Hell, I don't even have houseplants."

CJ put her coffee mug down on the scarred wooden table and said, "I've got you beat, then. I have a balcony at my condo, and lots of plants. I like to put in herbs, in pots, so I can have fresh ones in the summer."

"You cook?"

"I do," she said happily. "I'm pretty good, if I do say so myself."

Alex liked that she wasn't falsely modest. "Who do you cook for?"

"My wide circle of friends, old and new. You shall receive an invitation to my next dinner party."

"Not family?" Alex asked, returning the probing CJ had given her moments before.

CJ's face darkened and Alex was suddenly sorry she'd asked.

"No, it's all right," she said quickly, reacting to Alex's expression. "My family is a sore topic, that's all. A subject for another time."

Alex signaled for their tab. CJ began to dig in her purse and Alex said, "No, it's on me. I invited you."

A little to Alex's surprise, CJ said graciously, "Thank you. That's nice of you, welcoming the new girl."

Alex laughed. She couldn't remember the last person to make her laugh, either. "It's the least I can do. You did get yourself roughed up arresting my suspect, after all."

CJ sat back, her eyes bright. "I hope I don't have to go through that every time you want to go out and have a drink."

"No, next time we could just skip that part."

Alex saw her smile, and thought about how much she liked the thought of next time.

CJ looked at her sergeant and said, "Ya'll are not serious, are you?"

Chad McCarthy nodded solemnly and replied, "He actually did say that. Got a roomful of witnesses."

CJ ran her fingers through her hair. "Surely no one is that stupid," she muttered.

McCarthy studied his notes. "The instructor at sergeants' training said, 'Dealing with employees who are highly emotional or volatile can be a challenging part of the job.' And Reynolds said, and I quote, 'So the trick is not having any women on your team?' Unquote."

CJ didn't doubt it. In the month she'd been working with him, she'd discovered that McCarthy was very good at getting his facts absolutely correct.

"Well, that's just great," she said in mild disgust. "Let me check the file on prior disciplines and see what we're looking at here. Does he have any prior confirmed I.A.s?"

"Just one. I pulled the file for you. It's on your desk."

CJ looked doubtfully at the piles of files, papers and detritus on her desktop. McCarthy leaned forward, scrabbled around, and found it in the mess. CJ wondered how her desk could look like a disaster area so quickly.

"Thanks," she said. "I'll check this out and we can look at it after lunch."

He stood, looking at her uncertainly. "Um, Lieutenant?" he asked finally.

"Yes, Sergeant?"

"I was meaning to ask…just to know…" He rubbed the tiny bald spot just at the crown of his head.

CJ thought she knew where this might be going. "Yes, Chad?" she said, more gently.

"Are you, ah, married, or engaged or anything? I've had a couple of guys ask me, sort of, and I thought I'd…"

"Chad, I don't date guys."

He took a second to absorb that. "I…you're…uh, what?" He looked deeply puzzled.

"I wouldn't necessarily want you to post this in the men's locker room, but I'm gay, Chad."

She could almost, from experience, read his thoughts: She doesn't look gay. She sighed.

"You're…oh." It seemed to sink in. "Yes, right. Got it."

"If anyone asks, you can just tell them I'm not interested in dating, okay?"

He stood straighter. "Of course, Lieutenant."

She opened Reynolds' personnel file but after a few minutes found herself thinking instead about Alex Ryan. The evening they'd spent together had been the most enjoyable she'd had in a long time, and they'd only been sitting and talking.

It had just been a business meeting, but CJ tried, and failed, to recall the last actual date she'd had that had gone that well.

She sighed and closed the file. She'd been going over this for a couple of weeks. It was pointless to just sit around and wonder.

It was time to go upstairs and have a conversation with Captain Ryan.

The investigators worked in one large room, scattered among pairs of desks cluttered with files, computer monitors and coffee cups. The room was wrapped with windows on three sides, so the detectives had a decent view from the second floor of the Colfax Police station, including the distant purple-blue Rocky Mountains to the west. CJ glanced around. There were seven or eight officers in the room, working, along with a couple of civilians, and a pair of uniformed officers engaged in earnest conversation with one of the detectives.

The captain had a private office in one corner of the room, with windows on two sides and another window set into the wall overlooking the squad room. CJ put her head in the doorway, but Alex wasn't there. CJ saw the meticulous desktop, files carefully stacked, notepad centered on her blotter. There were three framed photographs, and she shamelessly crossed the room to pick them up.

The first showed a younger Alex, in her police uniform, hugging a woman who looked a great deal like her as they both smiled into the camera. The other woman was wearing a gown and a hood, and CJ had no trouble guessing this was her younger sister, at her law school graduation, probably.

The second photo was of a little boy, three or four years old, sitting in Alex's lap. He had dark hair and eyes, but he had the same face-transforming smile CJ saw on Alex's face. Her nephew, it had to be. CJ found herself smiling back at the photograph.

The third frame held a picture of a little girl, blonde, and missing a front tooth. Seven or eight, perhaps. It looked like a school photo. CJ couldn't guess who it might be, but she looked nothing like Alex or the other photographs.

Alex's jacket was neatly hung up behind the door, so CJ figured she must be in the building somewhere. She decided to cross the hall to the ladies' room.

She found Alex there, washing her hands. She was wearing navy blue slacks and a French blue blouse, and when she turned to grab a paper towel, CJ thought her eyes looked amazing. The quivering returned to her stomach, and she thought suddenly she might lose her nerve.

"Hi," she blurted.

"Hi," Alex said, drying her hands and tossing the towel into the wastebasket. "How are you?"

"The rib is getting better. Occasionally I'll turn wrong, in bed, and I'll get a twinge, but other than that..."

Her voice trailed off, and she wondered again if she was going to be able to have the conversation. What on earth was she so nervous about?

She glanced around to make sure the bathroom was empty, and when she returned to Alex's gaze, she saw a mixture of curiosity and faint amusement.

"Something on your mind?" Alex asked. "Other than using the facilities?"

CJ cleared her throat. "I really enjoyed talking with you the other evening," she began.

Brilliant, she thought. *Next you're going to tell her you saw her in homeroom and you think she's cute.*

"I enjoyed it too," Alex said, clearly a little puzzled.

"Look, Alex, would you like to go out sometime?" CJ took the plunge.

Alex was suddenly very still. "Out?" she said quietly, the word a question.

"Out. Dinner, a movie, miniature golf. A date."

Alex looked away for a moment, and then returned to meet CJ's eyes. "You're gay, I guess," she said.

"Wow, you really are a detective," CJ said lightly.

Alex frowned and CJ added, quickly, "Sorry. Sorry, I'm just a little nervous, I suppose."

Alex leaned back against the counter, and CJ couldn't keep her eyes from trailing down her trim body again.

"Why would you be nervous?" Alex asked, seriously. "I'm guessing that, as you're a lesbian and all, you've asked a woman or two out before."

CJ laughed, trying to release some of the tension building in her chest. "One or two," she admitted. "I think I'm nervous because I really want ya'll to say yes, and I'm not sure you're interested."

Alex had grown still again, and was looking at her with an expression she couldn't read.

"Because I was married?"

"Among other reasons, yes."

Alex didn't say anything else, and CJ waited, trying not to hyperventilate. She could not remember a moment like this since she was nineteen and she kissed her first woman.

Finally Alex said, "I'm sorry. This is…difficult for me."

CJ felt her stomach twist in disappointment. "It's all right," she said, quietly. "I just needed to ask. It's certainly okay to say no."

"It's not quite that simple," Alex admitted, with visible difficulty. "I don't date."

CJ waited for the end of the sentence: *I don't date women.* But Alex stopped, and CJ finally said, "You don't date? I don't understand."

Abruptly, Alex pushed away from the counter. "You don't have to," she said shortly. "I don't date. Anybody. Thanks for asking."

She brushed by CJ and pushed open the door. She was gone before CJ could even turn around.

A stunned CJ had expected a 'no,' hoped for a 'yes,' but this was confusing. *What the devil was that all about?*

Alex made it back to the safety of her office, closing the door behind her.

Closing the door, she thought ironically as she performed the act. *That was really true.*

She hadn't been ready for CJ to ask her out, not ready at all.

Coward, she berated herself. *Why didn't you just say no? Tell her you're straight, and politely decline. St. Clair is a grown-up, she would have accepted that. That would have been the end of it, the mature thing to do.*

But there was a better question: *Why didn't you just say yes?*

Alex dropped her head into her hands. "Oh, hell!" she said out loud.

There was a knock on her door, and she lifted her head. *Not her, not yet. I'm not ready to sort this out yet.*

"Who is it?" she called out.

Detective John Simon opened the door and said, "Captain? Have you heard?"

She shook her head, glad for the interruption. "Come in, John. What's up?"

Simon was a short man, somewhere over forty, and, as always, impeccably dressed. Alex sometimes wondered where he shopped to find suits that were tailored to his small frame.

"They got that guy," he said, excitedly. "The perp who killed that businessman, Ward, in the Springs last week, remember?"

She did remember. A local businessman, a former county commissioner in El Paso County, had been gunned down during what looked to be a failed robbery attempt as he left his office late one evening. Someone had gotten a license plate as the shooter fled the scene, and a BOLO had been issued across the state. Clearly, an alert officer had indeed been on the lookout.

"Who got him?" Alex demanded.

"We did," Simon answered. "One of our patrol officers pulled him over in a stolen car. The guy tried to run, and we arrested him over on University."

Alex smiled grimly. "Good news," she said. "Have we called CSPD yet?"

"Not that I know of."

"I'll call them myself. I'm very sure they'll want him down there first thing Monday morning." She looked at Simon, still bouncing on the balls of his feet.

"John, would you like to do the transport?" she asked him. Transporting suspects to other jurisdictions wasn't a desirable assignment, but there weren't many homicide suspects that passed through Colfax, so perhaps that was what was attracting him.

"That'd be great," he said enthusiastically. "Really great. Monday?"

"I imagine. I'll let you know."

She simultaneously picked up her phone and began to pull up the booking information to begin the creating the transport order, glad of something to take her mind off CJ St. Clair.

CHAPTER FOUR

Alex swirled the rest of the cabernet in her wineglass and looked up at the stars, just beginning to show in the sky at dusk. The sun had set not quite an hour ago, and the sky at the horizon was a deep blue, not black yet. She could see Venus overhead, a steady pinpoint of bright light.

"What on earth is the matter with you?" the voice across the patio demanded.

Alex sighed. "I'm fine," she said. "Just a long week."

She saw the figure shift forward in her chair across the table.

"All your weeks are long. Something's bothering you."

Alex smiled at her sister. Despite the years between them, they looked enough alike to be twins, except for the ten or so extra pounds Nicole Ryan carried. It actually made her look prettier, Alex thought, rounded out those sharp Ryan cheekbones.

"I'm not complaining to you," she said mildly. "You're the one working crazy hours and trying to raise a little boy. All I have to do in my spare time is mow my lawn."

Nicole looked at her closely and said, "I also have the world's best husband to help. Now tell me what's going on with you."

Alex drank some of her wine, deep and rich on her tongue. "Nic, I really don't want to talk about it."

This got her a disgusted snort.

"I am so tired of the stoic cop act," Nicole complained. "Dad was terrible, and you're worse. It will take David a good forty-five minutes to give Charlie his bath and read him a story, so it's just us. Tell me. You've been quiet and cranky all evening."

"I'm always quiet and cranky."

"Knock it off, Alex, or I'll start using my well-honed cross-examination skills on you. Is it something at work, I assume?"

Alex went back to staring at the stars. "It's not work," she admitted. "Something personal."

"Oh, my God!" Nicole exclaimed happily. "It's about time you had something personal to talk about."

Alex gave a little laugh. "Been a while, hasn't it?"

"More than a while. Sometime last decade, I think. I...Oh, no!" she cried.

"What?"

"It's not...tell me it's not Tony."

Alex turned and stared at her. "Why on earth would it be Tony?"

"Because the last time you were all torn up about something personal, you were getting ready to divorce him. He's not back in your life, is he?"

"You know he works across the street from me," Alex said, deliberately provoking her. "I see him once a month or so. He has never really been out of my life."

"Oh, my God!" Nicole was really agitated. "If you even consider going back to that selfish son of a bitch, I'm going to get a court order for a seventy-two hour psych evaluation on you."

Alex leaned forward and grabbed her hand. "Nic, I'm pulling your chain," she admitted. "It has nothing to do with Tony."

Nicole took a long drink as if she needed it. "Well, thank

God for that. But don't think I haven't noticed that you're not telling me what really is going on."

Alex let go of her hand and said, "It's not easy to talk about, Nicole."

Nicole frowned at her, concern creasing her face. "Alex, there's nothing you can't tell me, you know that, don't you? You're not sick, are you?"

Hearing the worry in her voice, Alex hastened to reassure her, "I'm fine. Just a little confused."

"About what?"

Alex leaned away from her again, picking up her glass. "Somebody asked me out," she began, reluctantly. She knew Nicole would not stop until she had the whole story, and Alex wasn't sure herself what the whole story was.

"And why is this confusing?" Nicole demanded.

Alex finally answered, "Because it was a woman," she admitted. "And because I wanted to say yes."

There was silence between them for a long time. From inside the house, there was the sound of happy laughter and splashing. Outside, a water sprinkler swooshed softly, a neighbor getting an early start on the diligent watering Colorado lawns required.

Alex was relieved and anxious at the same time. It was hard enough for her to admit her feelings to herself, but she was worried about what her sister would think, how she would react.

"Tell me about Jennie—what was her name? The tennis player, from college," Nicole said suddenly.

Startled, Alex answered, "Byers. Jennie Byers. I'm surprised you remembered her."

"I was thirteen and awash in hormones," Nicole answered dryly. "Anything remotely to do with sex was interesting. Did she know you had a crush on her?"

Alex laughed bitterly. "I hope not. I hardly admitted it to myself," she answered. "I'm amazed you figured it out."

Nicole drank some wine. "It wasn't that hard. You looked at her as if you would explode. Did you ever do anything about it?"

Alex shook her head in the darkness. "It was just...not an option for me."

"Dad would've blown sky-high," Nicole admitted. "After he promised Mom to raise two good Catholic girls and all." She took another drink, then said, "Jesus, Alex. Are you really a lesbian?"

The words said out loud, by someone else, made the possibility real to Alex.

"Honestly, I have no idea," she answered. "Maybe. Or maybe I'm attracted to both men and women. But if I am, it's only theoretical. I've never slept with a woman." Running a finger around the rim of her glass, she added, "Not that sleeping with men was ever very exciting."

"Then why did you marry that asshole Tony?"

Alex moved on to play with the base of her wineglass a moment. "I don't know. Part of it, I think, is that I was just lonely. You had David, Mom and Dad were gone."

Suddenly, Nicole got up and went around the table to gather Alex into her arms.

"Oh, Alex, I'm sorry," she said softly.

Alex returned the hug and said, "For what? It's no one's fault. If anyone is to blame, it's me. I made the wrong decision about Tony, and I just didn't have the nerve to admit this possibility to myself. I just tried to make it go away, by not ever getting involved with anyone. And now..."

Nicole sat back on her heels to look at her sister in the face. "And so, what? Do you like this woman, the one who asked you out?"

Alex chewed on her lower lip a moment. "That's not the point," she said. "God, Nic, isn't it a little late in the game for me to suddenly decide to do something like this?"

Nicole took Alex's hands in her own. "It's not too late. It's never too late to try to be happy. And whether or not you want to go out with her is exactly the point. You said you did. Do you, really?"

Alex thought about CJ acting nervous when she asked Alex out. For a woman so seemingly confident, the momentary shyness had been almost irresistible.

She took a deep breath and said, "I do."

"Then call her. Try. What do you have to lose?"

Alex searched the upturned face. "You won't hate me, Nic?" she whispered.

The grip on her hands tightened. "You listen to me," Nicole answered firmly. "You're my big sister, my family. You gave up everything for me, your scholarship, tennis, your education, to take care of me when Dad died. There's nothing you could do that would change the fact that I love you. Alex, stop second-guessing yourself and quit maintaining that wall you've been working on all these years. Just call her."

Saturday morning dawned gray and cold. On the balcony of her condo, CJ eyed the sky suspiciously as she tied her shoelaces, wondering if the rain would hold off until she finished her walk. She'd already switched from shorts to leggings, and decided to take a light jacket, just in case.

She was still standing in front of her hall closet, trying to decide which coat to take, when her cell phone rang.

She dug it out of her pocket. She didn't know the number, so she answered, "St. Clair."

"Hi. It's Alex. Alex Ryan."

CJ stopped looking at jackets and leaned back against the wall.

"Hello, Alex Ryan. How are you?"

"I'm, ah, fine. Look, I'd like to talk to you. Do you have time now, or are you doing something?"

CJ smiled into the phone. "I'm not doing anything that can't wait. Do you want to meet somewhere?"

"If it's okay with you, I could come over. If that's all right."

"That," CJ responded carefully, "would be quite all right."

She gave her the address, then hung up thoughtfully.

When there was a sharp knock, she glanced through her peephole before opening the door.

"Alex. Come in."

"I'm not interrupting you, am I?" Alex asked her again.

"No, not at all. I was just going to take a walk."

Alex seemed uncharacteristically anxious, and CJ tried to figure out why. She'd never actually seen Alex look uneasy before. Alex was wearing well-worn denim jeans and a light blue polo. But she looked good, even when she was edgy.

Nothing like a woman in a nice, snug pair of Levi's, CJ mused. Just looking at Alex sent a pleasant flood of warmth cascading down her body.

"I don't want to hold you up," Alex began.

Impulsively, CJ asked, "Do you want to come with me? I go at a pretty good pace, but I suspect you've already done your workout, haven't you?"

Alex nodded. "I did my three-mile run this morning, but I'm happy to go with you. There's something I want to say first."

CJ felt her heart speed up.

Alex cleared her throat and said, "I owe you an apology."

CJ gave a little sigh of relief. "Yes," she agreed. "You do."

Alex looked surprised, then she smiled. "Direct, aren't you?" she remarked.

CJ shrugged. "Not always, but I have a feeling you can handle direct. You do owe me an apology, and I want you to know I will accept it."

Alex seemed to be regaining her composure. "You still want me to do it formally?" she asked, a little amused.

CJ answered brightly, "I do, actually. I once lived with a woman whose idea of an apology was 'I'm sorry if I made you mad.' That is *not* an apology for bad behavior."

"Point taken. In that case, I'd like to say that I was rude to you when you asked me out, and I'm sorry. There is really no excuse for my bad manners, and I apologize."

CJ grinned at her. "That was a very good apology, and ya'll are completely forgiven," she responded happily. "Now we can forget about it and be friends."

Alex grew serious and CJ felt the pressure begin to build in her chest again, hope fluttering against her breastbone like a caged bird.

"Being friends is fine," Alex said slowly. "But I'm wondering if you'll let me reconsider my answer to your question. If the offer is still open, I'd like to go out with you."

"Really?" CJ heard the elation in her own voice.

Alex smiled at her. "If you're willing to take a chance on me, I'd like to give it a try."

"Why am I taking a chance?"

The smiled faded a little. Alex said, "I have some…history."

CJ reached across and squeezed her arm gently. "Alex, everybody over age sixteen has some kind of history. Believe me, I've got some baggage in the closet myself."

She saw Alex wince, and she said quickly, "What?"

After a moment, Alex answered, "You may have baggage, but I don't think it's in the closet, is it?"

Light began to dawn for CJ. She said, "It looks like it's going to rain anyway. I think I'll skip the walk today. Why don't ya'll come all the way inside, and I'll make us some coffee."

"I could use some, I think," Alex said.

CJ led her from the foyer. They stepped into the one large room that served as living room, dining room and kitchen. The furnishings were tasteful and expensive-looking, dark wood and brushed nickel against hardwood floors and a couple of beautiful Oriental rugs to add subtle color to the room. The windows were huge, with a magnificent view of downtown Denver several miles away to the north, and a panoramic vista of the mountains to the west.

There were signs of CJ's casual attitude toward housekeeping: a pile of newspapers on one table, and a massive leaning tower of magazines in the corner. There were books everywhere, on shelves, or stacked by the couch. One volume was open on top of the couch, a second lay open on the coffee table.

"This is a great place," Alex said. "Can I help you?"

"No, sit down. I'll just be a second."

Alex wandered over to look at the books: they were almost all nonfiction, history, biography, poetry, several books about psychology or sociology. The open book on the couch was a new Lincoln biography. On the coffee table was poetry, Emily Dickinson. It looked well-loved, the pages creased in places.

When CJ brought in a tray with coffeepot, cups and a small pitcher, she asked, "Is regular okay for ya'll? I don't actually have decaffeinated in the house."

Alex said, smiling, "It's still before noon, so regular is great. Do you always read two books at once?"

CJ laughed. "I do, actually. Sometimes three, even. Keeps me from getting bored. Do you like to read?"

Alex accepted a cup and saucer, and answered, "Very much. But I read junk."

"Junk?"

"Fiction. I get enough of reality at work. When I read for pleasure, I read mysteries, usually."

CJ gazed at her in amazement over her coffee cup. "Mysteries? Sounds like a busman's holiday."

"Not stories about cops, I hate those. No, I like the 'body in the library, little old lady detective' ones. Cozies, I think they're called. They're nothing like reality, and that's why I like them. Agatha Christie. I like that new series, the one set in Africa."

Stirring in her cream, CJ asked, "Do you like books better than movies?"

Alex cocked her head to one side, considering. Away from work, she seemed younger, vulnerable even. CJ thought she looked adorable.

"They're really different, aren't they?" she asked rhetorically. "With books the author can tell the reader so much, what characters are thinking or feeling. But with a good movie, actors can convey so much with just a look, sometimes things it would be hard to describe with words."

Alex drank coffee, and CJ had a moment of deep contentment. She was actually sitting in her living room, having coffee, and talking about books and movies with Alex Ryan.

She hated to ruin the mood, but she knew how much more she wanted from the relationship than friendship. Now that they were going to date—CJ could hardly believe her good fortune—she wanted to clear the air, sweep away any hesitations or objections Alex might have.

"Tell me," she began softly, "what you're worried about. About us going out, I mean."

Alex set her cup down with a small clatter, and CJ could see her uneasiness return.

"I told you I was married."

"Yes."

"I've never dated a woman before," Alex admitted.

CJ took a deep breath. "I'd sort of figured that out. Why have ya'll decided to do it now?"

Alex fidgeted with the cup, moving it against the rim on the saucer. "Because," she hesitated, then continued, "I've been attracted to women before. For a long time I didn't want to admit that to myself. And even when I did, I've just never done anything about it. And, as a result, I haven't been in any kind of relationship more serious than a few weeks since I got divorced."

"How long ago was that?" CJ asked quietly.

"Almost eight years."

CJ, a little surprised, tried to decide if she was more relieved or worried. "I suppose I should ask why you never acted on your attraction for women."

Alex's fidgeting continued. "My mother was a very devout Catholic," she began. "My father was sort of lukewarm about his religion, but he promised Mom to raise Nicole and me in the Church. I was just in denial, CJ. I just could not imagine giving in to what I thought was a sin, I suppose. I couldn't picture what it would be like to come out. Anyway, then Dad was killed, and I had to quit and go to work, take care of Nic, and, later, when she met David...I married Tony because he seemed to love me, and because I wanted someone of my own, I suppose. And, maybe, to prove to myself that I was totally and completely straight."

She lifted her eyes, dark blue and troubled, to CJ's gaze. "But I'm not," she finished.

"You sound pretty sure."

Alex gave a little ironic laugh. "As sure as I can be at this point," she said. "Apparently my sister figured me out a long time ago. And I've had enough lousy sex with men that...well, hell, if I don't at least try dating a woman, I'm doomed to a life of celibacy."

I certainly hope not, CJ thought. She said, "Are you sure you can overcome feeling like you're some kind of sinner? Because that's a tough one, I know. I was raised in a very conservative Protestant denomination myself."

Alex answered, "Honestly, I don't know. I think so. I'm not a kid anymore, afraid of what other people will think. And I fell off the Catholic wagon a long time ago, somewhere between using birth control and getting divorced. And neither of those made me feel like a sinner."

"Sex is different," CJ said gently. "I think you could be more troubled by that than by getting divorced."

Suddenly the air in the room seemed different, like electricity in the atmosphere before a storm.

Very softly, Alex replied, "Perhaps. But I need to try and find out."

CJ, her mouth suddenly dry, drank coffee. She recalled the feeling she was having, the intoxicating blend of intellectual attraction and physical desire forming an irresistible intoxicant.

It had been a very long time, but she remembered it well.

"Tonight," she managed. "Would you like to go out tonight?"

Alex looked at her steadily, and finally said, "Yes. I think it's a bit chilly for miniature golf, so I'll find a movie. There's a new Woody Allen. Okay?"

"Yes," CJ answered, trying to decide how difficult it would be to wait seven or eight hours to see her again.

As they were strolling toward a coffee place after the movie, Alex asked indignantly, "How the hell can you not love *Annie Hall?*"

CJ said, "I know it won all those awards and all, but I still don't like it as much as ya'll apparently do."

"Come on, CJ. It's one of the funniest movies ever."

"Well, that's high praise coming from you, Captain."

Alex lifted a sardonic eyebrow. "Are you saying I don't have a sense of humor?"

CJ, considering, answered, "Let's say I suspect your sense of humor is...highly selective."

"Very tactful. So why don't you think *Annie Hall* is funny?"

"Oh, it's very funny. Lobsters, and spiders the size of Buicks, and all. I just don't like it very much."

"Why not?"

"It doesn't have a happy ending."

"Excuse me?"

"At the end of the movie, they're not together. That is not my idea of a happy ending. I really, really like happy endings."

"What are you, eight years old?" Alex teased her.

"No," CJ said primly.

"You're a hopeless romantic," Alex guessed.

CJ didn't deny it. "It's mandatory for Southern girls."

The evening was milder than the day had been, with no wind. They took coffee to a small table outside, decaf black for Alex, latte for CJ. When CJ noticed Alex covering a yawn, she joked, "Past your bedtime? Or am I boring you?"

"Sorry. You are not remotely boring, but it is close to my bedtime. I'm normally asleep by ten. Usually on the couch."

CJ suddenly looked sad. She took a long drink and changed the subject. "Ah. Good coffee is one of life's great pleasures."

Alex answered, "Well, bad coffee is certainly one of life's great disappointments."

"Stop looking on the down side. Come on, what makes your list of life's greatest joys?" She lifted one eyebrow a little, and Alex wondered how anyone so beautiful could possibly be interested in her.

"Let me think," Alex began. "I love it when you have that moment, the second when you finally put the pieces together, and you've figured out the puzzle. I like when you put the cuffs on the perp and you know you got the bad guy."

CJ pulled a face and said, "I was hoping for something not related to work."

"Come on, you have great moments at work, don't you?"

CJ considered briefly, then smiled and responded, "I like figuring out how to approach people to get what we need. My favorite is when you're talking to someone, and you see them in the lie, and you know, just know, that you're going to get to the truth. I love that." She drank more coffee, and said, "Now, come on. Not work-related."

Alex really had to think for a couple of minutes. Finally she said, "I like when I turn the corner onto my street at the end of my run, and I can see the house. I know I'm almost done, that I've done something good for myself. I usually sprint the last hundred yards or so. In the winter the hot shower feels good. In the summer, it feels great to cool off. I like sitting outside, listening to music or a game on the radio, drinking a beer, and looking at the sky. And even though I can't cook, I do like a nice meal."

CJ smiled encouragingly and said, "See, that's a good list. I knew you could do it."

Alex shook her head in amusement and said dryly, "Okay, all right. Your turn."

CJ put her cup down and propped her chin in her hand. "Life's great pleasures. Let's see. Finding the perfect pair of shoes. Cooking a wonderful meal—and eating it with friends. Bubble baths. Sitting down with a new book you've been looking forward to reading."

"I like that one, too," Alex said.

"Um, what else? I like Christmas, all holidays, really. I like to drive fast."

That one got a smile from Alex. "Yeah, I noticed that on the way over. Got a lot of speeding tickets in our jacket, do we, Inspector?"

CJ gave her a dazzling smile. "Only a couple," she said. "I usually get out of them."

A sudden moment of discomfort tightened Alex's stomach.

CJ, reading the look, said quickly, "Alex. I was referring to my ability to charm the traffic officer. I would never badge my way out of a ticket. I'm in I.A. remember?"

Alex searched her face. "If we're going to date, you should know how much being a good cop, an honest cop, means to me," she said simply.

CJ reached across the table and laid her hand over Alex's. Even the casual touch sent a shock of pleasure up Alex's arm.

"Me, too," CJ said. "One of the things I like best about you is how seriously you take your job, how much you've accomplished in your career. I respect and admire you for it, Alex."

Alex, relieved, asked, "Is that why you wanted to go out with me?"

CJ sat back and her lids hooded her eyes a moment. "Among other reasons," she said, and her soft voice sent the same jolt of pleasure into Alex that her touch had done a moment before.

As they got in CJ's Lexus for the drive home, Alex asked, "Do you really charm your way out of speeding tickets?"

CJ laughed and said, "Yes, and here's the funny part. It always works with men, but I've been stopped twice by women and it didn't work either time."

Buckling her seat belt, Alex said, smiling, "Maybe they were straight."

CJ said, "Well, the first one, maybe, but the woman motorcycle cop up in Northminster...if she wasn't gay, I'm a Yankee."

Alex went up in the elevator to CJ's condo, her stomach tight with a pleasant tension.

CJ unlocked her door, and they stepped into her foyer. "I'm sorry," she said softly. "I'd invite you in, but I have to get up early tomorrow and go somewhere."

Alex felt a tiny surge of jealousy.

"Another date?" she tried to make it sound like a joke, not to sound as worried as she felt.

"No, Alex," CJ said quietly. "I never date more than one woman at a time. But one of my friends from Roosevelt, Rod Chavez, is having a birthday. His wife is throwing a surprise party, and I agreed to go over early, help with the cooking."

"Okay," Alex said, both in regret and relief.

"So it's good night, I guess," CJ said, clearly reluctant for her to leave. "I had a really nice time."

"I did, too," Alex said. "Can I ask you question?"

"Of course."

"Do you kiss on the first date?"

CJ said, smiling a little, "No. But by my calculations, this is our fourth date."

"Interesting math. How did you figure that out?"

"Coffee date this morning, drinks at the grill a couple of weeks ago. And then there was our first date, in the parking lot of K-Mart."

Alex laughed. *She's beautiful, and smart, and she makes me laugh. And she makes me want to touch her.*

"How do you figure that arrest was a date?" she asked, smiling.

CJ answered primly, "You saw me in my brassiere. Definitely a date."

Alex laughed again, then asked hopefully, "Do you kiss after the fourth date, then?"

"Absolutely," CJ said quietly, and Alex felt the knot in her stomach clench.

CJ stepped in close, looking her full in the eyes for a long moment. Alex could not bear to look away, and as the gaze continued, it flooded her with longing.

Alex stood still, waiting, her heart pounding in her throat.

CJ leaned in, bringing both of her hands up to Alex's face. She held her gently and brought her lips down until they were just touching Alex's own.

Alex felt CJ take a deep breath, and she took one of her own, taking in the sweet scent of CJ's skin, spring flowers after a rain.

CJ kissed her.

The kiss was both soft and firm, yielding and demanding, and Alex gave herself up to it, giving and receiving in turn.

Alex brought her hands up to CJ's waist, feeling her shape through the soft sweater, and pulled her in. She could feel CJ's body all along the length of her own. It felt odd at first, nothing like embracing a man, but electric at the same time.

Alex felt as if she had fallen into hot wax, melting into the embrace. CJ's breath drifted across her cheek, warm and soft.

Overwhelmed with touch and smell, Alex could hardly bear the additional sensation of the way CJ tasted, vanilla and spice and something else, something exquisitely unique to CJ herself.

Alex had no idea how long the kiss lasted, or the next one, or the one after that. She would willingly have spent a lifetime in the dark hall, hearing the sound of CJ's breathing, feeling CJ's body against her, smelling her scent, tasting her mouth.

When CJ finally released her face and stepped back, Alex was surprised that she could still stand. She was, literally, weak in the knees. Her whole body was alight with sweet, aching need, a feeling she could never remember having before, a feeling she'd never imagined she could have. She wanted to thrust her hands into the red hair and pull CJ to her again, taste her, feel her body.

The careful walls that had protected her heart for so long suddenly seemed very fragile.

CJ took one step back and asked hoarsely, "Do you feel like a sinner?"

Alex brushed CJ's lips lightly with one fingertip. "Not even a little."

"I'm glad. Goodnight, Alex."

It took her a long time sitting in the parking lot before Alex felt calm enough to drive home.

CHAPTER FIVE

Alex stood at the whiteboard in the Investigations conference room at exactly eight a.m. on Monday morning and looked at her squad. The uniformed officers downstairs were at a much more formal roll call, but Alex's version for the detectives was more casual, though it served the same purpose: a group update on what was happening.

Names of cases were written on the whiteboard in Alex's neat hand, with columns for the detectives assigned and a brief status note. Alex looked at her notes again, then said, "Let's get started."

Detective Roger Fullerton looked at the pastry in his hand and said, "God, I hate this jelly crap. Can't we have real doughnuts?"

Frank Morelli answered, "If you don't like the selection, Fullerton, why don't you buy them?"

Fullerton snorted, "I have a lot better things to do with my time than buy damn doughnuts. That's what I have a partner for."

He gave his partner, the innocuous Kelly Porter, a nasty smirk. Porter seemed to shrink a little in his chair, and Alex thought, not for the first time, what a pain in the ass Fullerton was. She really ought to figure out someone else to work with him, but the only person she could think of who could put up with him was Frank's partner, the easygoing Stan Rosenthal. But Stan was going to retire in a few months.

She shoved the problem to the back of her mind and said, "Knock it off, Fullerton. Since you've got the burglaries cleared, you and Porter are assigned to a high school break-in we had Saturday night at Prairie Hill."

Fullerton snorted his disgust. "Geez, what'd they steal? Geometry books?"

Alex fixed him with a look. "An interesting variety of items from the chem lab, actually."

Fullerton threw his half-eaten jelly doughnut into the trash can. "Burglary by a bunch of teenagers? That's our reward for clearing the biggest case of the year?"

The room was suddenly silent. Alex wasn't a particularly strict commanding officer, but while the free exchange of ideas was encouraged, insubordination was not. Morelli glared, seemingly ready to take Fullerton outside for a little chat, Kelly Porter looked like he wanted to crawl under the table, even Stan appeared dismayed. Everyone else found the carpet suddenly very interesting.

Alex very carefully laid her notes on the table and waited until Roger met her stare.

"Detective, if you can bring yourself to do some actual investigative work, we might be able to find a drug operation around somewhere. And as for clearing the burglaries," she added, her voice a lash, "you didn't actually arrest Mr. Milton, did you?"

Roger shifted his eyes angrily to Morelli. "We were the cops getting shot at," he complained, as if he expected support.

Morelli snorted in disgust. "But you weren't the ones who

got the shit beaten out of you, were you?" he said harshly. "And it was the new I.A. inspector who collared the guy, and she got plenty beaten up doing it, too, while you were busy getting your ass out of the way."

Roger's eyes narrowed. "You listen to me, you—" he began.

Alex snapped, "Stop right there. One more word, Fullerton, and you're looking at disciplinary action, is that clear?"

Roger turned his glare back to her, and she repeated. "Is that clear, Detective?"

A muscle worked in his jaw, but all he said, was, "Yeah."

"Good. Let's move on. Simon is doing a transport this morning on the homicide suspect for the Springs. You have the paperwork, John?"

"All set," Simon responded. He seemed almost ready to bolt out of the room, his hands shaking a little with suppressed excitement. Alex had never seen anyone so jazzed about driving a hundred and twenty miles back and forth on the interstate.

"Morelli, you and Rosenthal have the Hobart sexual assault to follow up on, right?"

She continued the meeting, as she had several hundred times before, but everything seemed brighter, sharper this morning. Not even the argument with Roger Fullerton could ruin her good mood.

Alex knew why. She'd been in bed last night when the phone rang.

"I didn't wake ya'll up, did I?" CJ had asked.

"No," Alex said, leaning back happily against the pillows. "I was just deciding whether or not to read another chapter."

"Want to get back to your book?"

Alex answered easily, "Nope. I'd rather talk to you. How was the party?"

"Pretty amazing. We actually surprised Rod, which is almost impossible to do. He spent the first hour wandering around saying, 'How the hell did this happen?'"

Alex smiled. "How was the food? Any good?"

In mock indignation, CJ answered, "It was wonderful, of course. Sort of a Mexican-Southern cuisine amalgam, which is to be expected when Ana Chavez and I are in the same kitchen."

"And what did that look like? Enchiladas with hush puppies?"

CJ laughed. A whole twenty-four hours, and Alex had almost forgotten how much she liked the sound of her laughter.

"No," she answered, still laughing. "More like chile chitlins."

"That sounds awful."

"Actually, it would be. That's why you have to have the cerveza and margueritas to wash it down."

"May I tell you…your Spanish accent is really terrible."

"So I have been told. I keep meaning to work on it."

"Anything else on your list to work on?" Alex asked, wondering what direction CJ would take the conversation.

"Oh, yes," CJ said softly, and Alex felt her breathing increase from the sound of her voice. "I think maybe I'd like to work on seeing you again, very soon."

Alex answered simply, "When?"

"I'd offer you breakfast, but I'm just not a morning person. I have enough trouble getting to work on time. Lunch?"

"Yes," Alex said, realizing that she was smiling into the receiver. "Lunch is good. But I think I need to ask—will that be our fifth date?"

CJ laughed again. "No, ya'll haven't figured out the math yet. That will be number six. This conversation counts as one, too."

"Does it?"

"It does. And that is important because that means dinner tomorrow evening will be date number seven."

Now Alex was having trouble getting enough air.

"What happens on date number seven?" she managed to ask.

There was a long pause, then CJ said, "Tell me if I'm moving too fast for you, Alex."

"Okay, I'll let you know. But I should tell you I'm really looking forward to dinner."

Now Alex looked up at the clock in the conference room and tried not to smile. Only three hours and fifteen minutes left before lunchtime.

At eleven forty-five a.m., CJ's office phone rang. She smiled at the interoffice caller ID and picked up with a happy, "Are we allowed to go to lunch early?"

Alex said grimly, "Change of plans. What's on your schedule for the afternoon?"

Normally the question would have pleased her, but Alex did not sound happy. CJ said quickly, "Nothing I can't reset or get Chad to handle. What's up?"

"I've got a missing homicide suspect and a detective in the emergency room in Castle Rock," she said, naming the small city halfway between Denver and Colorado Springs.

CJ asked, "You want me to go down with you, I assume?"

"Yes. You'll have to do an investigation sooner or later, so we might as well drive down together. Maybe we could drive through and eat on the road."

CJ was already opening drawers, trying to remember which one she'd stowed her purse in that morning.

"How badly is your detective hurt?"

"Don't know. He was doing a suspect transport to the Springs and something obviously went very wrong. Will you go?"

She spotted her purse hanging by its strap on the back of her office door. CJ got up, stretching the phone cord over her desk. "Of course. Do ya'll want me to drive?"

Alex, trying for a lighter tone, said, "No. I don't want to stop to watch you bat your eyelashes at some state trooper while you talk your way out of another speeding ticket. Besides, we can't have french fries all over your nice fancy car, can we? I'll meet you by the back door in five, okay?"

"I'll be there," CJ said, struggling into her jacket.

Lone Pine Regional Hospital was a modern facility, built to confuse visitors from the outside of the building and bewilder them once inside. A variety of color-coded signs indicated departments from radiology to obstetrics, but CJ found herself lost by the time they got a few feet inside.

Alex, however, marched with confidence around one corner, down a hall, and circled to a desk marked emergency.

A little winded, CJ asked, "Have you been here before, or do you have a GPS implanted on your body somewhere?"

Alex said crisply, "My sister lives nearby, and my nephew was born here." She showed her badge to the woman at the desk and asked, "Simon?"

"Cubicle Two."

Crowded into the small room were Simon, sitting up on an examining table, a physician and a nurse, both in purple scrub suits, and two uniformed officers wearing Castle Rock PD uniforms.

CJ eased back against a wall, prepared to watch and listen. The first priority was finding the escaped suspect; her investigation into any charges against Simon could wait.

Alex introduced herself to everyone, then asked Simon, "How are you, John?"

CJ noted that she asked Simon directly, not the doctor. Alex had already taken control of the room, perhaps without even knowing that she did it.

Watching Alex, CJ felt herself slip a little closer to the edge of a dangerous precipice. She already admired Alex, liked her, and God knew the physical spark was there, for her at least. It was too soon to think of anything else, much too soon.

Simon answered, "I feel like shit, Captain."

He looked a little groggy, but not badly hurt. His coat jacket was on the examining table, dirty but undamaged. CJ couldn't see any blood, or really any injury other than a small bump on his forehead. She relaxed a fraction—he didn't appear to be in any danger.

The doctor said, "We need to do a CAT scan. All head injuries are potentially serious."

Alex asked, "Blow to the head, then?"

Simon nodded, then added, "I feel like somebody used my head like a punching bag. Fuck."

"What do you remember?" Alex asked.

"I don't remember shit," he said in disgust, shaking his head. "I get the guy from County Detention, we're driving, and then…zip."

CJ watched the uniforms making notes, and heard the doctor making arrangements with the nurse for the scan, but she was watching the interaction between Alex and Simon. Something seemed off to her.

"John, what's the last thing you do remember?"

He stared off into space, cocking his head as if remembering, then answered, "Wolfensberger Road. The exit sign, I mean."

"Did you take the exit?" Alex persisted.

He shook his head. "I don't remember."

The doctor, attempting to regain control of his examination, said, "Retrograde amnesia is very common with head trauma. It could last from a few seconds to several hours. We really do need to get him to the CT scanner."

When Simon was transported out in a wheelchair, Alex turned to the uniformed officers and said, "What have you got?"

"A trucker called it in at ten fifty-one a.m.," the older man replied. "Saw a body by the side of the road. We responded, found him unconscious, called the paramedics. When we saw from his ID that he was a police officer, we secured his identification and weapon. It's locked in our unit outside."

Alex nodded. "Thanks. Where exactly was he?"

"On the shoulder out on Topeka Road." He gave her the location. "It's about fifteen minutes or so from the interstate. No witnesses yet. If you can give us the descriptions, we'll put out an APB right away."

Alex said, "We've already put one out for both the suspect and the car. Any information on what happened?"

The officer shrugged, and answered, "Looks like the guy got out of his cuffs somehow, hit your detective on the head, dumped him, and took the car."

When they had gone, Alex said, "I imagine John will be tied up for a while. Want to go for a ride?"

CJ pushed away from the wall and said, "Absolutely. Are we going to Topeka Road?"

"Oh, yes," Alex said grimly.

They sat in silence in Alex's SUV at the dead end of Topeka Road. A few minutes spent in examination of the scene had been enough—there was nothing to see, no tire tracks on the unpaved shoulder, nothing in the deep ditch beyond. The faint hum of afternoon traffic on the interstate a couple of miles away reached them, but this part of town, though it was within Castle Rock's city limits, was no more than an empty field. The nearest building was a fast-food place a good quarter mile away, the garish sign interestingly distorted through a meandering crack in the windshield.

CJ said mildly, "I'm going to assume this lovely truck is not your department-issued vehicle."

Alex laughed. "No. My official Ford is in the shop. They offered me a loaner, but I didn't want to have to swap out twice, so I'm driving my own car."

CJ surveyed the battered interior and said, "I think I would have taken the loaner from the pool myself."

"This wasn't my choice," Alex said. "It was a lovely parting gift from the ex."

"You've been driving this for eight years?"

"More like ten."

"Might be time for a visit to the dealership."

"Not everyone can buy this year's model," Alex said calmly, not wanting to sound envious.

"Of course not," CJ agreed gracefully, "but a new car once a decade might be all right."

Alex chuckled a little, then she sighed and said, dryly, "I'm having a little trouble with this scenario."

"I imagine so," CJ answered. "Want to do this out loud?"

Alex glanced at her, a little surprised, and said, "Okay. For starters, why here? The suspect, Perrault, wants to get away as fast as he can. Why drive out here?"

"To hide Simon, give himself more time before he's discovered," CJ supplied.

"Then why not dump him in the ditch instead of by the side of the road, where anybody can—and actually did—see him within a few minutes."

"He's not thinking clearly?" CJ suggested.

"All right," Alex conceded, then continued, "How did he get out of his cuffs? And what the hell did he hit Simon with that had him unconscious for most of an hour but doesn't leave more than the tiny bump we saw?"

"Simon's service weapon?" CJ mused, before adding, "No, that's not right. Castle Rock PD recovered his gun. He could have banged Simon's head against the car, or the ground."

"But there would be more than just the injury he seems to have. And that's another point. Why the hell didn't he take John's gun? Perrault allegedly murdered a man, surely he wouldn't balk at taking Simon's weapon." Alex shook her head. "Christ, he would have taken his wallet too. At least the cash in it. This is starting not to add up."

"I'm afraid I'll have to make it worse," CJ said. "Were you watching Simon in the emergency room? He was nodding or shaking his head as you questioned him. People with bad headaches don't do that, typically."

Alex looked at her for a long moment. "I didn't notice that," she admitted.

"And it is so very convenient," CJ added gently, "that Detective Simon can't remember what happened."

Alex stared out the windshield for a long moment. Her first instinct was to defend Simon, but she recognized the problems with his situation, and she wanted to trust that CJ would be fair.

"I don't know what happened, but we have got to find Perrault," Alex said at length. "He's dangerous as hell."

"You'll get him," CJ said, with quiet confidence.

Alex turned in the seat and met her eyes. "If Simon had anything at all to do with this…" she began.

"I know how you feel, Alex. Don't worry. I'll do everything I can to find out what happened. I promise."

Alex sighed and said, "Meantime, we've got to find this guy. I'm not feeling optimistic about our dinner tonight."

"Don't worry," CJ said reassuringly. "Why don't you call me when you're ready to leave? You have to eat sometime, and I hate for you to work too late."

An emotion Alex could hardly identify suddenly overpowered her. She'd been so used to managing everything alone, keeping her thoughts and her feelings private for so long, that just having someone who cared about what time she got home for dinner seemed overwhelming.

What was she feeling? Trust? Some of that, certainly. Or, perhaps for the first time in a very long time, she was just feeling that someone else truly cared about her.

CJ balanced a sack in her hands as she watched Alex unlock her front door. They stepped inside and Alex turned off her alarm system. The house was more like a cottage, really, compact but with period details like cove ceilings and a real working fireplace. CJ saw that Alex had done some nice things inside: Arts and Crafts furniture, a Tiffany lamp, muted green and gold paint colors. The place was clean and very tidy, not surprisingly, since Alex had the neatest desk CJ had ever seen for a police officer. CJ thought ruefully of her own condo, where nothing was ever in the right place.

Alex said, again, "You didn't have to do this. Drive all the way over here this late."

"It's fine," CJ answered. "You have to eat and I like to cook. Problem solved."

Alex led her into the small kitchen at the back, and CJ said, "Why don't you sit down? It'll just take a minute for me to reassemble this and heat it."

"Do you want a beer? Or some coffee?"

CJ gestured with her chin at the bag on the counter. "I brought half a bottle of wine, would that be all right?"

Alex got up to get a wineglass, asking, "Do you want some?"

"A small glass. I'm driving."

She busied herself with the food, then presented the plate to Alex with a flourish.

"Voilà. Clara Washington's famous meatloaf. Eat it while it's hot."

She sat with Alex at the small table in the kitchen and watched with pleasure while Alex took her first bite.

"Oh, my God," Alex murmured. "Who is Clara Washington, and can I marry her?"

CJ grinned. "Sorry, she has been happily married to Mason for the past forty-six years."

"Who is she, really?"

"Our cook when I was growing up. Before I emigrated from the state of Georgia, I tracked her down and got her best recipes."

"This is fantastic. What's in here?"

CJ waggled a finger, and answered, "I am sworn to secrecy. I can, however, hint that the other half of the burgundy went for a good cause."

"Is it in the meatloaf or in the cook?"

CJ laughed. "Well, most of it is in the meatloaf," she admitted.

She sat in a pleased silence while Alex ate with gusto, watching her. Everything about Alex attracted her, but more than anything she was drawn to her energy. Just being with her was exhilarating.

Finally, Alex pushed the empty plate away, sighing happily. "That was amazing," she said. "You weren't kidding about being a great cook."

CJ bowed her head. "All compliments gratefully accepted," she said.

Alex sat back in her chair and fingered her glass, her eyes fixed on the deep red depths of the wine.

Softly, CJ asked, "Do you want to talk? Or do you just want me to go home?"

Alex lifted her gaze and said, "It'll take me awhile to wind down enough to sleep. Would you mind staying awhile? We could just talk."

Deeply happy, CJ smiled and said, "I'd like that. Do you want to talk about work?"

Alex sighed and said, "Not much. Our murder suspect,

Perrault, has disappeared off the map. No sign of him or the car. I am very unhappy about having every law enforcement agency in the region looking for a murder suspect my department managed to lose, but mostly I'm pissed off that we've got a very dangerous man in the wind."

"What about Simon? Is he all right?"

"Apparently. They're keeping him overnight for observation, but the diagnosis is mild concussion. He still doesn't remember what happened." She rubbed a hand across her forehead and said, "You know, I really don't want to talk about it anymore tonight, CJ. Let's talk about something more interesting."

"What did you have in mind?"

Alex dropped her gaze to the table, then reached across for CJ's hand. She rubbed her thumb lightly across CJ's fingers, and said, "This looks like a professional manicure."

CJ liked the feel of Alex's hand on her. She answered, "Yes, mani-pedi once a week, without fail."

Alex stroked her fingertips across CJ's nails, with their cherry blossom pink color.

"Most women would keep much longer nails with that much attention, I would think."

CJ looked down at Alex holding her hand, still stroking the short, rounded nails. Clearing her throat, she waited until Alex looked up at her before saying, "Long nails interfere with a number of activities. Typing reports, firing my service weapon… and other things."

She stopped and Alex actually blushed. CJ smiled.

Alex asked, abruptly, "You have money, don't you?"

A little startled, CJ responded, "Yes. Does that bother you?"

"No, unless you got it doing something particularly illicit."

CJ sat back and said, "It's a long story. It involves my family, and why I left Georgia."

Alex withdrew her hand, finished her wine, and said, "I imagine you're not ready to tell me about that."

Surprisingly, CJ found herself more than ready. It was increasingly clear to her that the relationship with Alex was moving quickly into a place that could be serious, at least for her. She wanted Alex to know her deeply, and disclosing this was part of that desire.

"I would like to tell you, actually," she began. "But this could take a little while."

Alex got up and said, "The couch is a lot more comfortable. Do you want coffee now?"

CJ answered, "No, but thanks."

They sat together on the couch, but at opposite ends. Alex picked up a remote and Ella Fitzgerald began to sing softly into the room.

CJ said, "Ah, you like the classics."

"Absolutely. Frank, Ella, and, of course, Mel Torme."

"I can see I'll have to broaden my musical tastes."

Alex smiled and said, "I'll look forward to helping you with your education."

Suddenly every phrase seemed to be laden with double meanings.

"Are you flirting with me, Captain?" she asked.

Alex's smile broadened and she answered, "Absolutely. How's that going?"

"Just fine." Then CJ closed her eyes a moment, and finally asked, "You sure you want to hear all of this?"

Alex replied seriously, "Very sure."

CJ sat back and turned her body away slightly. She didn't want to watch Alex's face.

"I really didn't know," she began cryptically. "I'd dated a few boys when I was at prep school, nothing serious. There was one guy at college, but that wasn't serious, either. I was quite the romantic, I did believe in falling in love forever, finding your soul mate. I just never suspected I would fall in love with another woman. And when I did, I fell all the way. I thought it was the real thing, forever."

"What was her name?" Alex asked gently.

CJ sighed. "Laurel. Her name was Laurel." CJ wrapped her arms around her body, as if she were suddenly cold. "I was nineteen. I wanted her the moment we met, and I had no idea what to do with those feelings. She was older, sure of herself, sure of what she wanted. I would tell you she seduced me, but I was already so in love with her that it hardly took any effort."

"And she's what happened with your family," Alex said.

CJ gave a small, bitter laugh. "I waited almost a year to tell them, when Laurel and I were ready to move in together. I was apprehensive, but I figured they would accept it eventually. I could not have been more wrong. My father, I don't know—he was in shock, at first, but we might have reached some peace between us. But he just sat there, speechless, while my mother… she called me every name you can think of, and a few more besides. I really had no idea she even knew what some of those words meant. I was furious, shocked, hurt, and I flew out of the house. I haven't spoken to either one of them since that night. No one in my family will talk to me. My own brother wouldn't return my phone calls."

She realized as she spoke that the pain of it was always there with her, sometimes deeply buried, sometimes close to the surface.

She continued, "But I was still a romantic. It was just one more reason for me to be with Laurel. She *really* loved me, I thought, unlike my own family. They didn't attend my college graduation, but I didn't care. I had her.

"She was already a teaching assistant, and I got into the master's program. I had our lives planned. I would get my doctorate, and she'd teach somewhere." CJ fell silent a moment, steeling herself for the next words. It was harder to talk about than she'd even suspected.

"We'd been together almost four years. I was just about done with my degree," CJ continued, so softly she could hardly hear herself. "I came back to the apartment early that evening. I was supposed to be finishing up my thesis, but I was tired, and I wanted to be with her. I walked in to find her in bed with another woman, one of her undergraduate students."

"God, CJ."

"And you know what the terrible thing was? I just might have forgiven her, I really might have. If she'd gotten out of our bed and told me it was just a fling or something, I would have taken her back. I'd probably still be with her today, putting up with her unfaithfulness and telling myself that her affairs didn't mean anything, that I was the one she really loved. I think I could have fooled myself into thinking that."

She stopped for a moment. "But she didn't do that," CJ continued at last. "She laughed at me, and told me that I was a convenient rich girl to keep her warm at night while she looked around to find someone she really wanted. She said she knew how I felt about her, and she used me to get what she wanted. I snapped. I screamed at the woman she was with until the girl grabbed her clothes and ran out of the apartment. Then I put my hands on Laurel..." Her heart was pounding at the memory.

CJ said stiffly, "I wanted to kill her, I really did. I saw my love turn to hatred in the blink of an eye. She was taunting me, telling me she'd never loved me, trying to hurt me, and I wanted to kill her."

"But you didn't," Alex said.

CJ gave the bitter laugh again. "Not because I didn't want to, believe me."

CJ turned back to Alex for the first time, and saw unshed tears behind Alex's eyes. She realized that she was crying herself.

"I literally, physically, threw her out of the apartment. I'm not proud of it. I told her if I ever saw her again, I *would* kill her. My name was on the lease, she couldn't do anything. I actually got a restraining order, if you can believe that, although she certainly had much better grounds than I did. I just had more money and a lawyer." She laughed a little again, at the irony.

Alex said, "You didn't talk to your family after that?"

CJ shook her head. "They didn't object to Laurel specifically. They didn't know her. They objected to the fact that I was sleeping with a woman, and what happened with Laurel didn't change who I was. It was only later, much, much later, that I took what good I could from the relationship. She certainly helped me discover my sexuality, probably saved me from a disastrous marriage, a miserable life. The truth is...the truth is, that it was my mistake. She was the first woman I'd ever made love to, and I thought that *making* love was the same as *being* in love. I mistook sexual passion for love, and I'm hardly the first person in the world to have made that mistake."

Alex said, quietly, "I can't imagine how you felt."

CJ was still crying, tears running gently down her cheeks. "I've seen other women, since I've been here. I'm always careful—but even after all these years, I just haven't really…gotten all the way past it, I guess."

Alex moved next to her and said, softly, "Don't cry. I won't hurt you like that, I swear to God."

She put her hand on CJ's wet cheek. CJ leaned into the palm and closed her eyes, as if the touch could heal her.

They sat close together for a few moments, then CJ turned and kissed Alex's hand.

"Sorry," she murmured. "I'm sorry, I didn't know I'd get so emotional about telling you. It's a long time ago."

"It's okay," Alex said softly, brushing away the last tear with her thumb, gently.

"So…just to be clear," CJ said, trying to regain her composure, "if you change your mind, if you decide this isn't right for you, that's fine. Just tell me, okay?"

But as she said it, she knew she wouldn't be fine, not at all.

Alex moved even closer and said, her voice low, "I'm not going to change my mind."

She leaned in and carefully unbuttoned the top two buttons of CJ's blouse. CJ felt her heart lurch as Alex gently laid a warm cheek against the skin of her chest.

Then Alex traced her fingertips along the lace of CJ's bra, just slipping under the edge to stroke the skin at the top of her breast.

"So soft," Alex whispered. "I wanted to do this the first day I saw you."

CJ had never felt anything so sweetly erotic in her life. Instinct drove her to push into Alex's touch. Alex kissed the curve of her breast, then reluctantly pulled away.

"I know we haven't known each other very long," Alex said quietly. "But I don't want you to be frightened that I won't like being with a woman, or that I don't want you. I do want you, CJ. When we're both ready, I want to make love with you."

CJ felt her tears returning. Alex said quickly, "Jesus, don't cry. That's supposed to make you happy."

CJ smiled against the tears and said, "It did. It does." She kissed Alex softly, and said, "Soon, darlin'. It's all right. We have all the time in the world."

Alex walked her to the door, then, clearly reluctant to let her go, asked, "You never did tell me about the money thing."

CJ gave a little half smile and said, "Oh, sorry. My granddaddy, my mother's father, was richer than Croesus. I was his only granddaughter, and he didn't care about anything else, bless his soul. When my parents stopped talking to me, he decided to set up a nice little trust fund for me. Ever since he passed away his lawyer acts as my trustee, manages the investments and sends me an allowance. There's nothing my parents can do about it, much as they might want to."

"So you really don't have to work? You're a cop because you like it?"

"Something like that. I don't tell people. Money makes some people nervous."

Alex smiled and said, "Don't worry. Your secret is safe with me."

All the way home, CJ thought about the unexpected sweetness from Alex, the glimpse of soft heart. But she also remembered the tender touch of Alex's fingers on her skin and the thought made her tremble again.

CHAPTER SIX

For the third time, CJ asked Detective John Simon, "How did Perrault get out of his handcuffs, then?"

"Shit, I already told you. I don't remember! I don't know what the hell happened, so why do you keep asking me that?"

She folded her hands on top of a manila file folder. The label was blank, and she hadn't opened it yet. Simon kept looking down at it, and she could see his anxiety growing.

Finally, she leaned back in her chair and brought the folder with her. Opening it, she pursed her lips and looked inside at sheets of paper he couldn't see.

"You should have regained your memory of the incident by now," she told him. "I'm very concerned that you continue to be unable to answer my questions. You do remember the advisement I gave you earlier? You are required to respond to questions unless you're claiming your Fifth Amendment right against self-incrimination."

Simon glared at her. "Yeah, I remember. You also told me that if I claim the Fifth that you could fire me for that."

"That's true," she agreed calmly. "But really, it's much better if you just tell me what happened."

He dug at the tabletop with his fingers, and she looked down. His nails were bitten down to the quick on both hands. They looked odd with his carefully tailored suit and precisely knotted tie.

The two of them were in a small interview room near Internal Affairs, plain gray chairs on the gray carpet, and a gray metal table between them. It was an interior room, with no windows except the one in the observation room next door, and Simon looked gray himself after more than an hour alone with the Internal Affairs Inspector.

CJ waited, letting the silence work on him.

"I can't tell you what I don't remember," he repeated.

She shut the file folder and put it back on the table with a sharp slap. He jumped a little.

"Let me help you here," she said crisply. "You remember transporting the suspect, his hands cuffed behind him. He was securely in the backseat of your vehicle. You remember driving on I-25 approximately thirty miles south of town. You didn't talk to him, didn't discuss anything. Suddenly you end up on the side of the road in Castle Rock, no suspect, no car. And you don't remember anything, despite what the medical report says."

"What the fuck does the medical report know about what I remember?" he demanded defensively.

She tapped the file folder. "I think you know exactly what happened," she said firmly. "He didn't wrestle the wheel away from you at seventy-five miles an hour, so I think you screwed up, and you're trying to cover it up with this 'I don't remember' act. Your concussion wasn't nearly serious enough to keep you from regaining your memory for this long."

He glared up at her and muttered, "You don't know shit."

Now she patted the file folder with her palm. "It's not me," she said. "I'm just repeating what I read. You know what happened. I'm very unhappy you're not telling me the truth."

"God damn it, I don't—"

"He was handcuffed, John," she interrupted him. "When they released him from jail to your custody, he wasn't armed. How did he overpower you?"

"I told you, *honey*, I don't *fucking* remember."

She froze him with a look. "You can call me Lieutenant, or Inspector. You call me honey again and I'll add insubordination to the charges against you."

His face went even grayer. "Charges?"

She stood up, scooped up the file, and said, "You let a suspect, a dangerous one, escape when you were responsible for him. I'm recommending to the chief that he suspend you while I complete my investigation. If you are suspended, you are required to continue to make yourself available for interviews with me during regular business hours."

He looked shocked, as if it had never occurred to him that he might be charged. "Jesus, this is unbelievable!" he exclaimed. "I'm a cop, he assaults me, and you're fucking *suspending* me?"

"You had him in your custody, and now he's at large," CJ said succinctly. "Maybe you screwed up, or maybe you let him go. Either way, I'm recommending your suspension until we find out what happened or your memory returns."

He stood up angrily. She still was more than a head taller, so CJ held her ground as he came around the table, and she braced herself, watching his hands.

Simon raised a finger and put it an inch from her nose. "And maybe somebody else screwed up, huh? Maybe you don't know what the *fuck* you're talking about!"

"Are you accusing someone, Detective?" CJ asked coolly.

He glared at her. Finally, he took a deep breath and wagged the finger at her.

"Why don't you check that out, *Inspector?* Check out who signed the transport order, why don't you?"

She looked down at him and said, very quietly, "Get your hand out of my face right now."

Simon looked at his hand as if he hadn't known where it was. He dropped it, reluctantly, she thought.

He crossed to the door and jerked it open. "I'm out of here!" he snarled.

CJ sat down again, thoughtfully. A minute later, McCarthy entered from the observation room on the other side of the window.

"Well, that didn't go so good, Inspector," he remarked. "What the hell is in that file, anyway?"

She flipped it open to show him. "Nothing except his releases and acknowledgment of the advisement," she said. "I'm a little surprised an experienced detective would really think I had anything else."

McCarthy looked puzzled. "So you really didn't have any medical report that his memory should be back?"

She shook her head. "The doctor who treated him told me on the phone that he should have regained it by now, but you know doctors." She shrugged. "They're never able to say for sure.

"But he knows what happened," she added, with sudden vehemence. "He just wasn't hurt badly enough to have lost that much time. He screwed up, I just know it."

"So what's the plan?"

She sighed. "Oh, you know. The usual: good police work. Background check on him while I let him stew a bit. I'll get him back here in a couple of days and we'll go another round after he's had time to sit at home and worry for a while."

McCarthy scratched at the tiny bald patch on the crown of his head. "You gonna check out the transport order?"

"Oh, absolutely," she said grimly.

The computer monitor on CJ's desk had gone to her screen saver, a photograph of a Georgia bald cypress tree covered with Spanish moss. When she looked at the picture, she enjoyed both the feeling of nostalgia it gave her and her gratitude that she was no longer in the subtropical climate of her home state.

But she wasn't looking at the photograph. Printouts of John

Simon's financial records were spread out on the desk before her, but she wasn't looking at them anymore, either. She was staring out her window, over the parked cars, into a sky blue with springtime gray rain clouds beginning to build. She was thinking about Alex.

She had begun to daydream about Alex constantly: brushing her teeth would bring a memory of Alex's smile, just as the sky made her think of the color of Alex's gaze. CJ knew she could shut her eyes and remember the sandalwood scent, the taste of Alex's mouth, the feel of her arms.

Abruptly she turned and shoved the paperwork aside. She didn't want to think about the case anymore, about the nagging worry in the back of her mind. She lifted her phone and punched in Alex's extension.

Alex slipped her hands into her jacket pockets as she trotted across the parking lot into the park. The rain had held off, but the clouds still hovered above the mountains in the west, as if waiting for a signal to move across the Front Range.

She found CJ already at the bench near the walking path, tucked between two aspens. The sight of her, long legs stretched out in relaxation, made Alex's heart beat faster.

Alex couldn't remember ever feeling this way about anyone, ever. She laughed to herself at the idea of waiting half her life for this emotion, the excitement in just a glimpse of a familiar figure, the sudden lifting of the heart.

She sat down next to CJ and began to open the paper bag sitting on the bench between them. "What've we got?" she asked.

CJ said, "Deli, I'm afraid. I didn't think I'd have time to run home and whip up a gourmet picnic, although as it turns out, I would have had. Where have you been?"

"Sorry," Alex answered, already seizing a pickle and crunching down. "A couple of things came up."

"Don't they always," CJ said noncommittally. "Ham and cheese, or roast beef? I'll take either."

"Roast beef. Is there mustard?"

"Dijon is already on the sandwich."

"You," Alex said happily, "are my hero. Thanks for suggesting this."

CJ unwrapped her sandwich and pulled a piece of Swiss cheese free to munch. "You did have lunch, didn't you?" she asked.

"It's possible," Alex hedged.

"Try again."

"Do pretzels count?"

"Nope, darlin', they don't. There's pasta salad in there, too. Eat, please."

Alex ate with her usual enthusiasm, and they were quiet for a while, watching the joggers and strollers cross in front of them. Finally Alex crumpled the paper and stuffed it back in the bag, saying, "That was great. If I'd realized the benefits of having a girlfriend, I'd have gotten one years ago."

CJ turned to her, lifting her eyebrows. "Would you, indeed?"

Alex laughed, then impulsively reached across for CJ's hand. "Honestly? I think things happen when the time is right. I wasn't ready. Then, just when I believe it's never going to happen, there you are."

"'When the student is ready, the teacher appears,'" CJ murmured.

"Come again?"

"Zen Buddhism," CJ answered.

Alex gave her hand a squeeze, then released it. "I had no idea you were so...eclectic."

"Oh, darlin', was that our word of the day?" CJ teased.

"Shut up," Alex said, smiling. She leaned back and put her face toward the setting sun. "I do not want to go back to work," she muttered.

"Then don't. It's past quitting time, you know."

Alex sighed. "I'm waiting for a report from Forensics. They found Simon's department-issued car in a Park-n-Ride on South Broadway a few hours ago."

"No sign of Perrault, I guess."

"No such luck. I'm hoping they can tell us something. At least we're able to concentrate our efforts on the metro area. The problem is, he could have gotten light rail or a bus to almost anywhere."

CJ picked up the sack, walked over to the trash can, and tossed it in. She asked Alex thoughtfully, "Any idea why Perrault came toward Denver? I mean, he is from the Springs, right?"

Alex, frowning, answered, "Yes, and you're asking the right questions. The problem is we don't have any answers yet. The chief has got an all-out media saturation going, so I hope somebody will call something in soon and we can get him." She slid a glance at CJ and asked, "Did you talk to John today?"

CJ answered carefully, "Yes. He didn't tell me anything that would help you find Perrault. You know that if he does, I'll call you immediately."

"I know."

Alex knew better than to talk about CJ's investigation of Simon's misconduct, so she was surprised when CJ blurted, "Alex, I have to ask you something. About John Simon."

"Okay," Alex answered.

"Do you…is he a good detective? I mean, do you work well together?"

Surprised, Alex responded, "Yes. He's conscientious, a solid guy. Not a brilliant mind, but he does his job. Why?"

CJ looked away, clearly uncomfortable. Alex asked, "Is there a problem?"

"I don't know yet."

"That's not much of an answer."

Abruptly CJ returned to look at Alex full in the eyes.

"What?" Alex asked softly.

"You signed the transport order for Perrault," CJ said.

"Yes. I made the assignment."

"Tell me about that."

Frowning again, Alex related the story of Simon appearing in her office with the news that Perrault had been captured. When she was finished, she asked, "Will you tell me how the hell any of this is relevant?"

CJ said, still watching her, "Simon implied in my interview today that you were…involved in the escape."

Alex stared at her. "You are not serious," she finally managed.

CJ pursued the line of questioning with, "Can you think of any reason he might make something like this up?"

Alex, agitated, got up and began to pace, wondering how her earlier joyful mood could have been so quickly demolished.

"CJ, this is ludicrous. I've signed a couple of hundred transport orders over the years, and this one was no different."

"You can't think of a reason for Simon to involve you?" CJ persisted.

Alex stopped pacing and stood in front of her. "Hell, no, I can't! What did he say?"

CJ lifted a hand. "Nothing direct. Alex, let me handle this. I was putting a lot of pressure on him, and I think he was making it up as he went along, trying to divert attention. I'll talk to him again. Try not to let this make you crazy."

Alex sat down again, her stomach knotted. "You know I didn't have anything at all to do with this," she began. It surprised her that it was more important than anything else that CJ believe her.

CJ said firmly, "I do know that, darlin'. Don't worry, okay? Do ya'll think you'll be late tonight?"

Alex was still trying to calm down. "Yeah, probably. What are you doing tomorrow night?"

"My weekly manicure appointment."

Alex tried to smile, and said, "Sure you don't want to cancel it?"

CJ sighed and said, "I really can't. I go with my friend Vivian, and we catch up on the week's gossip."

Alex tried to tamp down her disappointment. Why was the thought of spending an evening alone a problem? She'd been doing that for years.

You know why.

Aloud she said, "I understand. Just tell me one thing."

"What, darlin'?"

"You're not...backing off from me, are you? Because you think you have a conflict of interest or something? You know I'd never interfere in your investigation involving Simon. Or anything else."

"Oh, Alex, no!" CJ exclaimed. "In fact, I was thinking of asking you something, but I don't want to make you uncomfortable."

You do, Alex thought, *but in a good way*. "What is it?"

The sudden shyness was back, and Alex found it as irresistible as before. Alex touched her hand in reassurance and said, "You can ask me anything."

She watched CJ take a breath, then say, "Would you like to go away this weekend? It doesn't matter where. The mountains, maybe. Just a couple of days, I thought…"

Alex wanted to grab her, right there on the bench, in front of the joggers and the strollers and the geese.

"Yes."

"Yes?" CJ asked.

"Wherever you want. Let's go."

CJ gave her a dazzling smile. "Yes. Good. I mean, we would, um…"

Alex grinned back at her, her good mood restored.

"I get it, CJ. One room, and I'll buy new lingerie for the occasion."

CJ's eyes went hazy, like smoke against green leaves in a forest. "Don't bother," she said, her voice low.

Her voice rubbed against Alex's skin like an electric current. She considered again throwing CJ against the park bench, but decided, reluctantly, that she could wait a few more days.

"There is one condition," she said as they walked back toward the police building.

"What's that?"

"You are going to have to tell me your name."

"I'll take that under advisement," CJ said primly.

"Hong Kong?" Vivian asked incredulously, examining the bottle of nail polish in her hand. "Christ in a uniform, what kind of name is that for a color?"

CJ laughed and said, "A nondescriptive one?"

"Well, no shit." She showed her the bottle and said, "Would

you have guessed this shade of blue? Or any shade of blue, for that matter?"

"Not in a million years," CJ answered.

"Jesus, where do they get these names?" Vivian persisted. She plucked another bottle from the manicurist's tray and wrapped her fingers around it. "Here, try to guess the color of this one from the name."

"May I trim the cuticle here?" the technician asked CJ.

"Of course," she answered before turning back to Vivian. "Okay, I'm game. What's it called?"

"Arabian."

CJ contemplated. "Blue, Arabian sea."

"No, please try again."

"Hmmm. Oh, tan, Arabian desert, like sand."

"Not close. Final guess."

"This is tough. I'm going…black. Arabian nights."

"Very creative. But wrong."

Vivian opened her hand to display a deep red bottle.

CJ laughed and said, "Clearly I'm terrible at this game. What was wrong with, oh, say, 'Dark Red'?"

Vivian said haughtily, "Obviously, you don't know anything about marketing. Names are supposed be exotic, mysterious, exciting. This one should be named…" she looked at it briefly, then declared, "Cinnabar."

"Very nice," CJ complimented her as the technician began stroking a light pink onto her nails. "You have the gift. You should give up mortgage banking and try fashion."

Vivian looked thoughtful. "The fashion industry. Good idea. I might meet more girls that way," she mused.

CJ tried not to laugh while her polish went on. "More girls?" she demanded. "My goodness, what would you do with more girls? You've already got them circling, waiting for a landing like a busy day at DIA."

Vivian smiled happily. "And that's just the way I like it."

CJ shook her head. "You are such a hound."

"Better than being celibate," Vivian retorted.

CJ simply smiled, and Vivian pounced in an instant. "Oh, thank God!" she exclaimed.

"What?" CJ asked innocently.

"You actually remembered what a lesbian is supposed to do!"

"Excuse me?" CJ said in surprise.

"You remember. Sleeping with women, that's what you should be up to."

The nail technician, who had apparently heard everything, simply continued to apply the topcoat calmly.

"Stop," CJ said.

"Hell, no! C'mon, sister, give. You haven't had a date since Christ was a corporal. Details, please, and leave nothing out."

"There's nothing to tell. Yet."

"Who are we talking about?" Vivian demanded. "The yummy-sounding older woman blue-eyed detective?"

"Alex," CJ supplied. "She's special, Vivian."

Vivian sat back in amazement. "Un-be-fucking-lievable. And how did I manage to miss dating this paragon of goodness and light?"

CJ put her nails under the dryer. "Because she wasn't out cruising the bar scene trying to get laid every night?" CJ asked innocently.

"Ha, ha. What was she doing instead?"

CJ stared at her nails and sighed. "Struggling," she answered briefly.

Vivian's eyes grew wide. "Oh, CJ. You haven't fallen for some 'bi-curious' weirdo, have you? Because she'll break your heart, sweetie."

"I'm going to try not to let that happen," CJ said. "But she's really somebody I could be serious about. I want her, and I'm sure she wants me too."

Vivian looked at her suspiciously. "At least tell me she's slept with another woman before," she said shrewdly.

CJ sighed again. "That's not the point," she began.

"Are you," Vivian exclaimed, "out of your mind? Why do you want to be her experiment?"

"Stop it!" CJ lashed out.

Vivian looked at her in shock. "CJ, what the hell?"

CJ took a deep breath. "She means a lot to me," she said at last. "I don't know what's going to happen, and I'm scared out of my mind that she's wrong, that she doesn't know what she wants, that…I don't know, that she'll cut and run, I guess."

Vivian leaned across and patted her on the arm. "Don't you worry, sweetie," she said reassuringly. "I'm sure one night between the sheets with you and she'll be firmly in the family."

CJ laughed shakily. "I just want to make her happy," she admitted.

"Oh, honey. You really do have it bad."

CHAPTER SEVEN

Simon was wearing a dark blue suit for his morning interview on Friday, his blue and green rep tie carefully knotted at the neck of a white oxford cloth shirt. The stripes on the tie ran from high on Simon's right diagonally down to his left, a design CJ's grandfather had once patiently explained to her was "American-style"—European rep ties usually went from high left to low right.

CJ had no idea why she was thinking about her grandfather's story at the moment, except that she had been staring at Simon's tie for thirty seconds or so, waiting for him to answer her question about his financial troubles.

"Look," he finally said, "I had a really bad divorce, all right? What money my ex-wife didn't get I had to pay to my damn lawyers."

CJ said, "John, you're not helping me here. We need to figure out what happened. You're the only one, other than our at-large suspect, who knows."

She watched him come to some decision. He folded his hands and sat up a little straighter, then met her eyes with a look that bordered on hostile.

"Inspector," he said. "I want some assurance from you that there won't be consequences to me if I tell you what I…remember now."

CJ sat back, both triumphant and concerned. "How can I make you any promises, John, when I don't know what you're going to say?"

"I'm just saying I know how things work." There was a trace of whine in his voice. "The working guys get blamed, and the brass walks away clean. I want to know that's not gonna happen if I tell you what really went down."

CJ felt a tremor of apprehension run up her spine. "Until you tell me," she repeated, "I can't promise you anything except this: I won't hide the truth. Not from anybody."

He folded his hands together again, cleared his throat and said, "I, ah, remembered what happened on Monday. With Perrault."

"Go on." McCarthy was out of the office, but she had the videotape running, and had already advised Simon of his rights.

"I was driving, like I told you, south on the Valley. When we got to Castle Rock, Perrault leaned forward and put a gun to my neck and told me to exit. What the fuck could I do? I pulled off. He made me let him out and walk over to the side of the road."

He stopped, and CJ said, "Was he still cuffed?"

"No, he'd gotten out of his handcuffs somehow."

"You didn't see him do that? Or where he got the gun?"

"Fuck no, I was driving at seventy-five miles an hour and there was a lot of traffic. I just looked up and there he was with a gun barrel sticking in me. The gun must'a been in the backseat, hidden somewhere, same with the handcuff key."

CJ watched him talk, watched his eyes. The facts were flowing easily enough, but the emotions were missing. She prodded him with, "You must have been terrified."

"Scared shitless is more like it. I figured he was gonna cap me right there. But he just hit me with the gun and that was it. Except..."

He hesitated and she tried to read him. Finally he said, "He did say something to me before he hit me."

One way or another, CJ knew he'd reached the point of his story. "What was that?" she asked.

Simon looked away, then forced himself to meet her eyes again. "He said, 'Be sure to thank your captain for me.'"

CJ felt as if she'd been punched hard in the stomach.

She managed to ask, "And what did you take that to mean?"

He shook his head angrily. "What the fuck do you think? She set me up. She got me to transport him, put the gun and the key in the car before I picked it up to do the transport. For all she knew, he could've blown my brains out, the bitch."

The turmoil in her stomach increased as she fought down a sudden surge of nausea. "You're referring to your commanding officer?" she said, through numb lips.

"Yeah, that's right. Captain Ryan. Alex Ryan."

CJ kept him for almost two hours, going over everything, asking a hundred more questions. Nothing he said changed, and in the end, she sent him away, reminding him that, even on suspension, he was required to make himself available for further interviews.

Then she went into the women's restroom on the first floor and threw up what was left in her stomach of breakfast.

She pressed her forehead against the cold tile wall, the thoughts chasing each other around and around in her mind: What was she going to do? Could Simon be telling the truth? Could she, somehow, protect Alex from the accusation? Should she?

She still felt sick, heartsick. She could not believe Alex had anything to do with Perrault's escape. Simon had to be lying.

But the question kept returning: Why?

She pushed herself to her feet, rinsed out her mouth. She

knew what she had to do, but it wasn't making the ache in her chest any easier to bear.

Alex looked up from the arrest report she was reading to see CJ in her doorway.

"Hey," she said happily. "What's the matter? Couldn't wait until tonight to see me?"

CJ, her face stiff, stepped inside the office and closed the door.

"Captain," she said, and Alex dropped the paperwork onto her desktop.

"What's wrong?" she asked sharply.

CJ said woodenly, "I am here to inform you that I have opened an investigation file on you today, related to the escape of Robert Perrault from custody on Monday. I will need for you to appear downstairs at one o'clock for a interview concerning this matter. At that time I will advise you of your rights under Garrity, which permit you to assert your Fifth Amendment right against self-incrimination but may subject you to disciplinary action, up to and including termination, if you decide to do so."

She turned on her heel, but Alex moved quickly around the desk to take her arm. "CJ! What the hell is going on?" she exclaimed.

CJ turned back to her. Her voice barely audible, she said, "Let go of me, Captain."

Alex stared at her. Even though she felt angry, confused, hurt, just touching CJ sent her blood thundering in her veins.

"Please," CJ whispered.

Alex dropped her hand and stepped away. "Whatever you say, Inspector," she replied, her tone a knife's edge.

CJ's footsteps were sharp and quick across the floor of the squad room as she walked away.

But even after CJ was gone, Alex could hear the sound, the sound of her world beginning to fall apart.

Alex signed the page, then shoved the written *Garrity* advisement across the gray table in the interview room.

"I understand my rights, Inspector," she said tersely.

CJ put the document carefully in the folder with Alex's name on it. Alex looked down at the file and said, "Did you find my personnel jacket interesting reading, Inspector?"

For an instant, the look on her face made Alex feel as if she were twisting a blade inside of CJ. Alex wanted to take the words back, take everything back to where they had been just a few hours ago, when she'd been looking forward to their weekend away, anticipating the time with CJ more than anything she'd ever wanted in her life.

Now CJ was some kind of icy stranger, all regulations and accusations—except for that momentary look of anguish. It was gone the next instant, and CJ said evenly, "I read all of your file, Captain. You have a very impressive record: two unit commendations, three individual commendations and a Distinguished Service Award."

"None of which means anything at this point, does it, Inspector?"

CJ straightened the file and papers inside carefully. Alex glanced down and saw that CJ's hands were shaking, but her voice was steady.

"It means a great deal, Captain," she replied. "But I need your statement concerning the Perrault escape."

Alex said fiercely, "Then this will be a short interview. I assigned Detective Simon to do the transport and signed the order as required by department regulations. My involvement began and ended there. You know everything that happened from Monday morning onward. I have been involved in the department's efforts since that time to locate the suspect. And that, Inspector, is all I know."

Alex sat back with an air of finality, wondering how much CJ would tell her, what interrogation games she might play.

To her surprise, CJ said simply, "Let me tell you what Detective Simon told me this morning."

She related the story. Alex could see CJ watching her, and she let her face show the anger and disbelief she was feeling.

"The only response I have," she said when CJ was finished, "is this: somebody's lying."

CJ sat back, and, for the first time, Alex caught a glimpse of the woman she cared for behind the green eyes.

"Either Simon made it up, or the suspect was lying for some reason of his own, is that what you're suggesting?"

"That's exactly what I'm saying. My response to this accusation is a flat denial. I had nothing to do with it. At. All."

CJ said, "Okay. Who's lying and why?"

Alex shook her head. "I'm not going to make stuff up, or guess, and you know it. I have no idea what's going on, but I will say this. Why would the suspect say anything to Simon? All he has to do is hit John and take off. Why would he bother to implicate me? It makes no sense to me." She was heartened for a moment by CJ's short nod.

"If Detective Simon is lying," CJ continued after a moment, "what's his motive? Does he dislike you personally? Did you deny him a promotion, or a transfer, perhaps?"

Alex was pretty certain CJ had already researched the answers to those questions. She shook her head again. "We get along fine. I've got a detective who's a pain in the ass, but it's not John. Simon was already a detective when I was promoted to captain and hasn't ever asked for a transfer. I have no idea why John would lie about this."

"Did you know Perrault? Ever met him?"

"No and no. I'll say this one last time. I did nothing to help him escape."

CJ looked at her steadily for a moment, then said, "I'm not recommending suspension for you at this time, Captain. I will be reporting to the chief, and he may make a different decision. In the meantime, I'd like for you to sign these."

She handed Alex another set of papers. Alex glanced down at them and said, "Releases? For what?"

"To examine your credit report and financial records. It's standard pro…"

She didn't finish the sentence. Alex felt a surge of anger as she slammed the papers down on the tabletop.

"You think somebody bribed me to let him escape?" she demanded in fury. "You think I would do something like that for *money*?"

CJ went pale, but said coolly, "It is standard procedure, Captain. Part of the background check Internal Affairs performs in cases like this."

Alex jumped to her feet, shoving her chair back so hard it bounced against the wall behind her. It fell with a clatter to the floor.

"I don't care. I'm not signing."

"Excuse me?"

"If you need a release, that means you can't access the information without my permission. You don't have my permission, is that clear?"

She stared at CJ, who returned the look without flinching. After a moment, CJ said, "We can get a search warrant."

"Then do it!" Alex snapped. "Turn off the tape."

CJ stood and said, "Interview terminated at one thirty-four p.m."

When she had shut off the videotape, Alex growled, "You do whatever you have to do, Inspector. When you've figured out what went wrong here, you can come and talk to me at that point. Until then, I think you and I should stay far, far away from each other."

Alex didn't know what she expected CJ to say, but to her faint shock, CJ didn't say anything. She gathered up her paperwork and left the room without another word.

Alex slumped against the table. Her anger was spent, replaced by raw, ragged fear.

Holy Mother of God. What have I done? What the hell have I done?

CHAPTER EIGHT

Deputy Chief Duncan said incredulously, "You don't really believe that, do you, Inspector?"

CJ lifted her arms helplessly and let them drop back to the arms of the chair. "It's not what I believe, sir. It's a matter of what the evidence shows."

"Evidence?" he snorted. "One sentence, uttered by some murder suspect who isn't even around to repeat it. It's hearsay and you know it."

CJ bristled at him. "I am very much aware of that," she said tersely. "But we both know I'm required to investigate this allegation, sir." She saw him frown a little at the subtle reminder that he wasn't her supervisor.

It was only twenty minutes into Monday's work day, and she'd already made Paul Duncan deeply unhappy. He couldn't be as unhappy as she was herself, CJ thought miserably. She couldn't remember a worse weekend in her life, not even after she'd thrown Laurel out eight years ago.

Emotions kept cycling through her, each bringing fresh waves of grief. Regret, for losing the weekend she'd wanted so much. Guilt, for putting Alex through the particular hell of an internal investigation. Anger at the situation, sometimes directed at Simon, sometimes at herself, sometimes even at Alex, for treating her so coldly. It wasn't CJ's fault that Simon had accused Alex—she was just doing her job, something she certainly would have expected Alex, of all people, to understand.

Then the circle of emotions would begin again, until she was a wreck. By Saturday night, she'd been unable to bear another moment, and she'd called Alex at home.

As she listened to phone ring, she thought Alex wasn't going to pick up. But at the last moment, she heard the connection and Alex said, "You really shouldn't be calling me."

"I'm well aware of that. I couldn't help it."

She heard Alex's sigh over the telephone. "CJ, whatever it is, just don't. I don't think I want to hear it."

"Alex." She gripped the phone so hard her fingers hurt. "I just wanted to say how sorry I am."

There was a long pause before Alex said, "What are you apologizing for? Doing your job? Or for thinking I'm a crooked cop?"

CJ felt her heart breaking. "Oh, darlin'," she cried, "you know I don't believe that, don't you?"

There was another pause before Alex responded quietly, "I have no idea what you think. Goodnight, CJ."

She'd hung up before CJ could say anything else.

"Inspector?" Duncan was saying, and she realized she'd missed his question.

"I'm sorry, sir."

"Are you all right, Inspector? You don't look well."

She grimaced. When she'd gotten out of bed this morning after a third restless night, she'd looked at herself in the mirror. Her naturally fair skin looked ghostly pale, emphasizing the dark smudges under her eyes. She'd tried to give herself a pep talk, convince herself that she could somehow find the truth and release Alex from suspicion, and that would let them return to their relationship without consequence.

But in her deepest heart, she feared that everything they had been working toward was already gone forever.

"Rough weekend," she answered him. "I couldn't eat, couldn't really sleep very well. A virus, perhaps."

"I asked why you had to get a warrant. Surely Captain Ryan—"

"She refused to sign the releases," she interrupted him. It was one of the things bothering her the most. Why would Alex refuse?

His frown deepened and he reached for his office phone. "I'll call her."

CJ said, "Don't, sir. I sent the affidavit for the warrant over to the DA already, and I expect the search warrant momentarily. I just want to get this over with."

He drummed his fingers on his desk. "Are you recommending to the chief that Captain Ryan be suspended?"

God, no, she could only imagine how much worse that would make it for Alex. "No, sir. I want to proceed with the warrant, then interview Detective Simon again."

Duncan looked at her straight in the eyes and said, "I cannot believe Captain Ryan had anything to do with this."

She was weary of everyone telling her that, of telling herself that. She didn't want to hear it anymore, she wanted to prove it and get this over with—no one had a better reason than she did.

Except Alex, perhaps.

"I hope I can clear this up soon," she said. "I'm going to call Simon in this afternoon for a third interview. I'm hoping after a couple of days thinking about it he'll have put together another, more convincing, story."

Duncan grunted. "I doubt it, frankly. Keep me informed, Inspector."

Alex was ten minutes late for the Monday morning squad meeting. No one commented, not even Roger Fullerton, when she came in quietly, saying only, "Let's get started. Gonzales, what's the update on your armed robbery?"

They went methodically through the open case files, and Alex assigned a few other cases that had come in over the weekend for follow-up. Then she turned to Frank Morelli and said, "Give us a summary of the search status on Perrault."

Morelli updated them with what they knew, which was pretty much nothing.

"No prints in the car except Simon's and Perrault's," he reported. "No other physical evidence, although they did find Simon's cell phone. Interestingly, the SIM card had been removed."

"What the hell is that?" Stan Rosenthal demanded.

Alex answered, "It's the computer chip that stores memory, makes it possible for the phone to work. Any ideas on why he'd take it out?"

Fullerton said, "You can sell those on the black market."

His partner Porter said, "Yeah, but why wouldn't he take the whole phone?"

Fullerton gave him a pitying look. "Because if the phone is activated, you can track them sometimes with GPS."

"That's a fairly sophisticated thought for a twenty-two-year-old guy who never finished high school and did day labor landscaping work," Morelli said mildly.

Fullerton glared at him. Alex preempted the upcoming argument with, "I agree. But there's another good reason to take the card."

"Yeah?" Fullerton said skeptically. "What's that?"

Alex answered, "Without the chip, there's no way to tell who he might have called on the phone."

Porter asked, "You think he called somebody?"

Alex leaned wearily against the whiteboard. "I think it's likely. Look, he's been gone a week, vanished off the planet. He had nothing, no ID, no money. How the hell has he been hidden all this time? Unless he's dead in a ditch somewhere, somebody's helping him. Maybe we should figure out who that is."

Morelli said, "CSPD talked to his family and known associates."

"I know." Alex shook her head in frustration. "And they're all in El Paso County, right? So why did he drive to Denver?"

No one had any answers. With a sigh, Alex said, "Okay, let's get back to work. Anybody has an idea on this, no matter how crazy, let me know."

Rosenthal said, "Don't you worry, Cap, we'll get this guy. He can't stay under the radar forever."

They filed out, Fullerton snagging the last of the doughnuts on the way. Frank Morelli hung back and watched Alex erase the whiteboard.

When she turned around, she asked, "Something on your mind?"

He tugged nervously at the sleeves of his jacket. They were just a little short on him. He had dark, thick black hair that always looked like he needed a trim. Alex thought involuntarily of John Simon, always perfectly tailored, impeccably groomed, and wondered, for the hundredth time, why he was throwing her under the bus.

"Frank?"

"Captain, are you all right?"

"I'm fine," she answered brusquely.

He fixed her with a kind look from chocolate brown eyes. "If you say so. But you don't look so good. And in all these years, I've never known you to be late for a meeting."

She sagged back against the board. She liked Frank, he was a nice guy and a hard-working one. She said, "I had a pretty bad weekend, that's all."

"No sleep?"

She laughed a little unpleasantly. "Obvious, is it?"

"Kinda. Anything I can do?"

The problem, Alex thought, was that there wasn't anything that she, or anyone else, could do. She wanted to run far, far away, from fear and doubt and confusion. And nothing confused her more than CJ St. Clair who was, she figured, working at that very moment to get her in even deeper trouble.

Alex sighed and said, "No, there's nothing. Thanks, though."

At ten thirty, an assistant at the district attorney's office called to tell Internal Affairs that the search warrant had been issued. By noon, CJ was staring at bank records, credit reports and account summaries for Alexandria Mary Ryan.

She said aloud to no one, "Alex, what the hell is going on?"

She pulled Alex's personnel file over the messy piles of paper on her desk and looked at it again. She checked the salary against Alex's checking and savings accounts, then found her checking account summary for the last three years.

Alex should have had a very comfortable living. Her mortgage was modest, her credit bills reasonably small. There weren't even any car payments, which was not surprising considering the ten-year-old junker she drove, CJ thought ruefully. No big cash withdrawals to tip off a gambling or drug problem, not that she suspected either one. There hadn't been a single deposit to her bank account in three years other than Alex's regular automatic salary deposit.

So why was there no money to speak of in either her savings or checking account?

CJ went back over the checking account summaries again and found it. There were two big transfers from savings to checking, one transfer two and half years ago, the other about a year after that. Alex had written a series of checks for varying amounts but always five figures, written at irregular intervals from checking, decimating the account.

Alex had paid someone just over a hundred and forty thousand dollars.

There had been no payments in more than a year. CJ's first thought was that the money had somehow been for her sister. Perhaps for her nephew? But the payments were so large, and so irregular, that CJ wondered. It hardly looked like a college fund contribution. Alex's parents were gone—what could she be spending that much money, her life savings, on?

Blackmail? But for what? And who pays their blackmailer with checks?

Was this the reason Alex refused the releases? CJ mused.

The now familiar longing to go upstairs and see Alex, or call her, returned once again. How could she have gotten so emotionally involved so quickly? It was unlike her—Vivian had kidded her for years about how slowly she moved in relationships, always cautious, never quite trusting herself.

But Alex was different, she'd known that from the first day. It wasn't only the physical attraction; there was some other powerful pull toward Alex that she couldn't define. Whatever the mystery was, she couldn't solve it, didn't want to solve it. She only wanted to finish this case.

CJ went back into the account summary and pulled up the payees on the checks. They were all made out to the same person: R.A. Bradford, Jr.

"And who are you?" CJ said to herself. "Let's find out."

Sergeant Chad McCarthy looked up from his desk and said, "Are you going out, Lieutenant?"

"Yes. Did you get lunch?"

"I brown-bagged it. Did you eat?"

CJ shook her head and said, "No, I'm not hungry," thinking that no symptom could be a clearer indication of her emotional state. "I'm going out on an interview. It's just at the DA's office, so I expect I'll be back in an hour or so. I have something I want you to check on."

"Sure. What is it?"

"First, call John Simon. I want to see him, today. Four o'clock should work."

"Okay. What else?"

"Call CSPD and get everything you can about the Perrault shooting. Not just about Perrault necessarily, but the original report on the murder, witness statements, anything you can get."

He made notes. "Okay. Are we trying to find him, too?"

CJ tapped her fingers against the edge of his desk. "In a way," she said. "I'll call you if I'm going to be late."

CJ sat in a small conference room in the Justice Center, waiting. The room had a surprisingly nice view, the same park CJ looked at from across the street, but without the parking lot in between, and from a higher floor. She could see the aspen leaves moving gently in the breeze.

Her appointment showed up, almost fifteen minutes late, bustling into the room.

"Sorry," he said briefly. "I got hung up on the phone with the Clerk of the Supreme Court. Some problem with a record on appeal apparently only I could straighten out. Are you Inspector Sinclair?"

CJ stood, recognizing the performance for what it was, an attempt to impress her with his importance. "It's St. Clair," she corrected him. "Thank you for meeting me on short notice."

He offered his hand. "Chief Deputy Anthony Bradford," he introduced himself.

He was, CJ thought, a little too handsome to be real. Dark blond, wavy hair, great tan, big brown eyes. He was wearing a very nice suit, and she caught a glint of cufflinks.

"Mr. Bradford, nice to meet ya'll."

He gave her a broad smile and the full up-and-down look. "The pleasure is mine. Sit, please."

She sat across him and noted his appreciative glance at her legs. She crossed them at the knee and said, "I don't plan to take up much of your time."

"As much as you need." He flashed her a smile, but tempered his words with a quick glance at his Rolex. "Are you new? I try to keep up with the major staff changes at the department, but I know I would have remembered you."

"I've been with the department about three months," she answered.

"I don't recall another case where the department went outside to hire command level staff," he said, making it sound as though they had done so without his approval.

She saw his eyes drop to her left hand. She added, "I was with the Roosevelt County Sheriff's Office before that, for almost eight years."

"Ah. Well, tell me, Lieutenant St. Clair, how can I help you?" Another quick look at his watch.

She decided bluntness might throw him off his game a bit. "You can tell me why Captain Ryan gave you a hundred and forty-one thousand dollars a couple of years ago."

His face flushed brick-red beneath his tan and he snapped, "Perhaps you can tell me why the hell that's any of your business."

"I'm investigating a complaint involving Captain Ryan, and her finances are part of that investigation."

"Complaint? What kind of complaint?"

She smiled unpleasantly at him. "Now, Mr. Bradford, you know I can't disclose details of an ongoing I.A. investigation."

"You had better tell me, or this conversation is going to end pretty quickly. What the hell did Alex allegedly do?"

CJ had been expecting it, yet it somehow bothered her for him to call her Alex. "I don't know that she did anything," she responded mildly. "That would be the point of an investigation."

The handsome face had gone surly. "What did Alex tell you about this?"

"Nothing at all."

"You mean you asked her and she refused, or that you haven't asked her yet?"

She said smoothly, "I'm asking you, Mr. Bradford. Is this a secret? Were you doing something illegal?"

"Don't be an idiot, Lieutenant."

She refused to rise to the bait, and continued, "Then you should tell me, shouldn't you? If it has nothing to do with the case…"

"It doesn't. And it's none of your business. Or the department's, for that matter."

He was bent over the table, glaring at her, using his voice and his body for maximum intimidation, his earlier flirting demeanor long gone. Instead of easing back, CJ deliberately leaned forward into his personal space.

"Don't do it this way, Mr. Bradford. Do I have to ask for another warrant, for your bank accounts? Do I have to drag ya'll across the street for another interview, or explain to your boss that you're refusing to cooperate in a police investigation? Do I have to cross-examine Captain Ryan to find out just what your relationship is?"

She knew she sounded calm, but inside the turmoil was tearing her apart. What had Alex done? Was it even possible that she was, somehow, involved with Perrault's escape?

CJ couldn't believe it, but she didn't know what to believe.

Bradford sat back, losing the game, but his eyes were still angry. "You are going to feel like a complete fool in about thirty seconds," he snarled.

"Wouldn't be the first time," she responded coolly.

He grunted and looked out the window over her head. "Alex gave me the money voluntarily," he began. "My niece was seriously ill, leukemia. My sister didn't have insurance, the kid's father was long gone. We scraped together everything we had for treatments. Alex gave us everything she could, because I asked her to. And that's it, Lieutenant. Your smoking gun. Alex was trying to save a nine-year-old girl's life."

CJ had a sudden memory of the picture on Alex's desk, the little girl with blond braids.

"Why didn't she just tell me?" CJ asked, half to herself.

"Maybe," he said bitingly, "she didn't think it was any of your goddamned business."

He stood up and said, "I think we're done here, Lieutenant. And for your information, as you continue your little witch-hunt, you might want to remember that Alex is a kind and loving person. Whatever the hell it is you think she did, she didn't do it. She's an honest and hard-working police officer, too much so for her own good, really. I can't imagine her doing anything wrong in any professional context."

He went to the door, but CJ said, "Wait. I still don't understand. I mean, why would Alex give you her life savings for your niece?"

Bradford leaned back against the door and said, "Why not? She was her niece, too, after all."

God damn it, CJ thought. I'm an idiot. Why didn't I figure this out before?

"You're her ex-husband," she said.

He smiled, his good humor restored.

"That would be me," he said. "And I hope to fix that 'ex' part someday."

"Hey," McCarthy said as CJ stalked back into her office. "That didn't take long. Any luck?"

"It was informative," CJ said tersely, "but not particularly productive. How are you doing?"

"Good and bad. The Springs Department is gonna fax us a bunch of stuff in the morning, and I've got a call into the lead detective. It'll probably be tomorrow before he gets back to us."

"Thanks. What's the bad part?"

"Can't get Simon on the phone. Home phone goes to voice mail, and his cell doesn't pick up at all. I even tried his email, but nothing."

"Damn it," she said, and then saw McCarthy grinning at her. "What?"

"Gee, Lieutenant, I don't think I've ever heard you cuss before."

She tried to smile back at him. "Nice Southern debutantes are not allowed to swear," she informed him. "I'm usually really bad at it. But some situations just call for swearing."

"This is one of them, I guess?"

"Yes. Keep trying Simon, and let me know."

She went into her office and shut the door wearily. After dropping her purse into her lower file drawer, she twisted the rod to close the blinds to her office, then slumped into her desk chair.

Nothing was making sense to her. Why would Simon lie? What if he was telling the truth, and Perrault had really accused Alex? Could Perrault possibly have been referring to someone else?

And why had Alex made her go through the charade of getting a warrant when she had nothing to hide?

CJ was exhausted from unanswered questions. She shoved Alex's file into an untidy pile on one corner of her desk and attacked another case file, trying not to think about it anymore.

When McCarthy appeared in her office door, she was amazed to see that it was almost six o'clock.

"Still no luck getting a hold of Detective Simon, Lieutenant. I've left messages for him."

"Chad, I'm sorry. You should have gone home an hour ago. It's fine, I'll see you in the morning."

He remained standing uneasily in the doorway, and she said, "What?"

"There's someone to see you, but I didn't want to disturb you."

She pushed the file away and ran her fingers through her hair. "Who is it?"

"Captain Ryan."

CJ felt both hope and fear wind around her like twin boa constrictors.

"Have her come in," she said, "and go home."

"See you in the morning, Lieutenant."

CJ stood up shakily as Alex came in. After seventy-two hours without seeing her at all, CJ thought she looked both beautiful and terrible.

"Captain," she began, but Alex shook her head and shut the door behind her.

"No," Alex said quietly. "It's just me."

CJ felt tears springing up behind her eyes. "Alex," she whispered.

"I was angry, and scared, and confused, and I'm still feeling all of those things," Alex said simply. "But I shouldn't have yelled at you."

"Okay," CJ murmured. "It's okay."

Alex shook her head again. "No, it wasn't. Look, I didn't want you to find out about some money I...money I gave away."

"I already know all about it. I talked to Bradford this afternoon."

"Did you?" Alex gave her a hard look. "I'm sure both you and Tony enjoyed that conversation."

"Why didn't you just tell me, Alex?" CJ asked in a rush. "You act as if you're ashamed of it."

Shaking her head angrily, Alex replied, "It was no one else's concern what I do with my money, not Paul or the department, not even yours."

The words stung CJ. "I thought," she said sadly, "that we might be past keeping secrets with each other."

Alex looked away for a long moment. When she returned to look at CJ she said in small voice, "Her name was Jennifer. She liked dogs and balloons and her favorite color was red. Even after Tony and I got divorced, I would see her every few months. We had her birthday party early because the doctors didn't think she'd make it to ten years old. They were right."

CJ blinked hard. How many people could Alex lose in one lifetime and still have enough courage to love someone else?

"Darlin', I'm so sorry."

"Don't," Alex said harshly.

Alex was looking at her closely, eyes bright with sorrow. CJ felt the gaze go through her as if she were falling into the ocean of blue.

Alex stepped around the desk, coming near. CJ could smell the hint of her cologne.

"I know this is still a bad idea," Alex began hoarsely, "but I don't think I can help it."

"Thank God," CJ said gratefully, and brought her head down.

Alex kissed her firmly, gently touched CJ's lips with just the tip of her tongue, then kissed CJ again, even harder. CJ responded, returning the pressure, parting her lips. Alex sought out the heat of her mouth, and CJ opened to her.

As they kissed, slowly, deeply, CJ lifted one hand to Alex's face, traced one sharp cheekbone with her fingertips.

Alex broke the kiss for a moment, and CJ said, "I wanted to touch you that way the first minute I saw you."

"Did you?" Alex asked, her voice low and soft. "What else?"

Heat went off inside CJ's body like a flare. She sat back on the edge of her desk and pulled Alex to her. Alex fit against her, her leg between CJ's thighs.

"Oh, God," CJ groaned as Alex began to move slowly against her.

The kissing became more heated, and the fire pulsed through CJ. She reached up and pulled Alex's blouse free, got her hands on the warm flesh of Alex's back.

Alex buried her mouth against CJ's throat, nipping at her, then lashing against the tender skin with her tongue.

CJ arched into her.

Then Alex stopped moving. After a moment of frustration, CJ sagged against her in acquiescence.

Alex murmured into her throat, "Jesus. I'm already in trouble. How much worse is it if I have sex with the Internal Affairs Inspector on top of her desk, for God's sake?"

CJ laughed in relief and regret, running her hands up Alex's back. "It's okay, it's all right," she said. "As long as you weren't stopping because you didn't want to go on."

Alex lifted her head. "You're kidding, right? Was I doing something wrong to give you that idea?"

CJ kissed her. "No, everything you did was right. Just the wrong time and place."

Alex brushed back a few strands of red hair from CJ's face and said, "Yes. But I want it to be the right time and place."

"Oh, yes," CJ said fervently. "Soon, please God."

Alex stayed against her, breathing into her shoulder. "What are we going to do?" she asked sadly. "I can't stay away from you, but we can't see each other, not while you're working an I.A. case involving me."

CJ tightened her grip, pulling Alex closer. She was surprised at how fragile Alex felt against her.

"I'm going to fix this," she said, firmly. "I'm going to get Simon in here, and I'm going to get him to tell me the truth, one way or another. I'm going to find out what happened. I swear I am."

Alex kissed her neck and let her go. "You'd better do it soon," she sighed. "I don't know how much longer I'm going to be able to stand being without you." She gave a sad little laugh.

"What?" CJ asked.

"It's just funny. A few months ago, I was alone most of the time when I wasn't at work, and it didn't really bother me. Now… Christ, CJ, I can hardly stand being away from you."

CJ said fervently, "I understand. Believe me, I do."

CHAPTER NINE

CJ threw her Lexus into park and twisted the key angrily in the ignition to turn off the engine. She grabbed her purse and slammed the door behind her.

In the lobby, she double-checked the number of Simon's apartment on the note McCarthy had given her and jabbed at the elevator button impatiently.

John Simon hadn't returned a phone call or email in almost twenty-four hours and she'd had enough. If he thought he could avoid the consequences of the investigation by ducking her, he was about to be thoroughly disabused of the idea.

She found the apartment and rapped sharply on the door. "Simon? It's Inspector St. Clair."

She half-expected to hear his voice immediately, claiming some illness. There was only silence.

She knocked again, calling loudly, "Simon! Open up."

Muttering to herself, she reached over and grasped the knob. It turned easily in her hand, and the door swung open a couple of inches.

She stepped away immediately, flattening herself against the hallway wall to one side of the doorway. She pulled out her weapon, pointing it toward the ground, and fumbled in her pocket for her cell phone.

Into the apartment, through the door ajar, she called again, "Simon! It's St. Clair! Are you in there?"

More silence. She thumbed open the phone and called McCarthy.

When he answered, she said, "Chad, get me a patrol unit to Simon's apartment right now. No, I don't know yet. Stay there, and I'll call you back."

CJ dropped the phone into her pocket and yelled, "Simon, I'm coming in!"

She brought her Sig into the firing position and used one foot to push open the door the rest of the way.

The hallway was clear. She said loudly, "Colfax Police Department!" but heard no response.

She eased down the hallway, gun up. Adrenaline racing through her made everything sharp and clear: the faint noises of the icemaker in the kitchen, the sound of a television in another apartment.

Then the smell hit her, and her stomach roiled in protest.

Blood smelled like nothing else, salty and metallic. She saw a dark red smear of it inside the doorway to the living room on her left. She stepped carefully over it into the room.

So much blood, soaking crimson into the carpet, sprayed scarlet on the walls.

CJ swept the room with her eyes, waiting for an assailant to spring at her, but nothing moved except a blinking cursor on the computer screen, the monitor sitting on a desk in one corner of the room.

In the middle of the mess was John Simon, one arm curled around his desk chair, splattered with gore. CJ crossed to him, stepping carefully to avoid as much of the blood as she could, and touched his neck lightly.

She didn't bother to feel for a pulse. His skin was cold. He must have been dead for hours.

"God damn it to hell!" she expelled. She stepped away from him, and the monitor caught her attention. A word processing program was on the screen, a white background with a single line of type.

She read the words in icy horror.

There were smears of blood on the keys, one streaking the edge of the monitor itself, but CJ could see nothing except the words typed there, the cursor blinking steadily at the end of the line.

Behind her from the hallway a loud voice called, "Colfax Police!"

CJ said loudly, "Lieutenant St. Clair. I'm in plainclothes and I've got my weapon out, so don't shoot me. We have a dead body in the living room, and I need for you to clear the rest of the apartment."

Two uniformed officers appeared in the doorway, weapons drawn. CJ, moving slowly, carefully showed them her shield, then said, "Check the kitchen, bathroom, bedroom. I think the perp is long gone, but make sure. Then call for a crime scene unit."

They scattered and she heard them calling out, opening doors. She returned to look at the computer screen. The 'delete' button was an inch from her fingertip. Just a couple of seconds, and the words would vanish.

Temptation almost overwhelmed her. It was another lie, in those words, and the lies were destroying everything.

What if it's not a lie? she asked herself.

Doubt frayed the edge of her certainty. In the end, she knew she could never destroy evidence, not even this most terrible three words.

One of the uniformed officers approached her and said, "Apartment is clear. Who's the vic, do you know?"

She turned away from the monitor in sorrow. "Detective John Simon," she said. "One of ours."

"Fuck almighty! Did he type something?"

She looked at him from the depth of misery. "Someone did, anyway."

"What's it say?"

Stiffly, painfully, she moved aside so that he could see the words typed on the screen.

ryan killed me

CJ was sitting in her car sideways on the passenger side, waiting in the parking lot of Simon's apartment. Her car door was open to the early summer morning. There were a few white clouds in the blue sky above her, so bright and fluffy that they looked artificial, like a painted backdrop.

She looked up at the sky, trying to figure out if she could just get in the car and drive away, drive and drive until she could forget the dead man, and the blood, and the ugly accusation.

If she drove away, she could leave all of it behind. But she would be leaving Alex behind too.

That's exactly what she should do, leave Alex behind, relegate her to the category of what could have been. How could she ever be with Alex now? Alex apparently wasn't the woman CJ thought she was. She'd been blinded by physical attraction. Chemistry had blocked her judgment. Again.

CJ's body was numb with ice-cold pain. The sun was shining but there was nothing that could warm her up.

That wasn't quite true, she admitted. Alex, if she were there, could do more than just thaw her frozen heart. She could have explained everything away, taken the tiny spark of hope CJ still felt and fan it into a fire that would warm and reassure her.

She watched Frank Morelli walk slowly away from the apartments, moving among the ambulance and patrol cars and crime scene van. He looked like she felt, she thought, raw and anguished.

He came over to her and said, "Lieutenant. Are you okay?"

She almost laughed. She was about as far from okay as

possible. She ignored his question for one of her own. "What did you find, anything?"

He sighed heavily and she knew, impossibly, it was going to get worse.

"Coroner's guy is giving a preliminary estimate that Simon's been dead thirty-six to forty-eight hours," he began. "On the canvass, we found a couple of witnesses who were here Sunday evening. One of them saw a woman knocking on Simon's door about eight o'clock. Another got a license plate of an old SUV that was in his parking space about that same time." He sighed again. "I called Deputy Chief Duncan. Stan and I are gonna have to work with an investigator from Denver PD on this because of the conflict of interest."

She just stared at him, unable to do anything else. "Conflict of interest," she repeated woodenly.

"I ran the plate myself," he said unhappily. "It was Captain Ryan's vehicle. The woman the neighbor saw matches her description."

Motive. Opportunity. Witnesses placing her on the scene, and a dying declaration by the victim. The tiny spark of hope, hope that Alex might be innocent, flared and died.

Alex could see the spot Frank Morelli had missed shaving that morning. She stared at the dark whiskers just under the angle of his jaw as she sat across from Frank and a detective named Edelman, someone she didn't know from Denver PD. She didn't know for certain who was behind the one-way mirror in the next room, but it wasn't hard to guess.

The last few hours had been surreal, unbelievable. She was sitting just yards from her own office in a interview room, a suspect in the murder of a colleague.

She was trying to remember the name of the novel, the one she'd read in a college literature class, the only college English class she'd actually had. Who had written it? A Russian author, or maybe German. All she could remember was the incredulous amazement of the protagonist, arrested and accused of some unnamed crime for which he was eventually executed, without ever knowing what he had done.

Unlike the character, she knew what the accusation against her was, even knew what at least some of the evidence was, but the horror she felt was the same.

When the Denver detective told her CJ had discovered the body, and the damning words of Simon's accusation against her, she had simply stared at him in stark disbelief.

In a daze, she'd waived her right to counsel, consented to a search of her house and vehicle, which she assumed was happening already. She had told her story four times, whole and in pieces, straightforward as it was.

Simon called her Sunday evening, demanded to see her.

She'd driven to his apartment, but he hadn't answered the door, or his phone, so she'd finally gone home.

No, she hadn't been inside the apartment.

No, she had no idea what he was going to tell her.

No, she didn't have an alibi for Sunday. She'd been alone all day, hadn't talked to anyone but Simon.

No, she hadn't stabbed him three times and left him to die.

And no, she had no idea why he'd typed that she was the killer.

The story was too simple for them to shake, but they didn't have to, she knew. All they needed was one piece of physical evidence linking her to the crime or putting her in Simon's apartment during the critical period, and she was going to be arrested and charged with murder.

Please, God, don't find anything in my truck or at my house.

After a while, Edelman switched gears, shifting to an incredulous summary of the evidence against her and demanding that she explain the inexplicable. Did she really expect them to believe the story about the phone call? Didn't she really have a good reason to silence him before he involved her further in accusation about the Perrault escape? Why would Simon type the words 'ryan killed me' if she hadn't done it?

The questions seemed halfhearted, Alex thought. She knew what he was doing, and he knew that she knew. It was as if it were a required exercise in police interrogation he was required to perform for the unseen watchers.

Finally, she ended it. She had nothing more she was going to tell them, and he'd run out of different ways to ask the same questions. Frank hadn't said a word, just sat watching her sadly. She half-expected them to arrest her on the spot anyway. She imagined the warrant, warm from the judge's signature, being sent across the street, handled by one of her own detectives, probably.

But Edelman just told her to stay in town, and they got up to leave. They left the door open, and before she could follow them out of the room, Deputy Chief Paul Duncan came in.

He looked as crushed as if someone had run over him with a truck. He told her the chief had placed her officially on administrative suspension pending the conclusion of the investigation. Then he asked her for her badge and service weapon. Alex took the badge from her lanyard, where it hung right over her heart, and handed it to him. Then she removed her Glock from the holster, carefully ejected the clip, and laid both the clip and the semi-automatic flat on the table, pointing the barrel of the gun away from him.

Paul asked about her backup weapon, and Alex could see that he was worried that she was going to go home and use it on herself. She reassured him woodenly, but when he tried to say something else to her, she interrupted and told him she didn't want to hear it. She got up and went into the hall without looking back at him.

The door to the observation room opened and CJ stepped out. Part of Alex couldn't believe that CJ could sit in the room and watch. Another part of her wondered why she was even surprised.

Alex waited for a moment in the hallway, wondering what CJ could possibly have to say. Alex knew, without a doubt, that whatever relationship they had was over, as dead as Simon was himself. CJ had certainly reacted badly enough to the implication that Alex had been involved in Perrault's escape—how would she react to Alex as a woman who had clearly knifed her colleague into a bloody corpse?

Alex lifted her chin a little, defiant, ready for whatever words CJ was going to hurl at her, ready for the anger, the revulsion.

She thought she was ready for anything, but she was wrong. CJ said nothing.

But her face was full of the naked emotion she wasn't even trying to hide. Alex saw everything in CJ's face, in her eyes.

Not anger. No revulsion. Just pain.

Everything in her face was deep, wrenching sorrow. Regret, longing, even mourning seemed threaded through her sadness as she looked at Alex.

It was more than Alex could bear. She tried to find something, anything, to say to wash away the anguish she saw in every line of CJ's face.

But CJ turned from her, silently, and walked away.

Alex wanted to reach for her, stop her, talk to her, hold her. She could do none of those things.

She could do nothing at all.

CJ looked up from the booth in the back of the Southside Tavern at the man in front of her.

"Rod," she said softly. "Thanks so much for coming."

He slid into the booth, maneuvering his bulky body across the red vinyl and shifting the table slightly toward CJ so that he could fit.

"You sounded kinda desperate," he said. "You all right, *pelirroja?*"

"No," she answered. "I've got your quesadilla on the way. You want a beer?"

"Just one," he said, as the waitress approached. "Whatever's on tap."

"I hope Ana wasn't too upset at me for calling you."

"Nah." He stroked his mustache. "She knew what she was gettin' when she married me. Besides, she's got book club until about ten, and the Rockies are off tonight, so I got nothin' better to do than hang out with you."

He grinned at her but didn't get the response he expected.

He squared his shoulders and said, "You better tell me what's goin' on."

"I need your advice," she began miserably.

"I got plenty of that. God knows I can't get my wife to take any of it. Are you lookin' for friend advice or cop advice?"

She shook her head. "I don't even know. Both, I guess."

The quesadilla arrived and he unrolled his napkin. "You talk," he said. "I'll eat and listen."

CJ looked at the food with indifference. "Oh, Rod, I don't even know where to start."

He pulled a wedge of quesadilla free and said, "Give me the one-sentence summary."

She stared at the table a moment. Finally she said, "I met a woman I think I could get serious about, finally. And she's probably going to be arrested for murder."

He stopped with the cheesy tortilla halfway to his mouth. "You are fuckin' with me, CJ. You've fallen for a perp?"

"No. She's a cop, Rod. The Captain of Detectives in my department. We've been dating a few months."

He put the quesadilla down and said, "Wait. She's a cop. You're serious about her. And she's a murder suspect?"

"Yes."

"What the fuck? Did she do it?"

"The evidence seems to say yes. I believe it, but I can't believe it."

"What do you need from me, *pelirroja*? You want me to talk you away from her? Or convince you she's innocent?"

CJ thrust long fingers through her hair. "I don't know. I don't know. I'm afraid she did it, yet...I just can't believe she did."

He picked up the tortilla wedge again. "Okay. Start at the top, and don't leave anything out."

She talked, and he ate, and he finally ordered a second beer.

"Okay," Rod said. "Try this. Could her story be true? Don't tell me how unlikely it is. Just tell me, I mean, is it at least possible? And if the answer's yes, let's poke some holes in the 'official version.'"

CJ looked at him warily. "We're the police," she said. "Our version is the official version."

"You're not the police now, *chica*. This time we're thinkin' like the other side."

She gave him a sad smile. "I'm not sure I know how to do that."

He picked up one of the jalapeños that had escaped. "You wanna give up?" he challenged her.

She drew a deep breath. "No, I don't. Okay," she answered. "I don't know of any reason why Alex's story couldn't be true. Unlikely, yes, but possible."

"Good enough for now." He leaned back. "What is the 'official version'?"

"Official version goes like this: Alex helped Perrault escape, and set Simon up. Perrault gives her involvement away to Simon, who in turn incriminates Alex by repeating the statement to me. Alex finds out, from me by the way, about Simon's accusation. She goes to his house Sunday evening, gets in, and stabs him to death with one of his kitchen knives, presumably so that she doesn't have to use her gun and alert the neighbors. She leaves, but Simon manages to crawl to his computer and type out his declaration before he dies."

He finished chewing and said, "So she killed him to cover up what she'd done, helping the murder suspect from the Springs to escape?"

CJ nodded unhappily.

"That make sense to you?"

She spread her hands in frustration. "Sort of. I mean, on some level it's closing the barn door after the horse is out. Simon's already told me what the suspect allegedly said, so it's too late for Alex to cover her complicity completely. On the other hand, if Simon is dead, he can't repeat the statement, and without some other evidence that Alex was involved, I doubt there's anything I can do. So killing Simon would probably get her off the hook. Unless we capture the escapee and he tells us Alex was involved."

"And what's your gut tellin' you about whether she was involved?"

She sighed. "I've got no evidence of any kind to suggest Alex would do such a thing. I can't trace a payment, nor can I find any connection between her and Perrault. It's just...I know her, Rod. She could make a mistake, anybody could. I could even imagine her killing Simon in a fit of anger, I suppose. We're all pretty much capable of killing if we're provoked. But helping a murder suspect escape...That's the kind of deliberate dishonesty I just don't feel she's capable of, under any circumstances." She sighed again. "That sounds bad. I'm saying I think she might be a murderer, but I can't imagine her taking a bribe."

Rod wicked a tiny piece of cheese from his mustache and said, "I think you've solved your own problem."

CJ looked at him, startled. "What do you mean?"

"Look, if we had another three or four hours I could poke all kinda holes in the official version, but here's the important thing. If she wasn't involved in the escape, she has no motive to kill the detective. I know you're not workin' the murder case, but you've still got an open I.A. file on her, right? So work your case, try to clear her on the corruption charge. If you can do that, the murder case kinda falls apart, I figure. Because then she's got no motive. She wouldn't have a reason to kill her detective if she didn't help the suspect escape."

CJ looked away, thinking, watching the waitresses bringing pitchers of beer and burgers to a big table of people across the room. Rock music was playing over the speakers above the bar, but she didn't hear it, really. "I can't work the I.A. case anymore, Rod," she said hesitantly. "We're involved now."

He lifted one dark eyebrow. "Involved? Like, um, involved?"

She tried to smile at him. "Not quite, but—"

"Wait a sec," he interrupted her sharply. "If you don't try to get her cleared, who the hell's gonna do it for you?"

"That's a point."

He sat forward. "Honey, lemme ask you this. Can you be objective? I mean, if you found out she helped this Perrault guy escape, would you turn her in?"

CJ remembered a conversation with Alex about how being an honest cop was important to her. If CJ discovered Alex was lying to her about that, she would report it in a second. "Yes," she answered. "I would."

"Well, that's the test, right? I mean, if you can be objective, then you don't have a conflict of interest."

For the first time she was feeling a tiny spark of hope. She turned back to him and said, "You're pretty great, you know that? Maybe I should go back to the house with you and tell Ana I'm taking you away from her."

He guffawed. "Only a couple of problems with that, *pelirroja*. She's not givin' me up without a fight, and you do not want to fight that woman. And also, correct me if my memory's playin' tricks, but you don't actually do guys."

"Those are two good points."

She drifted away into her thoughts, hope and fear warring again.

"Hey," he said, quietly. "You wanna tell me about her? Not the case, I mean. About her."

CJ said softly, "You don't want to hear this. It's just girly romantic stuff, and you big, tough guys hate that."

He pushed the empty plate away. "Yeah, we hate that, all right. Try me anyway. It's been a real long time since I heard you talk about anybody like you might get serious."

Every memory of Alex was bittersweet, but CJ wanted to pretend just a little longer, pretend that they could still be together. She said, "I'm pretty crazy about her. Alex is smart and strong and direct. She really cares about other people, but she doesn't want to show it. She likes books and movies and eating my cooking."

Rod grinned at her. "Gee, kiddo, sounds just like me."

She laughed a little. "Well, not exactly. No mustache, for one thing."

"Oh. You mean she's not as good-lookin' as me."

CJ could see that he was trying hard to cheer her up, and she wanted to make him think he was succeeding. Lightly she said, "You are incredibly handsome, but, as you will remember, I don't do guys."

"Oh, yeah. So she's pretty, then?"

The picture of Alex coming out of the doorway from the interview room that afternoon came back to her, unbidden. CJ knew she was devastated, but Alex had looked defiant, shoulders back, jaw set, eyes flashing. CJ had never wanted anything in her life more than to go to her, to take Alex in her arms.

"She's not pretty, exactly," CJ answered him. "But I think she's the most beautiful woman I've ever met."

Alex began picking up a pile of books that had been knocked over and lay scattered across her floor. She'd left her front door open to help air out the house, and the early evening sun showed the worn places on the hardwood floor.

Time to refinish them, Alex thought. *Well, I'll have plenty of time.*

There had been a lifetime of work, late nights and early mornings, bad coffee and missed meals, cases she couldn't solve, people she couldn't help, peppered with the occasional triumph: the victim avenged, the bad guy sent to prison. All of it had been wiped away as if it had never existed, all destroyed in a few words from Paul Duncan. The look on his face had been even worse than the words, his utter dismay at the realization that his protégé, a woman almost his own daughter, had done this terrible thing.

She had no doubt that he knew in his heart that she was guilty. And as terrible as that realization was, it faded next to her memory of CJ, the look of complete devastation on her face in the hallway.

She heard the front step creak, the one with the loose board. Then the screen door slammed open and she heard Nicole call out, "Alex? Where are you?"

"Living room."

Nicole stood in the doorway and exclaimed, "My God! What happened in here?"

Alex paused, grasping at one more moment of normal life. When she told her sister what had happened, she knew their relationship would change forever, that Nicole would never see her the same way again. She had lost Paul, lost her career, might soon lose her freedom. She had irrevocably lost CJ too, and she thought if Nicole walked away from her as well that she would be unable to bear the loss.

Alex replied, with a hint of bitter irony, "This is what happens after a very thorough police search."

Nicole looked around in astonishment. There was fingerprint powder, pearly gray-white on some surfaces, and Alex's usual tidy room was in complete disarray.

"Police search?" Nicole demanded. "What are you talking about?"

Alex put the books in her hands on the coffee table and said gravely, "I'm in serious trouble, Nic."

"What happened?" Nicole asked sharply.

"We'd better sit down for this. But first, I need to ask you if you know any really good criminal defense attorneys."

Nicole was staring at her. "For whom?"

"For me."

Nicole stepped toward Alex, her high heels making crisp taps on the hardwood. "Have you been charged?"

"Not yet. But it's just a matter of time."

"What will they charge you with?"

"Murder."

Some minutes later, Nicole said, "I just do not believe this."

Alex said, "I'm having trouble with it myself. You want more coffee?"

She shook her head. "I don't want more coffee," she said. "I want about three or four shots of straight whiskey."

Dryly, Alex said, "I think I have a bottle of something in the living room."

Nicole waved a hand. She'd taken off the gray suit jacket from her lawyer's power suit and hung it on the back of the kitchen chair.

"Tempting as that is," she answered, "I don't want to go home to my son smelling like a distillery. Alex, you don't really think they're going to arrest you, do you?"

"Honestly? I would arrest me if I were on this case. I'm sure they would like to have something else, like my fingerprints on the murder weapon, or a rag with Simon's blood on it in the trunk of my car, but they've got opportunity and motive."

Nicole shook her head angrily. "Why the hell didn't you call me right away? You really had no business making a statement and giving them consent to search before talking with a lawyer, at least."

Alex sighed. "They could've gotten a warrant easily. I've already tried the stonewalling technique with CJ, and it didn't work so well."

"Who is CJ?" Nicole demanded.

Grimacing, Alex got up to put the coffee cups in the sink.

Nicole persisted. "What aren't you telling me?"

With her back still to Nicole, Alex answered, "She's the I.A. inspector."

"Are you going to make me drag this out of you? Is she on this case too?"

"She was doing the investigation on Simon's allegation that I helped Perrault escape. She wanted my financial records and I refused."

"Why on earth would you...oh. Jennifer. I'd forgotten. I'm sorry, Alex."

Alex ran hot water into the mugs and began to wash them. "I'm pretty sure I don't have to worry much about the I.A. investigation now," she said bitterly. "Lieutenant St. Clair is no doubt busy helping my own officers build a case against me for killing Simon."

Part of her still couldn't grasp the truth of it, that CJ was actually working against her. It hurt more than the rest of the mess put together, and acknowledging the truth of that was killing her.

Behind her, Nicole said softly, "Alex?"

Alex felt tears beginning to build behind her eyes. Angrily she ripped the dishtowel from the refrigerator door and shoved it inside one of the mugs, twisting it fiercely.

Nicole got up and took the mug and towel away. "What is it?" she asked, her voice still quiet.

"I think I was about ready to fall in love with her," Alex blurted.

Startled, Nicole took a step backward. "What? Who?"

"CJ."

"I...the inspector?" Nicole was clearly scrambling to adjust to the change in topic. "Wait. She's the woman who asked you out?"

Alex sagged back against the kitchen counter. "It's only been a couple of months, but...Christ, Nic. What the hell am I going to do? She thinks I'm a crooked cop. She thinks I murdered one of my own detectives. God, I have no idea what she's thinking. I just know we're never going to be together, and I just don't think I can..."

She broke down completely. Nicole threw the mug and dishtowel down to pull Alex back into a chair. Alex put her arms on the tabletop and wept. She hated crying, she hated crying in front of Nicole, she hated being weak and vulnerable.

When she could control herself, she sat up again, wiping her wet cheeks. Nicole looked shell-shocked, almost dazed. Alex couldn't remember the last time she'd seen her cool and collected sister look like that. *Dad's funeral, probably.*

"Sorry," Alex managed. "I didn't mean to freak you out."

Nicole said, "No, it's okay. I'd have been crying long before now if I were in your position, I'm just...surprised."

"At what?"

Nicole sat down across from her and stretched out a hand to touch Alex's arm. "You told me about the suspension, about Paul, about the case against you, all of it without flinching. Then you started talking about CJ, and you just fell apart."

Alex dropped her head into her hand. "You're not going to believe this," she half-whispered, "but I'd give it all up to have her back. They can have my badge, they can think whatever they want, if I could just be with her."

She felt Nicole's hand tighten on her wrist. "Alex," Nicole said crisply, and Alex recognized her professional voice. "Tomorrow I'm going to make some calls and get you one of the best criminal defense lawyers in the state. Don't make any more statements, don't do anything until we retain an attorney for you, do you understand? And if anything else happens, if you need anything at all, call me. Any time."

Alex looked at her and said, "Aren't you going to ask me?"

"Ask you what?"

"If I did it."

Nicole's face twisted, and she stood abruptly. "No, I'm not going to ask you," she said harshly. "I'm not your lawyer. Don't confess to me, for God's sake, because this conversation isn't covered by the attorney-client privilege. I'm not going to give you any legal advice, but I am going to tell you what else to do right now."

Holy Christ, Alex thought in astonishment. *She thinks I'm guilty, too.*

"And what is that?" Alex managed.

"I've never seen you like this before. If this relationship means that much to you, for the love of God, fight for it. Fight for her."

CHAPTER TEN

The brief moments of hopeful enthusiasm CJ had after leaving Rod Chavez had disappeared by the time she arrived home. While they were talking, she thought she could see a way through the morass, a plan for at least a chance of saving Alex. All she had to do was prove that Alex was innocent of any involvement in Perrault's escape.

But the more she considered it, the more impossible it seemed. Simon was dead, and Perrault had seemingly vanished. Without either man, there was no way to prove—or disprove—the allegation against Alex.

CJ wearily unlocked the front door of her condo. She tossed her keys on the table in the front hall with a clatter and shut the door behind her. Surely Perrault would turn up eventually. When he did, what would he say? If he insisted that Alex had helped him escape, Alex would surely face a murder charge.

Every police agency in the Rocky Mountain region had been looking for Perrault for more than a week, and there had been not a single confirmed sighting, no leads at all. The car had yielded no evidence, and no leads had emerged from Perrault's family or friends. How was she going to find him when everyone else had failed?

She dumped her purse next to her keys and started down the hall toward her bedroom.

There was a single sharp knock on her door.

CJ put her hand on her holster and turned to face the front door. "Who is it?" she called.

From the other side she heard the muffled answer. "It's me," Alex said.

No, no, no. Not this, not now.

She went to the door and laid her cheek against the wood. "Alex," she said. "This is a bad idea. Go home."

There was a pause, and CJ thought for a moment that Alex had really gone away. Then she heard Alex say, "Let me in, CJ."

She shut her eyes. No. *I am not strong enough to see her.*

Aloud she said, "You should leave."

Alex said, so quietly CJ almost couldn't hear her, "Please, baby."

CJ unraveled inside. Her mind still told her to keep the door securely locked, keep Alex far, far away. She knew that what she was feeling, what she had felt from that first day, would betray her. She craved Alex's arms around her, her warmth, the sound of her voice, her mouth…

Her mind told her what to do, but her traitor body moved her fingers and she unlocked the door.

Alex stepped inside. She was wearing a lightweight track suit, a medium blue color that made her eyes look like bright sapphires. Her color was high, as if she had been running. CJ remembered vividly how she looked that first day, when Alex had run to help her.

"CJ," Alex began, and began to move toward her.

CJ backed up. She had to get away from her. She didn't want

to catch even a hint of her fragrance, feel even a single brush of her hand, or she knew she would be lost.

Alex took another step, and CJ felt the wall against her back.

"No, don't," she said, her voice pleading.

A shadow fell across Alex's face. "You're afraid of me," she said sadly.

The pain in Alex's voice broke her heart. "Oh, God, no!" CJ exclaimed. "Never! I'm not afraid of you. I'm afraid of myself."

Now Alex was right next to her, not quite touching, but close, so close. The sandalwood scent filled CJ. The heat began to rise within her, desire drowning her thoughts.

She tried one last time, desperate for control, to remind herself why she couldn't touch Alex, why they couldn't be together.

You can't trust her. She's not honest, she's a killer...

Alex asked softly, "Just answer this, and I'll go if you want me to."

"What?" She could feel Alex's breath on her cheek.

Alex whispered, "Do you still want me?"

This time it was her heart that betrayed her. CJ moaned, "Oh, God! You don't know how much I want you!"

Then Alex was kissing her, pressing against her so hard that CJ couldn't breathe. She didn't need to breathe, ever again. She only wanted Alex's mouth against hers, breathing for her, giving her the air she needed to live.

Alex broke away, panting, and murmured urgently, "Please. I need you. I'm in pieces without you. Please, CJ."

Desire flared up in CJ, white-hot, piercing her to the core. Her desire had immolated her judgment, destroyed everything except the frantic wanting, her own desperate need.

Alex kissed her again, a hungry kiss, and CJ opened herself to bring Alex in, get even closer to her body. Alex's hands were in her hair, her tongue in CJ's mouth. They pressed closer, and CJ pulled up on her own skirt until Alex could fit her thigh between CJ's legs, bending CJ to her.

Breaking the kiss again, Alex said, very low, "Bed. Take me to your bed."

CJ wasn't certain she could make it that far. Her legs were shaking, her hands unsteady, her body throbbing.

She had thought, when the time came for them to make love, that she would be guiding Alex, leading her, gently taking charge of that first encounter to reassure Alex, protect her. She hadn't counted on this, a complete loss of control.

CJ was on her bed, pulling Alex on top of her, trying to take off Alex's jacket and her own blouse at the same time. Alex sat up on her knees, straddling CJ's hips, and pulled both her jacket and T-shirt over her head with one motion.

Alex was naked from the waist up and CJ groaned. She brought her hands up to cup Alex's breasts and watched Alex's face change at the touch. CJ held her a moment, feeling the weight of the breasts in her palms, then brushed the stiff nipples lightly with her thumbs.

"Jesus," Alex hissed. She fumbled to unbutton CJ's blouse and finally exposed her bra. She knelt forward, kissing down from CJ's collarbone to the valley between her breasts, then pulled at CJ's nipples with her mouth through the lacy fabric of the bra cups.

Alex lay down on top of her, returning for another deep kiss, and CJ could feel Alex's heart beating against her own chest.

"Tell me," CJ whispered. "Tell me if something isn't right for you."

Alex looked at her with stormy eyes, dark blue. "You are right for me," Alex murmured. "I want you."

CJ felt the pressure of their bodies together, igniting heat that seemed to go all the way through her. She wondered if Alex could feel it.

She shut her eyes, focusing on the flood of sensations, the feel of Alex's breasts against her skin, the sound of Alex breathing hard above her.

Beyond desire, beyond relief, beyond anything in her life she had ever wanted, she wanted Alex's body to complete the commitment her emotions had begun.

Alex reached down and unzipped CJ's skirt, managed to pull it off. She pushed her leg again between CJ's thighs. CJ could feel liquid fire pouring into her, focused now between her legs.

She ran her hands down Alex's sides, smoothing the curve of

her waist into her hip, then tugged at the waistband of her pants and said, "Help me."

Alex struggled out of the rest of her clothes, then reached behind CJ to release her bra.

CJ caught Alex's hands and brought them to her chest.

"Front hook," she murmured.

Alex unhooked the bra, pushed it aside. She sat back a moment, filling her gaze with CJ so long that CJ felt a tremor of fear ripple through her desire.

"Alex," she began.

Alex lifted her eyes to CJ's face and said quietly, "You take my breath away."

Then there was only Alex, kissing her breasts, caressing her, pushing against her. CJ was filled with her touch, her scent, the taste of her mouth. She tried to memorize everything, afraid she might never feel this way again: Alex's skin, warm as sunlight, the curve of her neck, the sound of her voice, low and rough, in CJ's ear.

Finally CJ had to cry out, "Please, Alex, please! Touch me now!"

Alex slid her hand down, caressing her thoroughly. CJ thrust against her, then she found Alex's kiss on her mouth.

"Tell me," Alex whispered against her lips.

Tightening her fingers against Alex's back, CJ said, her voice raw, "In me. Please, God, go inside me..."

Alex entered her and CJ felt the world go away. There was nothing except Alex, touching her, thrusting within her.

She wanted to wait, make it last, but the climax overtook her. She arched upward, crying out, holding onto Alex's shoulders desperately.

Alex seemed to ride out the waves of pleasure with her, then relaxed against CJ. She laid her head on the damp skin between CJ's breasts, safely nestling, listening to CJ's heart begin to slow, with her hand gently stroking CJ's thighs.

When CJ could speak again, she managed, "Oh, darlin'."

Alex lifted her head a little and kissed the soft breast near her mouth. "Again," she said.

"I can't," CJ groaned.

Alex leaned over a little more and took a pale rose nipple into her mouth. She sucked gently and CJ pushed against her as the pleasure rose up again.

CJ heard Alex make a satisfied noise.

Lifting her mouth, Alex said, "I bet you're wrong."

She was.

Alex kissed one white shoulder and said, "Are you all right?"

CJ mumbled, "Depends on your definition, I suppose. I'm exhausted, if that was your objective."

Alex answered, "Not entirely."

CJ lifted a hand and pushed strands of red hair from her eyes. Alex met her look, saw her uncertainty.

"Why?" CJ asked simply.

Alex shifted against her, wrapping one leg around CJ. Because in the middle of the worst day of my life," she answered honestly, "I realized the one thing I couldn't bear to lose was you."

She saw CJ's eyes begin to blur with tears. She lifted her thumb and stroked her cheek. "Don't cry," she said softly. "I told you I wouldn't hurt you. I won't. I'm not trying to manipulate you, or just trying to forget everything. I needed to be with you. That's all."

"What else do you need?" CJ asked her.

Alex tried to remember the last time anyone asked her that question, and she couldn't. She searched herself, then responded, "I need to know that I'm not the only one feeling this way."

She trailed a hand slowly down CJ's long torso before letting it come to rest lightly, low on her belly. "I think about you all the time, CJ. I want to be with you, like this, and every other way. I was so damned afraid you were done with me after today, that we could never…"

She didn't finish the sentence because CJ laid long fingers against her lips. "Hush," she said.

Then she leaned up and kissed Alex, a hot and demanding

kiss, openly carnal. Alex groaned into her open mouth.

Then CJ was over her, pressing her into the bed. Alex felt herself unable to do anything except try to remember to keep breathing as CJ caressed her breasts, then kissed her.

The mouth on Alex became demanding, the hands possessive, and Alex felt hot, as if her skin were too tight.

CJ shifted her body a little, so that one long thigh slipped between Alex's legs. Then CJ gave a throaty murmur of pleasure and a moment later Alex realized why, as she felt her wetness against CJ's leg.

Desire poured into Alex's body with a rush. "Oh, God," she groaned into CJ's throat.

CJ kissed her way down the soft skin. Alex abandoned the idea that she had erogenous zones—every spot in her body seemed aroused, longing for CJ to touch and taste.

At last, CJ was running her mouth along the hairpin curve of Alex's inner thighs to the apex.

Even when she was expecting the feel of CJ's lips, Alex could not believe how much her body surged into the touch, seeking CJ's mouth against her.

Then there was nothing, nothing, except the hot, velvet strokes across her. She felt CJ's hands gripping her hips tightly, holding her in place against her mouth.

When she could bear it no longer, Alex reached down and thrust her fingers through CJ's silky hair. She heard herself groaning, as if from far away.

Then she felt the peak coming. She gripped CJ hard, clutching at her as she moved into the climax, consumed with the sensation of CJ's touch.

Alex lay under CJ, her body satisfied, her heart soothed. Whoever she was, whatever happened to her next, she knew she was where she belonged.

CJ moved her head and Alex felt the whisper of soft red hair against her legs. CJ stroked her gently across her belly, fingers light.

After a few minutes, Alex managed, "If I tell you something, promise not to laugh?"

"Not if you don't want me to."

"I've never felt more…this sounds stupid. I've never felt more like a woman in my life."

CJ kissed her. "I think that's the nicest thing anyone's ever said to me," she said softly.

"It seems silly," Alex said, running her hand gently down CJ's hip. "I'm not even the most beautiful woman in the bed."

CJ kissed her again, then punctuated her words with soft kisses down Alex's jaw. "You. Are. Beautiful."

Alex noticed that CJ wasn't comparing Alex to anyone else, just telling Alex how she felt. It made Alex feel beautiful, for the first time in her life.

They lay quietly together, Alex stroking with one hand down CJ's back. A thin sliver of silver light outlined the door. Alex tried to decide what emotion it was that was squeezing her heart. She felt as if she were no longer, somehow, a work in progress, as if she had been finished at last.

"It was what you wanted?" CJ asked her, at length.

Alex heard a tiny thread of apprehension in her voice and leaned down to touch her face.

"I want everything," Alex said, her voice throbbing. "Everything you have, every touch, every way, everything you can give me."

She felt CJ relax, felt her breathing ease into light sleep. Alex lay quietly in a night that was almost silent. Far away a dog barked somewhere, and the faint sound of music still sang from somewhere below.

How could I not have known that I needed this? Alex wondered. *How could I not have known that making love with the right person would feel like this?*

She didn't know how much later it was when she felt CJ stir against her.

CJ whispered to her. "Close your eyes."

Alex shut her eyes obediently. There was nothing to see in the darkness anyway, except the fear of what tomorrow might bring.

Now she focused on what she could feel. CJ's hand went trailing down her torso, stroking, caressing, touching her lightly everywhere: chest, ribs, stomach, the soft crease above her hip.

Alex inhaled and memory came to her. A bright spring afternoon, after the rain, with soft bed sheets hanging on the line, flapping against her, filling her with the fragrance of flowers and clean cotton. CJ smelled like that, and it made her feel safe.

CJ moved against her. Alex could feel the warmth of her body, and catch another scent, the deep, lush odor of woman. Alex reached down, seeking CJ's mouth. In the kiss she could taste CJ, rich flavors of vanilla and spice.

The featherlight touches continued, never demanding, but slowly becoming surer. CJ was murmuring soft words of passion into Alex's ear, and she shuddered with the joy of it.

There was no past, no present. Alex was only herself, in this moment, anchored into her body firmly by CJ's hands on her flesh. Need rose up from her belly, sharp and hot.

She reached for CJ, pulling her into her embrace, finding the warmth of her mouth again. CJ covered her, pressing her hand into Alex confidently.

As Alex lay on her back, spent and limp, CJ sprawled untidily across her body, one leg flung over Alex's thighs, one arm circling her waist. CJ's fingers traced a pattern on Alex's hip as Alex stroked her fingers lightly through CJ's damp hair.

CJ sighed, a deeply contented sound. "We should go to sleep," she murmured.

She felt Alex tighten her fingers.

"Yes. One of us has to go to work."

CJ sighed again into the night, her happiness fading. "Let's not talk about it."

Alex moved her hand away and said, "I think we have to talk about it."

CJ said, "No, we don't. It doesn't matter."

Alex remained still. CJ could feel her breathing. "Sweetheart," Alex tried.

CJ nestled closer. "I like that. 'Sweetheart.'"

Alex took a deep breath and said, "I talked to Nicole earlier. When I asked her if she wanted to know if I killed Simon or not, she told me not to confess to her. I think she actually believes I did it. I know Paul does."

CJ shifted up to look at Alex. "It will be okay."

Alex met her gaze. "How do you know that?" she asked, and CJ sensed the returning sadness marring the earlier feelings of joy. "They've got a pretty damn good case."

"We'll be all right," CJ repeated.

She felt Alex relax against her. In the moment before sleep overtook her, Alex murmured, "At least we don't have to worry about being together now that you're off the I.A. case. Silver lining."

CJ was quiet for a long time, lying back to stare into the darkness. There was no way now to rationalize her continued investigation into Alex's internal affairs case, was there?

Rod had asked her if she could be objective about Alex. Her feelings for Alex were far away from that, but could she be objective about the evidence? If she discovered that Alex was corrupt, she would turn her in. Wouldn't she?

You're fooling yourself, she grimaced at the thought. It's a conflict of interest and you know it. Turn the case over to McCarthy and stay out of it.

Another feeling tugged at her. CJ's heart told her Alex was innocent, and if that were true, then how could she abandon the investigation now? She might be the only one left who could destroy the murder case by proving that Alex lacked a motive to kill Simon.

CJ watched Alex sleeping in the dim light for a long time. CJ was looking for the truth, looking for the lie, but all she could see was the woman she wanted, the woman she needed.

CHAPTER ELEVEN

CJ didn't know Paul Duncan well, but she doubted that he'd ever sounded more discouraged in his life.

"Nathan's in Washington," he was saying into her ear, "but he wants me to report to him daily."

Well, no kidding, CJ thought. She wondered how much political pressure the police chief would be getting now that he'd suspended the head of his Investigations Division.

"I understand," CJ said into the phone. "I'll call you as I make progress. Obviously this has top priority right now."

Guilt jabbed at her again. She couldn't tell Duncan about her relationship with Alex and expect to still investigate the I.A. case against her, especially now that the I.A. matter was an integral part of the murder investigation—and she couldn't tell Alex she was continuing on the I.A. case, either. She suppressed a bitter laugh at the irony of the situation: if she told Alex the truth, Alex would be obligated to report CJ's conflict of interest herself.

Thin ice, very thin. But she couldn't stop now. She might be risking her career, but saving Alex's freedom, and their future, was the bigger risk she had to take.

"I'm on my way to the Springs now," she told him. "I'm going to interview some people, and talk to the CSPD about the Ward case. I think that's the key to this whole mess with Captain Ryan."

"I hope you find something," Duncan said, still sounding discouraged.

She said goodbye to Duncan and grabbed her purse.

CJ sat in a very uncomfortable plastic chair and watched the young woman at the desk in the reception room struggle with something on her computer monitor. The secretary looked to be twenty-two at the most, and she had been typing at a relaxed pace until a few moments ago, when she seemed to jab at something onscreen with the mouse.

The telephone rang, and she scooped it up, clearly happy at the interruption. "Front Range Land Consultants," she announced. "Oh, hi!"

She shot a look at CJ, the only person in the tiny waiting room, and half-turned away as if to insure privacy. CJ tried not to smile as she listened with scant attention to the secretary's half of the phone conversation. Clearly, it was a boyfriend on the other end. Giggles were punctuated with sighs of longing and expressions of undying devotion, as well as a complex discussion of where they would go tonight, and who else was going and who was driving.

CJ had called from the road as she left Denver to drive to Colorado Springs, an hour away. She'd arranged two appointments, the first with Arthur Gammon, the partner of the man allegedly murdered by Robert Perrault. Gammon had left her waiting twenty-two minutes past their scheduled time, and she wondered if he was busy, careless or deliberately rude.

She'd figure it out once she got in to see him. CJ had no idea whether any of this would lead anywhere, but she hadn't given up on the idea that finding out about the killing would, somehow, help Alex.

CJ knew she should be mentally preparing for the upcoming interview, but instead she allowed herself to drift off into the memory of the night before.

There had been other women, after Laurel, but no love-making had felt quite like it had with Alex. Glimpses came back to her, sights and sounds: Alex crying out her name, the sight of Alex arching with climax, Alex's arms holding her, Alex's mouth on her flesh. Every touch had been right, every moment felt like a gift.

Just the possibility that Alex might be arrested, convicted, sent to prison, made her physically sick. CJ knew she would do anything to prevent it. She wondered, wildly, if Alex had a passport, if there was anyplace they could flee and be safe.

She shook the thought off as the inner door opened. The man glared at the back of his secretary's head, then flashed a smile at CJ.

"She's pretty useless," he said, inclining his head toward the young woman, still on the telephone, "but she's decorative for the clients. Come in, Detective, uh…"

CJ stood and offered her hand, masking her distaste. Women as decoration. He'd managed to make her dislike him in the first ten seconds. "It's Lieutenant, actually," she said smoothly. "Lieutenant St. Clair. Thank you for seeing me on such short notice."

Arthur Gammon was losing the fight against middle-aged spread, flesh bulging above his collar and straining at the lower buttons of his shirt. Like him, his office was stuffed to overflowing, covered in pine wood paneling, furnished with purchases from office overstock supply stores: good quality but mismatched. On every wall was a framed picture, artists' representations of developments she presumed he'd been involved with at some point.

She settled into his visitor's chair, blessedly more padded than the one in the waiting room. "Are all these your projects?" she asked, wide-eyed. "You look like you've been real busy."

"We're the top land use consulting agency in El Paso County," he announced.

CJ wondered if this was equivalent to being the biggest frog in a very small pond.

"What is it exactly that ya'll do?" she asked.

He leaned back in his executive chair, which emitted a protesting squeak.

"Real estate developers come to us for help getting their projects off the ground. It's much more complex than you might think. Water rights, utility easements, flood plains. We had this one commercial development that required us to work with the Army Corps of Engineers to get a permit to move dirt near a navigable waterway. And, of course, there's local government approval."

"Oh," she said, green eyes wide. "City zoning, things like that?"

He nodded in approval, as if she were a bright intern. "Or county planning commission recommendations of approvals if the development is in the unincorporated areas of the county. Carl was especially helpful with getting through the applications and the public hearings and such."

"You must miss your partner," CJ said sympathetically.

"Yeah. So what is it that I can do for you, Lieutenant? You know I've already talked to Colorado Springs detectives. Twice."

CJ slipped a small, digital tape recorder from her purse and set it on the desk between them. He eyed it unhappily and she said, "Oh, I hope you don't mind. I have to tape all my interviews or the details just fly out of my head."

He laughed, revealing a mouth full of large, yellow-stained teeth. Smoker, she thought, catching a faint whiff of stale smoke.

"Sure." He waved a hand. "It's okay with me."

"Thank you, and I do appreciate ya'll taking the time to talk to me," she continued. "I'm actually not investigating the murder of Mr. Ward, but another matter related to that."

He gave her a shrewd look. He had blue eyes, pale and watery, and she thought briefly about how eyes of the same color could look so different. "What matter might that be?" he asked warily.

She crossed her legs and he gave them an appreciative glance. She answered, "As you may know, Robert Perrault escaped from custody last week when a Colfax Police detective was transporting him back to the Springs."

"I read about it," he said heavily.

"What you may not know is that the detective from whose custody he escaped was murdered a couple of days ago."

She let the statement hover between them, watching him carefully. He frowned at her and said, "You're investigating his murder?"

"I'm assigned to Internal Affairs," she told him. "I was investigating his involvement in the escape of Robert Perrault."

He tapped his pudgy fingers on the desk nervously, and she thought he probably wanted a cigarette. "You said you were investigating his involvement," Gammon said, after a moment. "Aren't you investigating it any more?"

"Actually, no," she admitted. "The death of the officer terminates the Internal Affairs investigation. I'm currently working on the possible involvement of another officer in the escape of Mr. Perrault. His superior, Captain Alex Ryan."

"You think she had something to do with Perrault's escape?" he asked.

CJ smiled, though she was far from cheerful. "That's what I'm trying to find out," she answered. "What can you tell me about Carl Ward?"

In response, he turned and grabbed a framed photograph from the bookshelf behind his desk. "Here," he said, pointing. "That's Carl, there, with his wife Elaine. That's their son, Mitchell, and that's me and my son Michael. The boys are within a few months of each other, just turned eighteen. This was taken at Carl and Elaine's twenty-fifth wedding anniversary in April."

CJ looked at the photo. The two men were in tuxedos, Elaine Ward was in a light blue cocktail dress, bright with sequins on the bodice. She looked very well maintained, a blonde, expensive hairdo, extensive makeup, a deep tan. The two boys were in suits and ties and looked vaguely bored. Drinks, dinner and dancing at the country club, CJ thought. Where, she wondered, was Mrs. Gammon?

"You were family," she said.

He nodded, gratified that she'd gotten it right. "Damn straight. He was like a brother to me, Elaine and Mitch like my own. You guys gotta catch the son of a bitch that killed him, okay? And this Captain Ryan of yours, if she helped him get away, you gotta arrest her, too."

CJ kept her face unexpressive, but the turmoil threatened her calm again.

He got one thing right, she thought, trying to comfort herself. *She is my captain.*

"Tell me," she began, "about the night Carl Ward was killed."

She led him through it, and he told her the story, well-practiced. The hysterical call from Elaine Ward, his identification of the body to spare her, the police investigation.

"Did you benefit financially from Ward's death?" CJ asked him casually.

He glared at her. "The other cops asked me that, too," he said with a touch of belligerence. "And I'll tell you what I told them. We had key man insurance on both of us. You know what that is?"

CJ suppressed her irritation at him again and nodded.

"Well, the policy was worth five hundred thousand dollars. So yes, I benefited financially. But I lost my business partner, and he'll be goddamned hard to replace. And I lost my friend, and he will be impossible to replace. And that's all I'm gonna say about that."

"Do you think Robert Perrault killed him as part of a robbery?"

"Hell, yes, that's what happened. Why would you think any different?"

CJ took the tape recorder, turned it off, and replaced it in her purse. She stood and said, "Thank you again for seeing me, Mr. Gammon. I'll walk myself out."

As she was leaving, a young man entered the reception room. He wore a denim shirt with 'Slade Real Estate' stitched across the front pocket, new-looking work boots, and jeans badly stained with dirt.

He ignored CJ and jerked his thumb at the office door.

"He in?" the kid asked the secretary brusquely.

"Yes, he's..."

Arthur Gammon appeared in the doorway and demanded, "What the hell's going on?"

The young man grumbled, "You would not believe the shit they pulled on me."

Gammon glanced quickly at CJ and said, "Get in here. Goodbye, Lieutenant."

He slammed his office door behind the boy. Despite the change of clothing, CJ had had no trouble recognizing him. CJ said casually to the secretary, "That's Michael Gammon, I take it."

"Oh, yeah," the secretary replied. "And he's a pain in the butt."

"You probably shouldn't let Mr. Gammon hear you say that," CJ said mildly. "Does he work here?"

She shook her head. "No, he works for some big client of Mr. Gammon's. If you can call it work. He's in here, like, every other day."

CJ walked thoughtfully to her car.

CJ dictated a few notes of her own into the recorder, her impressions and thoughts on the interview, and included the encounter with Michael Gammon. When she was finished, she glanced at her watch. She had two hours before her second appointment. It was almost eleven thirty, and she decided it was close enough to lunchtime to justify eating. She punched an address into her GPS and followed the directions given by the mechanical voice to the Edelweiss.

She was the first one in the door when the restaurant opened, and she read the menu with pleasure. There was no cuisine she didn't appreciate, and authentic German restaurants were in short supply in Colorado. She ordered sauerbraten and ate every bite of the meal, finishing off the dumpling and red cabbage, and mopping up the last of the sweet-and-sour sauce with the delicious bread.

Full and contented, she returned to her car in the parking lot and picked up her cell phone.

Alex answered on the second ring. "Hi. Where are you?"

"Out of the office. I just had lunch and it was spectacularly good." She'd have to figure out later what to tell Alex about where she went.

Alex's laugh came through the line and CJ felt her spirit grow brighter. She'd had to leave Alex in her bed early that morning, with just a brief kiss goodbye.

"There's a saying for that," Alex said. "The translation is 'Full Stomach, Happy Heart.' I'd give you the Spanish version but you'd just mangle it."

CJ snuggled happily back into her leather seat. "I have a happy heart," she said, "but it's not on account of lunch."

"Really," Alex said, and her voice dropped into a register that sent a shiver through CJ's body. "So why are you so happy today?"

"Guess."

"Hmmm. Is it because you got a really good night's sleep?"

"Not even close."

"This is tough. You went shopping this morning and bought a new pair of shoes?"

"You're getting colder. What kind of detective are you?"

There was a brief pause and CJ wished she could reach through the phone and touch Alex.

Finally Alex said, "I give up. Unless it was because you got some really good sex last night."

"Good doesn't even begin to describe it."

"Spectacular? Life-changing? Awe-inspiring?"

Now it was CJ's turn to laugh. "Pretty proud of ourselves, aren't we?" She grinned to herself.

Suddenly Alex's tone grew serious. "You left pretty quickly this morning. Was...is everything all right?"

"Oh, darlin', of course. I was just running late, as usual. What I wanted to do was crawl back in bed with you for a couple of days."

"I was afraid that I…I don't know, came on too strong, or something. I know the timing was awful, I just…I just needed you. I'm sorry."

CJ sat forward, gripping the phone tightly. "Don't you ever apologize for that," she said firmly. "Ever. I wanted you too, you know that. Making love with you was wonderful, however it happened. Stop worrying."

"I'll try. It's not something I'm particularly good at."

"I know," CJ said softly. "I told you last night. We'll figure this out." She hesitated another moment, trying to pick her words carefully. "Alex, would it be all right if we kept this—our relationship, I mean—private for a bit? Not talk about it until we're ready?"

CJ held her breath a moment until she heard Alex say slowly, "If that's what you want. But why?"

"I just want us to be more…oh, I don't know, settled, I suppose. People might treat you differently, and I want you to be ready for that."

Just until I can clear you, CJ thought. Then it will be all right.

Alex said again, "If that's what you want. I should tell you that Nicole already knows we've been seeing each other."

CJ shut her eyes. Every person who knew increased the risk that someone at the department would discover their relationship before she was ready. But what possible reason could she give Alex for not telling her sister?

"I understand," CJ conceded softly.

"Look, could we maybe talk more about this in person?" Alex asked. "I want to be in the same room with you when we talk."

"I'll come by tonight," she promised. "I have to do an interview at one thirty, then I'll probably stop back by the office on the way in. I'll call you when I'm done, okay?"

"Okay," Alex said, and CJ heard relief in her voice. "You want me to make dinner?"

CJ laughed. "No, darlin', I do not. We can go out, or I can pick something up. Let's decide when I call."

"All right. And CJ?"

"Yes?"

"Drive home carefully. I miss you."

CJ caught a reflection of herself, smiling, in the rearview mirror.

"Oh, Alex. I really miss you, too. See you tonight."

CJ used the GPS in her car to find Carl and Elaine Ward's house, a big two-story in an exclusive suburb of the city with winding roads, cul-de-sacs and street names that seemed designed to confuse. CJ had sympathy for a post office that had to distinguish among Pikes Peak Drive, Pikes Peak Street and Pikes Peak Way within a few blocks of each other.

She was early, so she parked on the street and looked over the house. The yard looked meticulously and professionally maintained, not unlike the picture she'd seen of Mrs. Ward herself, CJ reflected. There was a four-car garage, and CJ wondered if the late Mr. Ward liked to collect cars, or if he liked expensive toys, like boats or recreational vehicles.

After a few minutes her mind wandered away once again. She began to calculate how many hours it would be before she could see Alex this evening, and the thought of being back in her arms triggered a warm flicker of excitement inside her.

Vivian was right, she thought. *I've really got it bad.*

A silver Mercedes came speeding down the street, then turned into the Wards' driveway with a slight screech of tires. CJ watched the car pull into the garage, waited five minutes, then rang the doorbell.

The woman who opened the door was wearing a tennis dress, white with black piping, matching socks and very expensive court shoes. Diamond studs were in her ears, and several gold chains on her chest. She was so deeply tanned that CJ wondered if she had a tanning booth in her house.

"Yes?" she said. "Are you the detective?"

CJ showed her shield and said, "Lieutenant St. Clair. Mrs. Ward? Thank you for seeing me."

Elaine Ward made an unpleasant noise. "Like I have a choice," she spat. "My husband has the bad luck to get himself fucking murdered, and suddenly everybody wants some of my time. You may as well come in."

She left the door open and walked away, leaving a surprised CJ to shut the door and follow her into a large family room. The room was two stories tall, with huge windows reaching almost to the ceiling, like a cathedral. Through them CJ could see an impressive view of the mountains, the foothills looming close, and beyond them, just the top of Pike's Peak. In the room itself, the couches were white, the accessories were black, and a huge swath of zebra-striped rug covered the floor. In one corner a white grand piano had the air of a decoration rather than a well-used instrument.

It all looked expensive, tasteful, and like the yard outside, it seemed professionally decorated rather than lived in. CJ had been in plenty of fine homes with different décor but the same look, most of them when she was growing up. Rarely did police work lead her to places that looked like this one.

CJ managed to get a chair where the light would fall on Mrs. Ward's face and got out her recorder. The lady of the house sat on the couch, lit a cigarette with a gold lighter, and took in a big lungful of smoke.

"I needed that," she exhaled. "No smoking at the country club."

CJ noted the Adidas tennis bag tossed casually on the other end of the couch.

"Did you win?" she asked politely. She never knew what might break the ice.

Elaine Ward laughed. "Three sets, one tie-breaker. Barbara thinks she's pretty hot shit, club singles champion two of the last three years, but she can't play doubles worth crap. She only plays with Sharon because she can boss her around. We took them seven to five in the third set." She eyed CJ speculatively. "Do you play?"

"I have," CJ said neutrally. *Tennis lessons,* she thought, *not to mention dance lessons and horseback riding and anything else my mother thought a properly bred Southern girl should do.* "My job keeps me pretty busy, so I haven't played in a while."

"You should," Elaine said. "You look tall enough to have a

big serve, and I bet you can cover some ground at the net."

"Yes," CJ said, "I was always a serve-and-volley player."

"No doubt," Elaine said, inhaling cigarette smoke again. "I'm hoping the exercise somehow cancels out the tobacco." She laughed, an unpleasantly nasal sound. "It's funny, Carl was always on my ass about smoking, and he's the one who ends up dead in some stupid robbery."

CJ failed to see the humor, but she asked calmly, "Tell me, Mrs. Ward, do you believe it was a robbery?"

Elaine's eyes narrowed against the smoke. "Maybe you should tell me why you're doubting it."

CJ explained who she was, and what she was doing. Before she was quite done, a door slammed somewhere in the back of the house. Elaine Ward made a face. She stubbed out her cigarette and called out, "Mitch?"

After a moment, a young man sauntered into the room. He had his father's heavy features but was blond like his mother. He wore only long trunks and flip-flops, and carried a dark brown bottle of Michelob.

Elaine said, "It's a little early for that, isn't it?"

He took a long swig and said, "It stinks in here. And you know how much I love the smell of stale cigarette smoke in the morning."

CJ choked back a laugh at the reference to the line from *Apocalypse Now*, and Mitchell Ward shot her an appreciative glance.

The joke missed Elaine entirely. "It's not morning, it's almost two o'clock," she complained, "and you drink entirely too much beer. Where the hell have you been?"

He shrugged and drank some more. "Me and Buzz were over at Jen's, at the pool. It's hot out."

"Maybe you should try working for a living outside and see how hot is then, instead of loafing around all day and partying all night," Elaine snapped at him.

"Oh, right." He smirked at her. "Because that's so much worse than gossiping at the club all day and getting drunk every night. Skip it. I'm taking a shower."

He left the room without another word. Elaine jerked

another cigarette from her pack of Salems and lit it, snapping the lighter closed. "Fucking teenagers," she muttered. "You have any kids?"

"No," CJ answered. She considered that if she had ever spoken to her mother in the way Mitch Ward had just spoken to his, Lydia St. Clair would have had her permanently banished to Antarctica. Although, on second thought, her mother had pretty much done that anyway.

"He was a pain in the ass before Carl died," she remarked, "but at least Carl could talk to him. Since we buried his father, he's been impossible. He has no idea what I'm going through."

Cautiously, CJ ventured, "I'm sure you miss your husband very much."

The unpleasant nasal laugh returned. "Miss him? How the fuck can I miss him? Poor bastard was never here, always working. I thought when the real estate market went south a few years back and the developers ran for cover, he would at least be able to get home for dinner, but it was just as bad as ever."

"Was the business in trouble?"

She waved a hand, the smoke spiraling her around like a ghostly streamer. "I have no idea, but I doubt it. Carl had the contacts, brought in the clients, and massaged the local politicians, but Art is the money guy. I can't believe Art would let a single penny they ever earned out of his tight little fist."

"Were they old friends?" CJ asked.

"Yeah, since before the boys were born. Art was doing some small-time development and Carl was on the Board of County Commissioners. They hit it off, and when Carl was term-limited, he and Art started the business."

CJ let herself glance appreciatively around the room. "It must have done well," she said.

Another nasal laugh erupted as Elaine leaned forward to tap off ashes in a heavy black onyx ashtray on the coffee table. "This wasn't from the firm," she said. "The business barely paid the country club dues. It was just to keep Carl busy, and God knows it did that."

"Family money?" CJ ventured.

Elaine's eyes narrowed. "Cops. You're so subtle. The Springs detectives have already been through this with me, believe it. Carl comes from money, and a lot of it is still in the family. But I've got enough, at least for now. The problem is that you have no fucking idea how hard it is to be a widow in our circle. I'm not going to be a fifth wheel the rest of my life, count on that."

Not much grieving going on here, CJ mused. She abruptly changed tactics and said, "Did you know Robert Perrault?"

Elaine sat back and smoked, looking at CJ for a moment.

"I never heard of him before he murdered Carl," she said. "And you can ask the Springs cops about that, too. At the time of my unfortunate husband's murder, I was playing bridge with seven other women at the club. Carl was a pain in the ass sometimes, but I'm a lot worse without him than I was with him, so I'd be very happy if you'd quit sitting here asking me the same goddamned questions and go out and find the son of a bitch who killed him."

CJ called Duncan on the way back to the office. Her interview with the CSPD detective on the Ward homicide had taken longer than she'd expected, and she wasn't sure whether she would make it back before he left.

"How'd it go?" he grunted at her, sounding no happier than he had that morning.

"Nothing clear-cut, but I know more than I did this morning. The interview with the CSPD detective was interesting. They are not completely convinced that Ward's murder was quite as random as it appeared. And I tend to agree."

"Really?" Duncan said, with interest. "Why not?"

"I went to Ward's office to interview his partner. The night he was killed, he was supposedly leaving his business after working late, and I've got to tell you, it's a weird place for a mugging. No retail or residential, just office space and light industrial. No sane armed robber would just hang around the parking lot on the off chance that someone would be leaving late. And Ward was carrying a couple of hundred dollars in cash, credits cards, a Rolex, an unusually nice haul for a mugger. A bit too much coincidence. That's one reason the Springs detective really, really wanted to talk to Perrault."

After Duncan grunted again to show he was still listening, CJ continued. "I'll give all my interview notes to Chad when I get back, and I'll go over the transcriptions of the recordings tomorrow. There's something I just can't quite articulate yet."

"Well, find it, Inspector," Duncan muttered. "We're going to run out of time real fast."

CHAPTER TWELVE

Alex sat on her back porch, legs stretched out to the sun. In her right hand was a glass of iced tea, half empty. It was a beautiful afternoon, she thought: the usual puffy white clouds were beginning to dot the bright blue Colorado summer sky, and far off to the west was a giant thunderhead just beginning to gather itself for a march across the eastern plains. Maybe the rain would hold off until after dark, though whenever it came it would be welcome.

If she were just having an afternoon off, it would be perfect. Well, perfect if it were CJ in the other lounge chair instead of Nicole, and if she weren't in the midst of a strategy session about what would happen when one of her own officers would show up and give her a copy of an arrest warrant with her name on it.

Nicole said, with some asperity, "Are you listening?"

"Yes," Alex said. "I've got Whitefield's number, and I'll phone him as soon as I hear anything. It's probable that they'll just call me, let me turn myself in at the station for booking. I'll make sure Whitefield goes with me."

"Good," Nicole said crisply. "And listen to me, Alex. Do whatever he says. If he tells you to shut up, shut up. He's the best criminal defense attorney in the region, but it doesn't matter how good he is if you don't take his advice."

Alex said, "And how is it, exactly, that we can afford the best criminal attorney in the region?"

Nicole waved a dismissive hand. "I'm getting the professional courtesy rate. He's an old fraternity brother of my senior partner."

"Even at that, this is going to cost us a hell of a lot. I don't want you going into debt for me, Nic. You've got my nephew to consider."

Nicole drained the last of her iced tea and said, "You make me crazy. You supported me for ten years, Alex, and you don't want me to pay a legal bill?"

"It wasn't just me. There was Dad's insurance."

"I know exactly how much money that was, and it didn't begin to touch my tuition. You took overtime every chance you got so I didn't have to work during the school year, and I never once heard you complain about it."

"Nic. You're my sister, remember?"

"And that's my point. You're my sister. Let me handle this, all right? Now, we have to talk about..."

Alex heard the side gate open, metal scraping against the ground. She got up and looked at her watch, surprised to see that it was after six o'clock. To her delight, CJ came around the corner, her suit jacket draped over one arm.

"Hi," CJ greeted them. "No one answered the front door, but I saw the Volvo out front."

There was brief moment of awkwardness as she stood, a few feet away. Alex knew what she was feeling and so she crossed to meet her.

"Hi," she said softly, and leaned in to kiss CJ, lightly and briefly, on the mouth.

She saw CJ's lips curve up happily. Alex took her free hand and led her to the chairs on the porch. She said, "CJ, this is my favorite sister, Nicole."

Nicole stood, offered her hand, and said, "I'm her only sister as well. I am very happy to meet you at last, Ms. St. Clair. I hope I'm not supposed to call you lieutenant."

CJ laughed and said, "Please, no. It's CJ."

They all sat down, and Alex watched with both trepidation and amusement as sister and lover eyed each other covertly.

"Would you like some iced tea?" she asked CJ. "Sorry I don't have any sweet tea."

CJ smiled and said, "Nobody in Colorado makes sweet tea, so I'm used to it. Plain old regular is just fine."

"Okay. Nic, you need a refill?"

"Yes, thanks."

Alex went inside and busied herself with ice cubes, pitcher and glasses, listening through the open kitchen window as best she could.

"I saw a photo of your son in Alex's office," CJ began. "He's a doll."

Nice opening, Alex thought.

She could hear pride in Nicole's voice as she said, "He's a great little boy. He looks just like his father. I'd like for you to come over some weekend and meet both of them."

"I would love that," CJ said warmly.

"I think," Nicole said after a moment, "it's time for all of us to get to know you."

Alex could hear a slight creak in the chair as CJ sat forward and said, "Nicole, what do you want to know?"

"I...what?"

Alex smiled as she sliced lemon. *Oh, nice job, sweetheart*, she thought.

CJ continued, "You must have a lot of questions, about me, about Alex with me. I know Alex hasn't dated a woman before."

"Are you always this direct?" Nicole sounded a little stiff.

"Only when it's important," CJ answered. "Ask me anything you need to, Nicole. If Alex were my sister, I'd have a lot of concerns, too."

"Concerns? Like, are you just screwing around with her? Are you going to dump her and break her heart? Are you trying to put her in prison for something she didn't do? Concerns like those?"

Alex threw down the paring knife and turned to go outside, but then she heard CJ say calmly, "Fair enough. I don't sleep with women only for sport, and I never have. I'm like a lot of other people, Nicole, trying to find someone I can be with and spend a lifetime loving. I don't know yet if that person is Alex, but I hope very much that it is. And as for trying to put her in prison...that is the last thing I want."

Alex waited in the kitchen, tense and listening. After a very long moment, she heard Nicole say, "Then on that, at least, we agree."

Alex gathered up the tray and came out again. "How's it going?" she asked innocently.

"Just fine," they answered together, then began to laugh, easing the tension.

"How was your day?" Alex asked CJ as the three women drank tea.

"Long," CJ answered. "How's it going here?" she asked.

Her question included Nicole, and they talked for a few minutes about Alex's legal representation. Eventually, CJ asked quietly, "Have you thought about bond?"

Nicole said tensely, "Thought about it, yes. Solved the problem, no. Not yet."

Alex felt her stomach clench. Jail was a special kind of hell for police officers, and she didn't mind admitting, to herself at least, that she was terrified of being there. She couldn't even begin to think about prison.

CJ said to Alex, "How much is the bail likely to be, do you think?"

Alex shrugged. "Depends on how good a job my attorney does convincing the judge I'm not a threat to the population generally. For a murder charge, it could be fifty thousand dollars. It could be a hundred thousand dollars. Christ, it could be more."

She heard Nicole's sudden intake of breath. "I had no idea it could be so much," she admitted. "We can pay a bail bondsman, though, right?"

"Yes," Alex said, "but they typically want at least ten percent up front, and you don't get that back."

Nicole was frowning, clearly thinking frantically, when CJ interrupted softly, "It's not a problem."

Alex said, a little harshly, "Surprisingly, I don't have ten or twenty thousand dollars lying around. But you would know that."

CJ winced, and Alex said contritely, "Sorry, sweetheart. I didn't mean it like that."

CJ said, "I thought about this as I was driving up. I called Roger Edgarton."

Nicole demanded, "Who is that?"

"He's the trustee of my grandfather's trust. My trust, really."

"There aren't other beneficiaries?"

Alex said, "Nicole, don't lawyer up on us here."

CJ said, "It's all right. No, I'm the only beneficiary. He's arranging a letter of credit for me. It should be here tomorrow, so if Alex is arrested, we'll be able to post bail as soon as she's arraigned. I don't want her spending one minute in the county jail."

Alex said, "You don't have to do that."

CJ reached across and took her hand firmly.

"Yes, I do. I want to, darlin'. I'm not risking anything. You're not going to jump bail, are you?"

She said it lightly, but Nicole interrupted, "You're going to pay for a bond?"

CJ said, "No, I'll secure all of it myself, whatever it is."

"Even if it's a hundred thousand dollars?" Nicole persisted.

CJ met her eyes. "The letter of credit is for a million," she answered finally. "I can get more if we need it."

Silence fell on them. When Alex found her voice at last, she said, "You have a million dollars in your trust fund?"

CJ answered with a smile, "No, I have more than that. But you're not with me for my money, are you?"

Alex walked Nicole to her car, then returned to find CJ putting the glasses in the sink. She crossed to her and said, "I'd like a proper greeting now, please."

CJ turned happily and said, "My pleasure."

She kicked off her shoes and Alex brought her hands to CJ's face and kissed her thoroughly.

"I missed you today," Alex said.

"Apparently," CJ said with a little smile. "When you kiss me like that, it almost makes going to work worth it."

"What do you want first? You want to talk, or get some dinner?"

CJ smirked and answered, "Neither one."

Alex said, with mock severity, "I thought you tried never to miss a meal."

CJ leaned close and said, "Every rule has its exception. I think I'd like a house tour."

"You've seen the house."

"Not all of it. I haven't seen the bedroom."

"Oh. We should fix that right away, then," Alex responded.

Alex lay half-asleep, lying on her side. She could hear the faint rumble of thunder in the distance to the west.

She felt a soft touch trailing down her back.

"CJ, I'm begging you for mercy," Alex muttered happily. "I'm completely exhausted."

CJ murmured, "I'm just touching you."

"That's what got me exhausted in the first place."

"Stop it. We can enjoy touching without making love."

"Can we?"

"Smart mouth. Yes. Just relax."

CJ's hand traced down the sinuous curve of spine, then slipped down to briefly clasp one firm buttock. She ran the back of her hand down Alex's neck across her shoulder, then trailed fingers gently down to caress the side of one breast. She stroked the flare from waist to hip and back again.

Alex whispered, "What exactly are you doing?"

"I'm trying to decide which of your curves is my favorite. So many nice ones to chose from."

Alex rolled over and smiled at her.

CJ said softly, "Ah. That's it."

"What?"

CJ said, "This one is my favorite," and leaned down to kiss the upward curve of Alex's mouth.

Long minutes later, Alex murmured, "You're being very brave, but I know you're starving. Let's raid the kitchen."

"Is there anything in there?"

"Not much. Betty Duncan stopped by earlier today and brought me a tuna casserole, if you can believe it."

CJ sat up against the headboard, amused. "Really? A casserole?"

Alex shook her head. "Yeah. She was pretty pissed off at Paul for suspending me, I think, and just wanted to reassure me I was still part of the family. God knows Nic and I ate a lot of tuna noodle casseroles at her house after Mom died."

CJ stroked the back of her hand down Alex's side. "You're not angry at Paul, are you?"

Alex shook her head again. "Not really. What was he supposed to do? He could hardly give me special treatment, and you have to admit, the evidence looks bad. I just wish I felt like everybody—Paul, Nicole, Frank—looked like they believed I didn't kill somebody."

CJ said gravely, "You know that I believe you, don't you?"

Alex looked at her closely. "You had your doubts, too."

"I did," CJ admitted. "But I don't any more."

Alex leaned forward and kissed her. "Thank you," she whispered.

"Come on," CJ said. "Feed me."

CJ showered first, then borrowed the longest T-shirt Alex

owned, which still ended several inches above her knees. Alex watched her from the bed and said, "You have unbelievably beautiful legs."

CJ leaned over and flashed her. "Just my legs?" she asked innocently.

"Come over here," Alex growled.

CJ laughed and said, "Food first. I don't know about you, but I need some energy."

"You seemed plenty energetic an hour ago."

"Well, ya'll wore me out. In a good way."

Alex jumped into the shower. When she got out, she quickly dressed in sweatpants, socks and a faded Colfax PD T-shirt.

CJ was in her tiny kitchen, putting finishing touches on a huge, elaborate plate of nachos.

"Wow, this looks great," Alex exclaimed. "How did you manage that from my pantry?"

CJ said, "It's just a knack. I keep telling you, I'm all about the food. Beer, wine, or something stronger?"

"Beer with nachos, I think."

CJ grabbed two Michelob Lights from the refrigerator and Alex carried the plates into the living room. She settled on the couch, beer and food within easy reach, and CJ curled into the rocking chair nearby.

Alex munched happily. "Man, this is good."

"Easy to do," CJ said, pleased. "Chips, salsa, some leftover black beans, grate the cheese on top, microwave for a minute and a half. I would have added sour cream if you'd had any. You really don't cook much, I take it."

Alex laughed. "I live on coffee, toast, cereal and takeout. I wasn't kidding when I said I can't cook."

"Trust me, you can learn. I'd never made anything in my life more complicated than a peanut butter sandwich until I was twenty."

"What turned you into Julia Child?"

CJ swallowed and said, "I moved out of the sorority house and started living with Laurel, who couldn't cook worth a lick. I had to learn or we were both going to starve."

Alex said, "You know, I really should be grateful to her."

"What?" CJ asked, startled.

"Absolutely. She forced you to learn how to cook, she acted like an asshole and compelled you to move to Colorado, and she helped you understand that you're a lesbian. And now I'm the beneficiary of all three."

CJ shook her head in amazement. "I never thought I would say this," she said, "but you're right. Perhaps I should send her a thank you note."

"On second thought, maybe not," Alex said. "I do not want you to be thinking about the dozens of ex-girlfriends you undoubtedly have littering your past."

CJ sat back and said, "Is this the conversation we're going to have?"

"Which one is that?"

"The sexual history conversation."

Alex set her beer bottle down on the coffee table. "Okay," she said. "I'll go first. I was too busy running the household and taking care of Nicole to date much in high school. I met Tony when I was in uniform. He was prosecuting a case where I was the arresting officer. He was the first man I ever slept with, and I think I felt morally obligated to marry him after that. And after the divorce, I made several other attempts to enjoy sex with men and pretty much failed miserably. I haven't been with anyone else in almost two years."

CJ ran a fingernail across the top of her bottle. "Alex," she said softly. "Are you happy?"

"About us? Hell, yes. Being in bed with you is unbelievable, if that's what you're asking. Were you having trouble figuring that out?"

"No. Just checking."

Alex picked up her beer again and said, "Your turn. Or do I want to hear this?"

CJ answered, "The story is just about as brief. After Laurel, I dated some, but didn't really get serious about anyone. Until I met a woman, one Vivian introduced me to, if you can believe it. I liked her. I thought I loved her. We lived together for two years."

"Why did you break up? Did she cheat as well?"

CJ sighed. "No. Not exactly, anyway. She worked a lot. She was in real estate, and that's pretty much a twenty-four seven job if you let it become one. When things began to go bad with us, she had an interesting approach to solving the problem I wasn't interested in pursuing. So she moved out."

Alex ate silently for a moment, and pushed her plate away. "I think you should tell me," she said at length. "Did she want to go to counseling?"

CJ laughed, a little bitterly. "Oh, darlin', no. I would have gone to couples counseling in a minute. I suggested it, in fact. But Steph decided the problem was our sex life, so she suggested we find a friend to help us out with that."

She looked at Alex for her reaction, and Alex felt her eyebrows go up. "She wanted another woman in bed with you?"

"Yes. In truth, she just wanted my permission to cheat, and apparently wanted me to watch her doing it as well. I was emphatically not interested."

She could see CJ looking at her, a little question in her eyes. "Um, just for the record, CJ, I'm not interested in a threesome." She watched CJ relax again.

"Glad to hear it," CJ said lightly.

She picked up the empty plates and carried them to the kitchen. Alex followed her and took the plates away, placing them in the sink, then turned CJ to face her.

"That's why you doubted me," Alex said. "You're questioning your own judgment about women, aren't you?"

CJ looked away. "Wouldn't you?"

"Probably," Alex admitted. "But I heard what you said to Nicole this afternoon. I know you're a romantic, I know you're still looking for the right woman. CJ, I want it to be me."

CJ met her eyes, searching.

"Do you?" she whispered.

Alex kissed her and said, "I do. And we have plenty of time to find out. Assuming I can stay out of prison."

CHAPTER THIRTEEN

CJ walked into her office and Chad McCarthy said, "Good morning, Inspector. And happy hump day."

She stopped and stared at him. "Excuse me?"

"Wednesday, you know. Getting past the middle of the week. The hump. After lunch on Wednesday, you're on the downhill slide to the weekend."

She recovered herself and asked, smiling, "How long have you been a police officer, Sergeant?"

"Lemme see. About sixteen years. Why?"

CJ, still smiling, shook her head and said, "There aren't weekends for cops, you should know that by now. How are my transcripts from yesterday's interviews coming along?"

"They should be up here by noon. I'll bring them in when they get here. Meantime, there are two new files on your desk."

CJ sighed. She knew she didn't have the luxury of working only on clearing Alex, but she didn't think her concentration was going to extend very far on other cases.

"Okay," she said. "Come in and we'll divide up the workload. But give me ten minutes—I want to make a call first."

She closed the door to her office and got Frank Morelli on the phone.

"How are you?" she asked him.

"I've had better weeks," he confessed. "I feel awful about this, and so does Stan. Actually helping on a murder investigation where my captain is the main suspect really stinks."

"I want you to know I'm still on the I.A. case," she said. "I'm trying to establish whether Alex really was involved in the Perrault escape."

"Good luck," he grunted. He knew she couldn't tell him anything about her investigation, and he didn't ask. "Jesus, I wish we could find that guy. It's gotta help, one way or the other."

"No trace of him yet, I guess."

"You got that right. Guy has disappeared but good."

She felt less than honest about her motives in asking, but she inquired, "Did you find anything else on the searches?"

"Edelman told me they didn't find anything at Alex's house or in her car," he said. "No trace of Simon's or Perrault's prints anywhere, not that I expected any. I don't know whether I'm relieved or frustrated. And more important, there was nothing in Simon's apartment we could trace to Alex, no prints or other evidence. There's no proof she was ever inside."

CJ exhaled in relief. "That's something. You know, Frank," she continued, lobbying gently, "Alex could be telling us the complete truth."

"I would love to believe that," he said. "I've known Alex for twelve years, and I just can't believe this. In fact, I don't believe it. The problem is that I don't think Edelman agrees with us. There was this one weird thing, though, that's really bugging him."

She found herself gripping the phone tightly. "What was that?"

"The computer keyboard didn't have any prints on it. There was a smear of blood, but no fingerprints at all. Wiped clean."

"What?" She could scarcely believe what he'd said.

"Yeah," he repeated heavily. "You think Simon typed out the name of his killer so we could see it and then wiped the keys down so it'd be all nice and neat before he died? I'm telling you, Inspector, I'm thinking this is a frame, big time. I just cannot figure out who the hell is doing it. I'm hoping to bring Edelman around to my way of thinking soon."

CJ closed her eyes, happiness surging up from her chest. If the chief investigator could believe that Alex was being framed, things were going to look better and better.

"Frank," she dared to ask, "is Edelman getting an arrest warrant for her?"

He snorted into the phone. "Hell, no, Inspector. We're a long way from that yet. There is no physical evidence we can use to tie her to the killing, just a lot of circumstantial stuff. Other than the line on the computer screen, of course. And I gotta tell you, I am very, very suspicious of that right now. Listen, you let me know whatever you can tell us that might help, will you?"

"Oh, don't worry," she promised. "I will. You, too."

CJ hung up, feeling better than she had in days. Chad knocked on the door and said, "Ready for me, Inspector?"

She grabbed the new case files and said, "Ready as I'll ever be. What have we got?"

He pointed at one of the files, chuckling. "Let's do the fun one first," he suggested. "We got a uniformed officer who practices his marksmanship by firing his service weapon into telephone books. In his apartment. At night."

CJ rolled her eyes and opened the folder.

By six o'clock, CJ's eyes were blurry with reading. She'd been over every word of every file, interrogation, and her own notes on John Simon and Robert Perrault. She'd looked at the crime scene photos of Simon's apartment and gone over the transcripts of yesterday's interviews. She was hungry, tired, and more than anything else, she wanted to see Alex. She shoveled all the materials into an untidy pile and left it in the middle of her desk.

In the car, she used her hands-free link to call Alex from her cell phone.

"How was your day?" Alex asked her.

"Long. Frustrating. Boring in spots. I would tell you the kind of idiocy some police officers can get up to, but it's all confidential, so then I'd have to kill you."

Alex laughed sadly and said, "Well, whatever it was, I'm sure it was more interesting than my day."

She sounded more than a little melancholy. CJ said lightly, "I'm guessing you didn't just lounge around on the back deck all day drinking mai tais and reading trashy novels."

"Not even close. I scrubbed, polished, washed, waxed and otherwise cleaned my house to the point that I think I could use it as an operating room."

As CJ ran a yellow light, she answered, "Is that your usual reaction to stress?"

Alex, as usual, took the question seriously and answered, "Typically. When I couldn't get a case solved, I used to take everything out of my desk and reorganize it. I still have to have everything neat and tidy before I can really think. Weird, huh?"

"Only a little bit."

"What do you do? When you're stressed out?"

CJ swerved around a slow moving truck on Broadway and said, "Depends on the reason. If it's something personal, I'll go for a drive or go home and cook, sometimes."

"And if it's work-related?"

CJ smiled and said in a sultry tone, "Ya'll really want to know?"

"I do. Are you going to talk dirty?"

"Let's just say that I prefer to be distracted as pleasantly as possible. Nothing like a good night's, um, sleep to put work problems into perspective."

There was beat of silence, then Alex said, "So...you had a tough day at work, right?"

CJ laughed. Then, a little tentatively, she said, "I wondered if you might need an evening to yourself, maybe."

Alex said firmly, "We already tried backing off and that

didn't work out so well. Instead, I think we should spend as much time as possible together and see if that works."

"Are you sure, darlin'?"

"Aren't you?"

CJ braked, forced to actually stop at a traffic light. She ran fingers through her hair and finally asked, "Am I smothering you, Alex?"

"No," Alex answered emphatically. "Now, do you want me to come over?"

CJ smiled and responded, "Let me put it this way. My maid service is coming tomorrow and they haven't been at the condo in two weeks. I'm not sure it's fit for human habitation. I'd much rather spend the evening in someone's sparkling clean operating room. Assuming I'm invited."

"Only if you bring dinner."

"Done. Do you care what I get?"

"You know me. I'll eat anything."

"Oh, are we talking dirty again?"

"I don't want to just talk about it. I want to do it, so get dinner and get over here."

"Yes, ma'am."

Alex sat back, blue eyes sparkling in satisfaction.

"That was awesome," she pronounced.

"Glad you liked it," CJ said, lightly licking her lips.

"What did you call that again?"

"Chicken tikka masala," she said. "It's chicken marinated in yogurt and spices, including curry."

Alex began to pick up their plates.

"I thought all curries were spicy hot," she said.

"Curries are like chile peppers," CJ answered. "You can go as mild or hot as you like, pretty much."

Alex handed her a plastic container for leftovers and began to rinse the plates.

"And what," she kidded, "would you know about chile peppers, you Southern belle?"

CJ jerked in surprise, spilling grains of jasmine rice over the table. Alex glared at her and grabbed a couple of paper towels.

"Hey, don't throw food on my newly sterilized kitchen floor," Alex said, wiping the tabletop carefully.

"Sorry."

"What did I say? You can't take a little teasing tonight?"

CJ took a deep breath and released it. "Sorry," she said again. "No one has called me Belle in a long time."

"I didn't...wait. Are you telling me your name is Belle?"

"All my secrets are about to be revealed." She smiled wryly.

Alex stopped cleaning the table for a moment and raised her eyebrows. "My God, you have other secrets I haven't discovered? Clearly, I haven't explored enough. Let's go to bed and I'll…"

"Stop," CJ said, frowning. "This is hard."

Alex threw the paper towel away, then came back to sit down next to CJ. "Tell me," she urged.

"I'm sorry," she said. "I told you what happened with my family and all. Belle is what everybody called me, growing up. It just takes me back there to hear it, I guess. When I moved to Colorado I decided to use my initials. I didn't like my given names anyway, so it was an easy transition."

Alex threaded her fingers through CJ's, and said, "You've got me confused. How do you get 'Belle' from CJ?"

"Belle is from…" CJ drew a breath and took the plunge, "it's from Christabelle."

Alex stared at her.

"Go ahead, say it," CJ said. "It's really old-fashioned."

Alex swallowed hard and said, "Um, it's...unusual."

"Please. It's a two-hundred-year-old family name. And it gets worse. Some great-great ancestor was a Civil War hero named 'Stovepipe' Johnson, and I'm named after him too. So that's it. Christabelle Johnson St. Clair."

All Alex could say was, "Oh. My. God."

"Exactly. I never liked Belle very much, but it beat Christabelle all to pieces. The only name I really ever liked was what my grandfather called me, my mother's father, the one who left me all the money. He called me Jo. It reminded me of Little Women, but my mother hated it, so Belle it was until I left Georgia. After that, I could do what I liked."

She eyed Alex closely. "So, what do you think?"

"Would it hurt your feelings to say I like CJ better?"

CJ laughed.

"Not a bit. I like it a lot better myself. And I hardly need to tell you, this is a deep, dark secret. I haven't even told Vivian or Rod, so no revealing it."

Alex lifted their joined hands and kissed CJ's fingers. "Okay. Can I call you Christabelle in the throes of passion?"

"Only if you'd like to sleep alone."

"I've slept alone quite a bit, and sleeping with you is a lot more fun. And just so you know, I feel privileged to be in on the secret."

CJ said playfully, "You know what this means, don't you?"

"No, what?"

"We're going steady."

Her voice was light, but Alex read the serious question behind the green eyes. Alex tightened her fingers against CJ's hand and said, "I have something to tell you too, though I don't think it's much of a secret."

"What's that?"

"I'm in love with you."

She heard CJ's breath catch. "What?"

"Were you not listening?"

"I was listening. I just wanted to hear you say it again."

"I'm in love with you, CJ. This may be the world's least romantic setting, and I know the timing is lousy, but I wanted you to know."

CJ leaned across the kitchen table and kissed Alex on the mouth. "There is never a bad time or place to say that," she whispered.

Alex said, "I'm not scaring you off, am I?"

"Oh, no, darlin'. And I'm going to tell you the same thing. In the morning."

"In the morning?" Alex asked, amused.

"Yes. If I tell ya'll now, you'll think it's just an automatic response. I'll wait for just the right moment tomorrow, and surprise you, like when you're brushing your teeth or something."

Alex laughed. "Why don't you go outside and get some air? It should be nice and cool. I'll bring the coffee out when it's brewed."

CJ kicked off her shoes in the front hallway and stepped out onto the front porch. She considered turning on the porch light against the night, but decided to enjoy the darkness. The light from the house behind her cast a dim rectangle of yellow onto the porch. The shadows were deep, with the sky just a shade lighter than black. Remnants of clouds streaked the deep navy blue with wisps of milky white. The moon had risen, almost full, bright silvery light in the night sky.

She wiggled her toes against the wooden decking and tried to remember when in her life she had felt like this. It was like floating and being fully anchored at the same time, completely unbound and completely attached. She was weightless, free of fear, free of pain and yet safe, secure.

Alex Ryan loved her, and nothing in the world could be as wonderful.

CJ tried to remind herself of all the problems they still faced, the ominous threat of a murder charge looming over them like a dark mountain on the horizon; but in this moment, she couldn't see anything but Alex's eyes, couldn't hear anything except Alex, saying 'I'm in love with you.'

Whatever happened, Alex belonged to her. And she belonged to Alex.

A cool breeze brushed against her cheek. A few houses away, a dog barked because someone was walking along the sidewalk. In the dark, she could tell only that the figure was a man. He was going slowly, not as if he were out for his post-dinner exercise, but as if he were looking for something. A moment later, she realized he was looking at addresses.

When he got in front of Alex's house, he stopped for a moment. Then he began to cross the lawn toward her.

Some instinct tightened her belly, and she put her hand on her weapon, drawing it and pointing it toward the ground. It seemed as if he hadn't seen her, standing in the dark. As he drew closer, she saw that his hands were in his jacket pockets.

Did he really need a jacket? She wondered, her protective instinct growing stronger.

CJ stepped into the patch of light that came through the screen door, putting herself between him and the house.

"Who are you looking for?" she asked.

His voice floated across to her in the night. She could see his face a little in the light from the streetlamp at the end of the street. Something about his features seemed vaguely familiar to her.

"Alex Ryan," he replied.

Her nerves were tingling. "Why?" she said.

She saw him take his hands out of his pockets, saw him lift his arm toward her.

Then she saw the gun.

CJ yelled, "Police officer!" and raised her own weapon.

She saw the muzzle flash as he fired.

Alex had just added a very generous splash of cream to CJ's mug, and picked up one mug in each hand when a gunshot boomed through the house.

She dropped both mugs and they shattered at her feet.

"CJ!" she yelled.

No answer, no other shots.

Alex raced into her bedroom, jerked open the nightstand drawer and grabbed her backup gun, a .38 revolver. She ran toward the front door, making sure the gun was loaded, yelling again, "CJ!"

Alex flattened herself against the hallway wall, crouching to be as small a target as possible. The porch light was out, and she couldn't see CJ, she couldn't see anyone.

"CJ?" she said again, more softly.

There was no noise, almost no light. Heart pounding, she

gently pushed open the screen door and eased carefully onto the front porch.

CJ was propped against the wall, long legs sprawled in front of her as if she'd suddenly gotten tired and had to sit down. Alex crept nearer, and her foot kicked against something hard and metal.

CJ's weapon.

Alex could hardly breathe. She touched CJ's arm, then her chest, felt the sticky, warm gush of fluid.

"Oh, God, no!" Alex exclaimed.

Behind her, the front step creaked. Alex pivoted, gun up. In the moment between one heartbeat and the next, she saw him, coming toward her, aiming a weapon.

She fired three times as fast as she could pull the trigger.

CHAPTER FOURTEEN

The first help to reach them was a pair of Colfax PD patrol units, one approaching from each direction, sirens screaming, lights ablaze. Alex had turned the porch light on when she called 911, and she had carefully put her gun down before the officers arrived.

One of them knew her, thank God, so when she said, "First shooter is down. I don't know if there was more than one," they immediately followed her orders to search and secure the perimeter.

She had asked for the paramedics first, but they arrived three minutes later. Waiting for them felt like torture.

There were two of them, moving as quickly as they could without running, up to the front porch. They stopped at the first victim they saw, the man Alex had shot.

She barked at them, "Leave him. He's the perp. We have a cop down."

The younger paramedic, a woman, looked up at her in surprise, but the older man nodded at once and said to her, "Cops come first. Come on."

Alex had to let go of CJ so that they could work. She had been trying to stop the blood pumping out of CJ's chest, and she was soaked with bright red blood, T-shirt, jeans, even her socks. The younger paramedic looked at her and said, "Are you hurt?"

Alex shook her head, then whispered, "No. Just her."

She desperately wanted to demand answers, insist on the reassurances that she needed, the promise that they could save CJ. She knew better. There was nothing they could tell her. Alex had never seen so much blood from a living person.

"Eighty over fifty," the older paramedic said. "Saline, now."

She watched them set up the IV, heard them calling out numbers, blood pressure, pulse.

At one point the male paramedic glanced over at her and asked, "Single GSW?"

Alex nodded. "I just heard one shot."

He jerked his head at the other man, lying still across the porch steps. "What about him?"

"I shot him," Alex said. "More than once."

He nodded again, then said to his partner, "Keep the pressure on the wound. We gotta transport as soon as we can. She's bleeding out."

His words froze Alex from the inside, even though she'd already known it was happening.

A third patrol car pulled up, then a fourth. The street was bright with red and blue flashing lights, bright white headlights. The first two officers returned, claiming that there was no one else on the property. A few neighbors had emerged from their homes into the summer evening to see what the fuss was about.

Alex wanted to tell the officers what to do, but she couldn't think anymore, she couldn't see anything but CJ bleeding to death on her front porch.

A patrol supervisor showed up, then another set of paramedics, who immediately began to work on the second victim. The first two continued to labor over CJ as Alex stood and watched and saw her life slipping away.

Finally she heard someone calling her name, and turned to see Frank Morelli standing next to her. She hadn't seen him arrive.

"Jesus, Captain," he said, looking at the blood on her clothes. "Are you hit?"

"No," she said, irritated that everyone kept asking her that. "What are you doing here?"

"What do you think, Cap? Patrol recognized the address, Sergeant called me in. Are you sure you're okay?"

The paramedics were trying to load CJ onto the gurney, but her blood pressure kept plummeting.

"Alex," Frank was saying.

"What?" She was angry at him, angry for talking to her when she wanted to be quiet and listen to CJ's breathing. She was so pale.

Still breathing.

"Captain," Frank said firmly. "For God's sake, tell me what happened."

"I don't know," she said. "I was inside, I heard just the one gunshot. He must have shot her. Her gun was out, but I don't think she had time to return fire."

"What did you do?"

She finally managed to turn away long enough to look at him. "Hell, Frank, aren't you going to give me my Miranda rights first?"

"Do I need to?" he retorted. "Christ, Alex, talk to me."

"What the hell do you think I did?" She was close to shouting at him and everyone was looking at them. "He shot her, Frank! I got my backup weapon and came out here. When he came at me with a gun I returned fire, and I fucking shot him. Okay?"

He looked at her and she could see he was a little pale.

"Okay," he said.

They finally got CJ onto the stretcher and were lifting her over the steps to get her into the ambulance. Alex started after them and Frank said, "Captain. You have to wait."

She turned on him angrily. "You have my statement,

Sergeant. The Sig on the porch belongs to Inspector St. Clair, the Smith & Wesson thirty-eight caliber there is mine, and I have no idea what he was carrying. It's on the lawn somewhere. I'm going with her."

Frank made a last attempt. "Do you know him?"

"I don't think so. I have no idea why he was here, or why he was carrying a gun, or why he was at my house, or why he shot CJ. I'm going with her."

Frank let her go, then.

Keep breathing, baby.

They had lost her heartbeat for a minute in the ambulance, and Alex had to shout at CJ, telling her that she had to breathe again. CJ was in the trauma room, a few minutes ahead of a second stretcher carrying the man from Alex's front porch. She saw both of them go into emergency, and wondered if there were some great cosmic scale she could unbalance, to sacrifice his life for CJ's.

Just don't stop breathing. I'm here.

Then automatically she began reciting the rosary, silently.

Our Father, who art in heaven, hallowed be Thy name…

What was she going to do if CJ died?

Thy kingdom come, Thy will be done…

No, please don't take her, please.

She continued with the decade, the prayers coming by rote.

Hail Mary, full of grace, the Lord is with thee…

Please…

World without end…

Breathe, sweetheart, just keep breathing.

There was a code, they were calling over the intercom for resuscitation in ER She saw two people running, she could hear distant shouting, orders barked.

After a few minutes, she could hear the silence under the activity, and she felt the tension seep out of the air: futility acknowledged, defeat accepted.

Alex knew in the moment that CJ was dead, that she must be

dead. She wondered why she couldn't feel it yet, couldn't feel CJ's absence from the world the second her soul had slipped away. She couldn't feel anything, and knew she was in shock. The pain, the crushing grief, the agony of loss was coming. Later.

Alex didn't know if she would survive it, when it finally came.

Thy will be done…

No more praying. God was continuing to play some cruel cosmic joke on her, giving her people to love so that they could be jerked away again. She was done with God.

A large person came into the small waiting room, almost filling it. Alex didn't look up. If she didn't actually hear someone saying the words, "She's dead," then she could still pretend that CJ was alive, that they were going to be together.

"Alex," a man said.

She looked up anyway. Paul Duncan was standing in front of her, wearing his usual off-duty outfit of khakis and polo shirt. He looked solid as a brick wall. He was real and he was there.

She got up and went into his arms.

"I think she's gone," she said into his shoulder, and she couldn't stop the first tremor of grief that ran through her.

Paul sat her down and sat next to her, holding onto her shoulders.

He didn't ask her any questions, and Alex was grateful. Paul wasn't being her boss, or a cop, just her friend.

At length, she managed, "Frank called you?"

"Yeah."

"Sorry to drag you away from Bible study."

"Oh, Alex," he said heavily. "Frank told me you shot the guy."

"I shot the guy. He had a gun, he had already shot CJ, and he was going to shoot me. I'd do it again. I hope he dies."

Paul remained impassive.

A woman in scrubs came into the room, a doctor, a nurse, she couldn't tell. She looked at the two of them and said, "Are you here with the man who came in, the multiple gunshot wounds?"

Paul stood up and fished the leather wallet with his badge out of his back pocket.

"Deputy Chief Duncan, Colfax PD," he identified himself. "The man is a shooting suspect."

She eyed him and said, "I'm sorry to tell you he died a few minutes ago. Do you know who he is? We didn't find any identification on the body."

The words penetrated Alex's heart.

"The woman," she said, her voice shaking. "The redhead, who came in just before he did, is she..."

"We're still treating her," the woman answered. "Do you have identification for her?"

Hope poured into her with a rush.

She's alive.

Keep breathing, love.

Paul looked down at Alex, then said to the woman, "Yes. Her name is St. Clair, CJ St. Clair. She's a police officer. If you bring us the forms, we'll start on them."

"How...how is she?" Alex asked, afraid of the answer.

The woman looked as if she were about to refuse to respond, then she looked at Alex's face and said, "We're trying to stop the bleeding. I can't tell you much more yet. You should contact the next of kin."

She left, and Paul said, "I'll call HR and find out her nearest family."

Alex said, "Not her family. They're estranged."

He stared at her in surprise and finally said, "Well, somebody's listed as her emergency contact."

He took out his phone and made a couple of calls. Alex sat, numb, trying to send her presence into the trauma room.

I'm here, CJ. Breathe, keep breathing.

Paul returned and sat next to her. "Alex," he said. "You want to tell me what's going on?"

"Jesus, Paul, what else do you need to know right now?" she asked, irritated.

"I talked to HR, and I called Rod Chavez as well. He said he'd get in touch with a couple of people, her friends. Some family lawyer back in Georgia is her emergency contact."

She remembered CJ talking about her trustee, an old friend. "Good."

Paul asked, his voice heavy, "Why was she at your house, Alex? Were you discussing your case?"

She snapped, "No, we weren't discussing my case. She's not on my case anymore, remember?"

His brows drew together heavily. "What are you talking about?"

Alex drew in a deep breath, and her courage at the same time. Even if CJ wanted to keep their relationship private, she had to tell Paul now.

"She turned the case over to her sergeant," Alex said. "She couldn't do it anymore because we're...we're dating, Paul."

She watched his expression run from shock to disbelief several times in the space of a few seconds.

Finally he said, "And when were you planning on telling me?"

"Someday. I don't know. I was afraid to tell you."

"Afraid? Alex, you're like my own daughter."

"Oh, come on, Paul. Did I have any reason to think you'd be open and accepting of me if I came out?"

"Alex, I've known you all your life and...I had no idea."

"I didn't have very much of one myself."

"I don't know what to say to you. I mean, I gave you away at your wedding."

"Paul, listen to me. I was never intentionally lying to you, or to Tony, or to anybody else. Myself, perhaps. Never to anyone else."

Paul scrubbed a hand over his gleaming bald head. "Alex. What would Charlie say?"

"Hell, Paul, do you feel as though you have to disapprove because you think my father would have? Because I'm telling you, whatever faults he may have had, he loved me. He would want me to be happy, I know that."

He looked at Alex, and finally asked, "And this makes you happy?"

"Yes. God, yes. It's who I am."

Paul sat back and the plastic chair squeaked in protest. "We've got a problem here, Alex."

She didn't want to hear it. "My personal life is my own

business, Paul. She doesn't report to me, so there's no violation of the fraternization policy."

"She was working your I.A.," Paul said heavily.

"No, she…" Alex stopped at the expression on his face. "What?"

"She was in Colorado Springs day before yesterday interviewing witnesses. She didn't mention a word of this to me."

Me, either, Alex thought, stunned. What could CJ have been thinking?

"How could she do that?" she half-whispered. "She had to know about the conflict of interest. Hell, Paul, she and I talked about it before. I just assumed…"

He was staring her down. "Are you telling me you didn't know?"

Anger flared suddenly, and she said fiercely, "Of course not, damn it! She didn't tell me. I thought she'd transferred the case." She stopped then after a moment, she continued, "Of course she didn't tell me. She was protecting me. She was trying to clear me of the corruption charge so the murder case would fall apart. Damn it to hell!"

She was angry at the disregard of procedure, she was hurt at CJ's deception, but beneath both emotions she felt a surge of tenderness. CJ was putting her own career on the line, breaking the rules to save her because she loved her. Her head felt too heavy, buffeted with a storm of so many strong emotions. She dropped her head into her hands.

Paul looked at her, then put his arm around her shoulders again and said, "St. Clair is a tough character. She'll pull through this, wait and see."

Alex knew the reassurance didn't mean a damn thing, but it still made her feel better to hear him say it.

Come on, baby. Breathe.

Rod Chavez showed up within the hour, with a lovely woman in her forties he introduced as his wife, Ana. A few minutes later, a small, beautifully dressed woman rushed in.

"Where is CJ?" she demanded. "How is she? What happened, for Christ's sake?"

She looked at Rod Chavez, who stood and said, "She's still in the emergency room, Vivian. We don't really know much."

She'd apparently met Rod and Ana before, and she shook Paul's hand perfunctorily before turning to Alex.

"Who are you?" she demanded.

"Alex Ryan."

Vivian looked at her closely. "Alex," she repeated. "You're the one."

"Yes," Alex said, knowing what she meant. "I'm the one."

"Were you with her?" she asked, eyeing Alex's bloodstained clothing.

"Yes."

"Then why the hell didn't you take care of her?" Vivian demanded. "She's crazy in love with you, didn't you know that?"

The words stung Alex. "Yes," she answered, her voice barely above a whisper. "I know that."

Vivian seemed to collapse at the admission. Rod got her into a chair and she slumped over. "What the fuck is happening in there?" she cried.

They looked at each other. There was no answer, so they sat together, waiting.

After another endless hour, another woman came into the waiting room. She was wearing scrubs, and a smear of blood that she had missed ran across the hem of her scrub shirt. She had dark hair, and dark, deep-set eyes that reflected weariness.

Alex stood when she entered, searching her face, looking for life and death.

"St. Clair?" the woman asked. "I'm Doctor Kovacs."

They all stood, Paul right behind her, Rod on one side, Vivian on the other, surrounding her, ready to catch her if she fell.

"Yes," Alex answered. "What's her condition?"

You're still breathing, right? Breathe.

"I will tell you frankly: it's very grave. We are having difficulty keeping her blood pressure up. She's lost a great deal of blood, and is still bleeding internally. We were trying to get her stable enough for surgery..."

"*Trying?*" Alex's voice was broken glass.

The woman looked warily at her and said, "The bullet damaged some major blood vessels and we're going to have to do surgery to repair the damage. The surgeons are already prepping. The scans show that the bullet apparently struck a rib and a fragment of it is lodged in or near her heart. They have to remove it."

Beside her, Alex heard Vivian gasp.

"I want to see her," Alex said. "Before she goes in."

"She's not conscious. I don't think..."

"I need to see her. Thirty seconds. I won't get in your way, or delay you. I have to see her."

The doctor finally nodded shortly and turned to lead Alex to the trauma room.

Behind her, Rod said, "Tell her we're here, will you?"

"Please," Vivian added.

"Yes," Alex said. "I will."

CJ looked impossibly young, her hair under a cap, her skin so white Alex wondered how she could still be alive. There were bloodstained drapes and clothes and instruments all around, but CJ looked like a sleeping angel, Alex thought, wrapped in white, and peaceful. This sight of her, at least, was a better memory than the bloodied form she had last seen in front of her house.

Don't let her become just a memory.

Alex leaned in close, and murmured, "I'm here, baby. We're all here, Rod and Ana and Paul. Vivian told me to tell you to get your ass out of here as soon as possible."

She leaned in closer and whispered, "Remember I love you. Come back to me, sweetheart. Just breathe. I'm waiting for you."

She didn't care who was watching or what they were doing. She kissed CJ lightly on the lips.

Then they took her away.

Frank Morelli came in just before midnight, looking exhausted, his dark eyes the color of mud. He asked Alex for her clothes, and she looked down in surprise to see that they were stiff and dark with dried blood. They found a cubicle for her to change, and one of the nurses gave her a light blue scrub suit. It was too large, but at least it was clean. Her bra and panties were also soaked and stained. She kept only her shoes, though they, too, were smeared with blood.

When she came out, she saw Paul talking to Frank in the hall. She handed him the clothes, and he put them carefully in a large evidence bag.

"What do you know?" she asked.

Frank cleared his throat uncomfortably, unsure what he could say.

Paul answered for him, "We're running the guy's prints as we stand here. You want to look at him, make sure you don't know him?"

She wasn't looking forward to it. She had been so focused on CJ that it occurred to her, for the first time, that she had killed someone tonight.

She pushed the thought away for a moment, and she said to Paul, "Yes, all right."

The three of them went downstairs and checked in with the night attendant. He rolled a gurney toward them, checking the tag, and said, "This is the John Doe."

He pulled the sheet down to the man's shoulders.

Alex leaned over and looked at him. It always amazed her how different people looked after death, when the light of life was gone from their eyes. He was young, just a kid really. Or rather, he had been young. He wouldn't be getting any older.

He was dead because she'd killed him. She let the reality of it slip into her, unwillingly.

She stared at him a long time, then turned to Frank.

"I don't believe this," she said. "This makes no sense. Look at him."

"What?" Frank sounded as confused as she felt.

"Just look at him carefully."

Frank peered down, then muttered, "Holy fuck."

"What?" Paul demanded.

Alex said grimly to Frank, "Well, at least one good thing came out of this nightmare. We can stop looking."

"This is unbelievable," Frank said, still clearly baffled.

Paul growled, "Either one of you want to let me on the joke, detectives?"

Alex answered, her voice grave, "It's no joke. This is the guy we've been looking for the last ten days."

Paul stared. "Are you sure?"

"I am," Alex said, and Frank nodded. "God knows we've been seeing his mug shot long enough. This is—or was— Robert Perrault."

CHAPTER FIFTEEN

Paul Duncan drove Alex home soon after dawn. He stopped his car behind CJ's Lexus, still parked at the curb.

"Will you be all right?" he asked as he dropped her off. Bright yellow police tape was still surrounding her yard.

She nodded wearily. "I'm going to take a shower and sleep for a couple of hours before I go back," she said. "The doctors said they won't let me see her before noon at the earliest."

"Alex," he said. "She made it through the surgery. You have to be hopeful."

She looked back at him. She ached all over, her head, her back, her heart. She felt drained, and she never wanted a shower more in her life.

"I'm trying to be," she answered him. "She means everything to me, Paul."

He was silent a moment, and she wondered what he was thinking. After a moment, he said, "I'm glad you told me, Alex, about you and St. Clair. We'll figure out the policy violation problems later. We want you to be happy, you know that, don't you?"

She smiled wanly. "I know," she responded. "I just hope I get the chance to be."

There was dried blood, dark and rusty, on her front sidewalk. She stepped around the stains and the wobbly board on the second step creaked under her foot. She stopped a moment and looked down at it in wonder.

A loose board she hadn't fixed. It had probably saved her life.

CJ's blood covered her front porch. Someone had taken away the towels Alex had used to try to stop her bleeding. The guns were gone too.

Nothing left but the bloody decking.

Alex went wearily inside the house. CJ's shoes were lying in the front hall. She picked them up, and then stood in the kitchen door and looked down at the floor. The shattered remnants of coffee mugs and the dark brown puddles of cold coffee awaited her.

She knew she should clean it up right away, but it didn't really seem to matter enough. She left the mess and put her own stained shoes on the back porch. Then she dragged herself to her bedroom to strip off the borrowed scrubs.

Adjusting the temperature in the shower, she turned on the water as hot as she could bear, and she stayed in until the hot water tank was empty. She scrubbed every inch of herself to take the blood away. She washed her hair twice, letting the water run down her face like a thousand tears.

In her robe, she sat on the edge of her bed and checked the clock. Nicole should be on her way to work by now, so Alex called her cell phone.

"Alex, what's wrong?" Nicole demanded when she heard her voice.

Alex told her as calmly as she could manage.

"For God's sake, why didn't you call last night?" Nicole exploded.

"I wasn't going to wake all of you up. What was the point? There was nothing you could have done."

"Jesus, Alex, I could have been with you!"

"Paul was there. So were CJ's friends. I wasn't alone."

There was a pause, then Nicole said, more calmly, "Alex, when this is all over, we're going to have a conversation about your insistence on doing everything without help. I'm not a kid anymore. You don't need to take care of me, or protect me, all right?"

"I know that," Alex answered tiredly.

"Do you? Because you don't act that way. Tell me how she is."

"They took the bullet fragments out and stopped the bleeding, finally. The surgeon told me she'd lost about a third of her blood. They're still saying she's in critical condition. She could start bleeding again, or have heart failure, or get an infection."

"Don't do this to yourself. Think positively."

"That's what Paul said."

She paused again and asked, "Did you tell him? About you and CJ, I mean?"

"Yes."

"How did he...I mean, was he..."

"Nic," Alex said, suddenly unable to keep her eyes open one more minute, "why don't you call him yourself and ask? He was completely kind and supportive last night. If he's got some religious problem with me being in a lesbian relationship, he didn't tell me about it. Now, I've got to sleep a little. I've just got nothing left, and I have to see her as soon as they'll let me."

"Yes, of course," Nicole said. "What do you need?"

She hadn't cried yet and she wasn't going to start now. "I just need for her to be all right again. Nothing else really matters."

She took off the robe and crawled naked between the clean sheets.

Clean sheets. She was sorry she'd washed them yesterday. If she hadn't, they would still smell like CJ, still smell like their lovemaking.

She got up again and went back into the kitchen. CJ's jacket was hanging on the back of one of the kitchen chairs. She picked it up and took it back to bed, falling asleep with it wrapped in her arms.

The phone jolted her out of dreamless sleep.

Hospital, she thought, fumbling frantically for the cordless receiver.

"Is this Alex Ryan?" a man's deep voice asked her.

"Yes." *She's all right, she has to be.*

"The hospital gave me your number," he explained. "My name is Roger Edgarton."

Her brain clumsy from slumber, it took her a few seconds to place the name. "CJ's trustee," she finally placed it.

"CJ?" He sounded baffled.

"Belle," she amended. "She uses her initials in Colorado."

"I see," and she heard a brief rumble that she decided was a sound of faint amusement. "I shouldn't be surprised. She always did dislike her name. Miss Ryan, I spoke to a Mr. Chavez late last evening, and he informed me my client was in the hospital, but he didn't supply many details. The hospital, and rightly so, refused to give me any information on the telephone. What can you tell me?"

She sat up, trying to gather her thoughts. She'd been asleep just about the two hours she'd allowed herself, she figured, and she still felt exhausted.

"She was shot last evening," Alex explained. It still felt unreal, as though it happened to someone else. "She was in surgery most of last night to remove the bullet and stop the bleeding. Her condition is still critical. I'm going to see her in Intensive Care later, and I hope I'll have more information soon. Are you going to call her family?"

He hesitated, then said, "I will contact them, but I don't expect a response."

"She was shot?" he sounded shocked. "Was it a robbery?"

"No," Alex answered, wondering why he was so surprised that a police officer had been shot. "She wasn't on duty, she was at my home. We're still trying to figure out why the assailant shot her. He may have been looking for me."

As she said it, she realized it was true. It was her house he'd come to, with a gun. Why in God's name had Robert Perrault been looking for her?

"I don't understand," Edgarton said. "On duty?"

Alex frowned. "I meant she wasn't at work. She's a police detective with the Colfax Police Department. Didn't you know that?"

"Police? My word, I had no idea."

"When did you last speak with her?" Alex asked suspiciously. Perhaps this man wasn't who he said he was.

"We had an extensive telephone conversation last month," he answered dryly. "We spoke at some length about her portfolio and some private matters, but she never mentioned a job to me."

Of course not, Alex thought. She didn't have to work, after all.

"She was at your home, you said?" he continued. "Are you a co-worker, or a friend or..."

He let it dangle and Alex wondered a moment exactly what to say. She finally settled for, "We're dating."

There was a beat of silence, then he said, "Have you known Belle a long time?"

She thought this was an odd time for him to do a background check, but she answered, "A few months. We met at work. I'm a captain in the same department. Not her superior officer, a colleague."

Another silence, longer this time. She didn't want to be rude, but she wanted to be done with this, get to the hospital, see for herself that CJ was still breathing.

"You're probably curious about my questions," he said heavily. "I'm on the horns of a dilemma here. You, or someone, will need a durable power of attorney to consent to any future treatment Belle may need. I have her medical POA, but I am, obviously, not there, and my own health will not permit me to travel at this time. I can delegate the power of attorney to someone, but it's difficult to determine who would be the most appropriate person."

Alex closed her eyes. My God, she thought, she'd never heard anyone sound more like a lawyer. Aloud she said, "She has a couple of close friends here, Mr. Edgarton, and if you want to give one of them the authority, I understand. But I will tell you this: I love her, and I will do anything I can to make sure she's all right."

A third pause. Alex could almost hear him thinking. Finally he said, "I will have my assistant fax you the documents you need right away. Do you have the number?"

She almost gave him the number at the office before she remembered that she was on suspension. On an impulse, she said, "My sister is an attorney. Why don't you send them to her at the office? She'll be in a better position than I am to check them over and see if there's anything else we need."

"That would be most satisfactory." She heard relief in his voice. He obviously preferred to deal with another lawyer.

Alex told him the name of Nicole's firm, and he assured her that he would be able to locate their number and send the documents. She, in turn, promised to call him with any news about CJ. She could tell that CJ was more than a client to him, and that he was genuinely worried about her.

She called Nicole, who was in a conference, and left her a message. Then she found some clean Levi's and got ready to go back to the hospital.

Five minutes, that was the rule in ICU, and then she had to go away again for an hour to wait for her next five minutes.

When they finally let her into the cubicle, Alex carefully stepped around all the tubes and monitors so she could hold CJ's hand.

CJ had awakened briefly in recovery, responded to spoken commands, they told her. She was still unconscious. Alex didn't care, she just wanted to be in the room with her.

When they sent her out, Alex found a cup of coffee, then called Rod and Vivian. Nicole phoned, and said the forms from Roger Edgarton looked all right, and that she was coming to the hospital to make sure everything was properly recorded on the chart and with the hospital administration.

"You don't have to do that, Nic," Alex told her. "I know you're busy."

Nicole said, exasperated, "Do you ever listen to me? This is me helping you. Let me. You paid for most of my law school education, you may as well take advantage of it."

Alex said humbly, "Thank you."

Then she sat in the waiting room until they let her in to see CJ again.

CJ wasn't awake, but it didn't matter in this moment. Alex took her hand, and told her she was strong and beautiful and wonderful and brave. And every other minute, she reminded CJ that she loved her, that she was right there with her. CJ seemed peaceful, at least for a while.

But just after dinnertime, Alex noticed that CJ was restless. When Alex touched her face, she thought CJ seemed warm.

A nurse came to take her vital signs, frowning. Within minutes, they had paged the on-call resident and Alex had to wait in the hall, impatiently, for someone to come and tell her what was happening.

Finally, the resident appeared and explained. He needed her consent to start CJ on antibiotics immediately.

"She appears to have an infection, not unexpected given the nature of the injury. The problem is that an infection of the lining of the heart is very grave, and she's already very weak." He looked grimly at Alex.

"I don't mean to frighten you, but you should call her family. She may not survive the infection in her condition."

Alex went icy cold. "I'm her family."

He said, "I'm sorry," and went away.

Alex sat down, her body numb from anxiety, her mind racing.

No, not now. Please, no.

She fumbled for her cell phone and began making the calls.

"When did you last eat?" Nicole asked her around ten that evening.

When? Alex couldn't remember eating anything today. When had she last eaten?

Chicken tikka masala.

"I'm not hungry," she answered.

"That wasn't what I asked. I'm going to go get us something. I assume you don't want to leave."

How had her world gotten so small? Alex asked herself. Just this waiting room, and the tiny cubicle where CJ lay fighting.

Alex didn't leave the hospital for three days. For a few hours, they let her sleep in an on-call room, a concession, she thought, they probably made because she was a cop. CJ's fever spiked and they pumped antibiotics and fluid into her, desperately trying to reduce her temperature. Paul sent his pastor to see her, and Alex sat with him, reciting the Twenty-Third Psalm. She couldn't quite get through the part about walking through the valley of death.

Memories had become dreams, dreams were memories.

Her brother Clay sitting on top of her. Six, seven years old? He was pressing into her chest, heavier, taller. She beat against him with her fists, scratching and clawing.

"Get off of me!"

Laurel, getting out of their bed with another woman in it, laughing in her face. "I never loved you." Pushing her in the chest.

"Get out!"

Stephanie, cool and detached, calling her a fool.

"Get away from me."

She was so hot. There was hot pain, pain crushing her chest.

She ran away from the pain, her feet never touching the ground. *The ocean rose on the horizon before her, blue and welcoming.*

She plunged into the water. It was cool, a cocoon of relief from the heat surrounding her, the tide drawing her away from pain, deeper, deeper.

Blue water. Blue eyes. The salty taste of ocean became the sea salt taste of a woman in her mouth, on her tongue.

Cool and safe. Salty. Blue, so blue.

And from somewhere, she could smell the faintest hint of sandalwood.

Her.

Alex.

"CJ, I'm here."

The only response was the steady beeping of the monitors. The sound didn't bother Alex. It was the sound of CJ's heart still beating, so Alex wanted to hear it as she had never wanted to hear anything else in her life.

How long had she been here? A month, a year, a lifetime? The universe had narrowed to this room, tile and metal and beeping machines. The only vivid color in the room was the flame-colored hair fanned across the pillow, and the spray of flowers on the bedside table. A bouquet had arrived from Roger Edgarton, but there had been nothing from CJ's family.

Just above the pale blue hospital gown, Alex could see the top of her bulky bandages, the ones covering the incision over her heart. They made Alex leave when they changed the dressings, or when they washed her, but Alex spent every other moment she could in the chair, watching, waiting, talking to her. Even Nicole had given up trying to get her to leave, settling for making sure that Alex ate something every few hours and calling five or six times a day. Alex answered her calls between the daily phone calls from Vivian, Rod and Paul.

A miracle that CJ had survived that first night, made it through the surgery. Another miracle that the infection had been overcome, finally. Alex was waiting on the third miracle, that CJ would wake up, be all right again.

She said again, "I'm here, CJ."

This time, for the first time, she heard a quiet, rusty voice.

"Alex?"

Alex was at her bedside in a moment, gripping the hand that wasn't pincushioned with IV lines and monitor leads.

"CJ, it's okay. I'm right here."

And best of all, her eyes opened, those amazing emerald eyes Alex had feared she would never see again. CJ tried to focus and Alex reached over to dim the lights.

"You're all right now, CJ."

"Alex," CJ said again, the name less of a question this time.

Alex brushed back a copper-colored strand from her face. "Yes, it's me. Welcome back."

CJ tried to swallow, and Alex got her some ice chips, held her head. Just that seemed to exhaust her, and Alex helped ease her head back on the pillow.

"Alex," she said a third time. "Dying?"

Alex's heart broke like a wave against the rocks. She leaned down and put her lips near CJ's ear. Even with the odors of antiseptics, Alex could still smell her scent.

"No. No. You've been really sick, but you're all right now. You're all right, I promise. Trust me."

"I do," CJ whispered, and drifted off again.

"Alex." Hours later.

"I'm here."

"Hospital?"

"Hospital," Alex confirmed. "Doctors, surgery, tubes."

"Surgery?" CJ seemed limited to one word questions.

"The perp shot you. They had to take the bullet out." Alex was trying to keep things simple.

"Out?"

"Yeah, it's out, sweetheart. You're fine."

"'kay."

"Alex, where…?" Bright green eyes fastened onto her.

"University Trauma Center. The hospital."

"No." CJ struggled a moment, then managed, "Where was I shot?"

Alex touched the bandages lightly over CJ's chest. "He aimed at the biggest target. He shot you in the heart."

CJ closed her eyes, and Alex thought she'd gone away again, but after a moment Alex saw just the ghost of a smile.

"No," CJ said. "Biggest target…would'a been…mouth."

Alex laughed out loud for the first time in what seemed like a very long time.

CHAPTER SIXTEEN

Alex's cell phone rang, and she stepped out into the hall to answer it. She recognized the number.

Paul said, "How are you holding up? How's St. Clair?"

"We're okay," Alex answered. "She ate most of her lunch, and complained about it the whole time, which I think is progress. On this afternoon's exciting docket is a very slow walk up and down the hall. Thrilling stuff."

"Do you think somebody else could cover that?" Paul asked, and her pulse quickened.

"Yes, if need be. The physical therapist will be here. What's up?"

"I made an appointment for you with Doctor Amaya. It's at two, so you'll need to leave pretty soon."

"The department shrink? Why am I going to see him right

away?" Alex asked. "They're talking about releasing CJ home in a day or two, and then I can…"

"I need you here as soon as possible," Paul interrupted her. "And I can't take you off the administrative suspension until you've had a fitness for duty examination, because of the shooting. You know the regulations. So if Amaya clears you this afternoon, you can report back first thing in the morning."

Alex thought she would crush the cell phone in her hand. "The chief is taking me off suspension?" she demanded.

"He is as soon as you get the go-ahead from Amaya."

She sank into a waiting room chair, unable to believe it. "What happened?"

"Well, this morning the DA's office officially cleared you of any criminal wrongdoing in the death of Robert Perrault, and in record time, I might add. The fact that you shot a suspect who was a suspected murderer, a fugitive from justice, and who had just shot a police officer, weighed heavily in that decision."

She still could not believe it. "But what about Simon's murder?"

"We have a lot of work to do, Captain," he said crisply. "So get yourself back in here in the morning, ready to concentrate on the job. Sergeant Morelli will fill you in with what Denver's been doing on the case. But I can also tell you that you are officially off the suspect list in the Simon homicide. Be on time to see Amaya. I don't want you missing the appointment."

"No, sir. I wouldn't want to do that."

Frank Morelli sat with his partner, Stan Rosenthal, in Alex's office, drinking coffee and trying not to grin at her. She sat back in her chair and said, "Well, that was embarrassing."

"What?" Stan said. "You don't like parties?"

"I'm not sure being cleared of suspicion in two homicides is a classic reason for a party," Alex said dryly.

"Nah, it wasn't because of that," Stan said. "It was just a little welcome back party. Like you had been on vacation or something."

She had stood in the meeting room, eating cake, watching her detectives, wondering what they might be thinking about her. She'd assumed, department gossip being what it was, that it was generally known that she was in a relationship with CJ. Did they feel differently about her? Was she about to encounter prejudice, subtle or blatant, because of her sexual orientation?

Everyone had seemed the same to her. Whatever everyone might be thinking, she couldn't see a difference. Not yet, anyway.

Alex shook her head ruefully. "I'm going to need a vacation to recover from my vacation, then," she said. "It feels like I've been gone forever." She looked at Frank. "And would either of you fine detectives want to tell me who murdered John Simon?"

Stan and Frank exchanged a look, then Frank said, "Let me take it from the top, Cap. After we confirmed the ID on Perrault from his prints, we did a search of your neighborhood. Eventually the Denver guys found a stolen car parked a couple blocks away. When they searched it, they found some interesting stuff. Like a city map, a note with your name and address on it and few hundred bucks in cash."

"There was a motel key on the body," Stan interjected. "Edelman finally tracked down the place he'd been hiding out in, one of the cheaper establishments on Colorado Boulevard, right near the light rail line. And guess what they found when we executed the search warrant on his room?"

Alex looked from one man to the other and answered, "Some evidence that he killed Simon."

Frank smiled at Stan and said, "I told you she'd get it. We got him cold, Cap. We found a bloody T-shirt stuffed in a drawer at the motel. He must have pulled it off when he got back from Simon's place. Results came in yesterday morning. It was covered in Simon's blood. Perrault killed him. We think Perrault got Simon to call you that night so you'd be on the scene. Then Perrault stabbed Simon to death and typed the words on the computer to set you up. A nice little frame with you right in the picture."

"Does Edelman agree with this theory?"

"Absolutely," Frank reassured her.

Alex tipped her head up for a moment and looked at he ceiling. "Okay," she said. "So what have we got? Perrault kills Simon, tries to set me up for the murder, then suddenly shows up at my house to, presumably, kill me. Why would he bother to try and frame me, and then kill me?"

Stan answered, "Maybe he wasn't there to kill you."

Frank frowned. "Well, Jesus, what else would he be there for?"

Alex shook her head. "No. She…Inspector St. Clair said the only thing he did was say my name. When she answered, he shot her. He probably thought she was me. When I showed up a few seconds later, he was going to shoot me too, no conversation. He definitely came over to kill me. The question remains: why? What changed between Sunday night, when he killed Simon and set me up, and Wednesday night, when he's trying to kill me?"

The trio sat in silence for a moment, then Stan said, "Did you do anything while you were out on leave, Captain? On the case, I mean?"

"Absolutely not," Alex said firmly. "Let's go at this another way. How did Perrault escape custody in the first place?"

Frank answered, "It was Simon, had to be. If he wasn't involved, why would Perrault even bother to kill him? Perrault must have talked to John, promised him something, money, I bet. John had a worse divorce than I did, believe it or not. He was really strapped."

"I agree that makes the most sense," Alex said. "Do we have any actual evidence that Simon was involved in the escape?"

"Yep," Stan said. "When Edelman did a more complete search of Simon's apartment, he found eight thousand dollars wrapped in plastic food bags and stuffed into a couple of empty frozen pizza boxes. And the gun Perrault was carrying the night he shot the Inspector was Simon's backup weapon. He musta been carrying it when he was doing the transport and gave it to Perrault when he let him go."

"Fucking moron," Frank said forcefully. "A cop who sells his soul for a few thousand bucks, and gives a murderer his gun. Guy almost deserved to get whacked."

She didn't disagree. "But we've still got a lot of unanswered questions," Alex pointed out. "Where did Perrault get the money to pay for his motel room, eat, live? Why did he kill Simon? Why did he frame me? And why did he try to kill me?"

Frank said, "No idea. To all that."

Alex said thoughtfully, "A couple of days before the shooting, Inspector St. Clair told me she'd talked to the Springs detective on the case. They thought that the murder that Perrault had been arrested for was, perhaps, not really a random mugging."

"What else could it be?" Stan asked.

"Murder for hire," Alex answered succinctly. "And if somebody hired Perrault to kill...what was his name?"

"Ward," Frank supplied.

"Then whoever wanted Ward dead probably paid off Perrault, and also paid off Simon after he let Perrault go."

"I still can't figure why Perrault tried to frame you," Stan complained.

Alex smiled a little and said, "Actually, I think that was John's idea."

"Simon planned for Perrault to murder him?"

Frank, excited, said, "Don't be an idiot, Stan." Then to Alex he said, "It was Simon who was trying to frame you! He tried to implicate you to the inspector."

Alex said, the smile grim, "And he did a hell of a good job of it."

"I get it," Stan said. "To divert attention from himself?"

"Exactly," Alex agreed. "And it worked. Perrault just took advantage of the setup Simon had already constructed to have someone else blamed for Simon's murder. I wonder, though, why he didn't take the eight thousand dollars after he killed Simon."

Stan explained, "You'd have had to be pretty smart to find that money, or have hours to search. Edelman said it was buried under a pile of other stuff in the freezer. There were signs that Simon's place had been searched, the guy just did a lousy job of it."

Frank tossed his empty coffee cup into Alex's wastebasket. "So somebody else was pulling Perrault's strings?" he asked.

Alex felt energized, the way she always felt when a case began to make sense to her.

"Yes. He—or she—paid off Simon, got Perrault enough money to hole up, and probably told Perrault to kill Simon. Maybe John wanted more money, maybe our killer just wanted to tie off that loose end. Either way, I don't think a twenty-two year old who did day labor hauling landscaping materials planned how to frame me. Somebody a lot smarter was in charge."

"This all makes sense, and fits with what we've got," Frank mused. "But it still doesn't explain why Perrault showed up and tried to kill you."

"I'm not sure we'll find out until we figure out who's behind this. But at least now we know what we're looking for. Frank, talk to Edelman and suggest that he should go talk to the CSPD detective again. If we can figure out who wanted Mr. Ward dead, maybe we can unravel this whole mess."

The two men got up to leave, but Frank turned in the doorway and said, "How's the inspector, by the way? Have you heard?"

Something emerged in Alex's memory at the same moment. Absently, she said to Frank, "She's great. They're sending her home this afternoon if her blood work is clear."

Frank looked at her curiously, but just closed the door behind him as he left.

She made a brief phone call downstairs, and then checked the clock. She was picking up CJ from the hospital, and she wanted to make very sure she was on time.

Several hours to go. She sighed and began to attack the giant pile of papers waiting on her desk.

CJ eased herself onto the leather couch in her living room.

"I'm fine," she said to Alex. "Quit acting like you're assigned to the Patient Protection Program."

"You're a riot," Alex said dryly. "I'm so sorry that bullet couldn't have ricocheted and taken a chip out of your funny bone."

CJ began to laugh and then grasped her sides.

"Ow!" she exclaimed. "I told you not to make me laugh!"

Alex was kneeling on the floor beside her in a moment. "I'm sorry. Relax, baby, just breathe."

CJ caught her breath, and said, "You keep saying that to me. Breathe."

Alex said, "That first night, when it happened…I figured if you just kept breathing, everything would be okay."

CJ pulled Alex to her and kissed her. "Everything is okay," she answered. "I'm sorry I scared you so much. If our positions had been reversed, I would have been completely insane. I'm sure you handled it better than I would have."

Alex stood up and looked down at her, shaking her head. "I bet you wouldn't have been reduced to saying the rosary in the emergency waiting room."

CJ, more than a little surprised, managed, "No, you're right. I hadn't realized it was quite that serious."

"Didn't you?" Alex said gravely. "They told me twice they didn't think you were going to make it. Your heart stopped in the ambulance. I thought you were leaving me, sweetheart."

CJ tried not to cry. "Never," she whispered. "I promise."

Alex ran her fingers down CJ's cheek, and CJ shuddered at the touch.

"Ya'll behave, all right?" CJ said softly. "I have about as much energy as an old dishrag. I have to go back to the doctor before I can get my final okay for…physical activity."

Alex dropped her hand and smiled. "Occupational therapy, that sort of thing?"

"Well, yes. Sort of that sort of thing."

"Okay," Alex said. "I'll make you some soup."

"Can't I have a steak?" CJ asked.

"Nope. Not yet. Couple of days yet."

"I can't have anything I want," CJ pouted.

After dinner, CJ turned on a jazz station and let the music wander around the corners of the room. Alex made coffee and sat with her, listening, needing no conversation, needing nothing but to be in the room together.

About ten, Alex said, "Do you want to talk about it?"

CJ answered, "No." She sighed, and then said, "I guess I don't really have a choice."

"You have a choice. Now, or tomorrow. But it's not going to go away."

"Yes, all right."

Alex said, reluctantly, "I think I understand why you continued to work on the case, and it's not that I'm ungrateful. But you lied to me."

CJ shifted in discomfort. "Not exactly. But I didn't tell you the truth, I admit."

"Should I ask you why not?"

"It was bad enough that I was playing fast and loose with the rules, Alex. How could I involve you in that? If I told you what I was doing, that made you as guilty as I was."

"So you're telling me you lied to me to protect me, is that it?"

In a small voice, CJ replied, "It's not much of an excuse, but it's the only one I can give ya'll."

Alex reached across the sofa cushion and took her hand.

"Here's the deal," she said quietly. "I'm not going to have a relationship with you if we can't tell each other the truth, good or bad. You have to promise me that you won't ever do something like that again."

"What was I supposed to do?" CJ asked sadly, her eyes searching Alex's face.

"You should have told me," Alex said simply.

"And what would you have done?"

"Talked you out of it," Alex said firmly. "We would have found another way. You're in a lot of trouble now, you know. Once you're off medical leave, the chief is going to be asking you some very hard questions. You could get transferred out of I.A. You could lose your job."

"I know," CJ said softly. "But don't you see? It was worth it. You're cleared of all the charges, and you're safe."

Alex shook her head. "You can't break the rules whenever you think your cause is worth it."

"Apparently, you don't believe the ends justify the means," CJ said, trying to keep her tone light.

"Sweetheart, for a cop, the means and the ends are the same thing. How we do things is as important as what we do. If we don't follow the rules, who will?"

Was it possible to love Alex any more? she wondered. Her fingers tightened on Alex's hand and she whispered, "Will you stay with me tonight?"

"If you want me to," Alex said, leaning in to nuzzle her hair. "Guest room?"

CJ snorted gently. "Don't be silly."

"I don't know," Alex sighed, "if I can be in the bed with you and remain chaste."

"I didn't know ya'll were chaste to begin with."

"You know what I mean."

They listened to the music another minute, then CJ said, "You can go, if you need to."

"No, I want to stay," Alex said. "But there are rules."

"Rules?"

"Rule one: everybody wears sufficient clothing to bed."

"Spoilsport."

"Rule two: no excessive touching."

"Excessive? And who will be the judge of that?"

"I will," Alex said sternly. "You're still on disability leave. Third rule: beds are for sleeping. You're still healing, sweetheart. Okay?"

"Yes, ma'am," CJ agreed meekly.

Sometime deep in the night Alex felt CJ stir against her back. She rolled over and said groggily, "You all right?"

CJ said quietly, "I think I need some pain medication."

Alex was awake instantly, sitting up and snapping on the bedside lamp.

Blinking in the sudden flood of light, CJ said, "It's no big deal, darlin'. They said it would take a while for everything to feel normal again."

Alex carefully ran her hands over CJ's T-shirt, checking her still-bandaged chest and ribcage. "Any sharp pains?"

"No. It's okay. And, by the way, that was very close to excessive touching."

Alex got up and padded into the bathroom for water and a single white pill. She waited until CJ took the drug, then returned to bed, turning out the light.

"Let me hold you a minute," Alex murmured, and she got CJ settled against her shoulder. CJ nestled in and wrapped her arm around Alex's waist.

"I feel better already," she whispered.

"Me, too," Alex said.

"Alex?"

"Hmm?"

"Is it morning yet?"

Alex glanced over her shoulder at the bright red numbers on the clock. "Well, technically it's morning, I guess. Why?"

"I told you," CJ muttered, her voice already thickening with sleep. "I said I would."

"Baby, what are you talking about?"

"In the morning. I told you I would tell you in the morning that I loved you. It was supposed to be a surprise, remember?"

Alex laughed softly into the darkness. "Yes. You overshot it by a few weeks, though."

"I know. Sorry. I wanted to say it."

"It's okay, sweetheart. Go to sleep."

"No. Want to say it out loud."

"I already know."

"Don't be stubborn. I'm in love with you, too Alex."

"I'm really glad."

CHAPTER SEVENTEEN

Sergeant McCarthy appeared in Alex's office at eight o'clock the next morning.

"Captain," he greeted her. "I brought the stuff you wanted."

"Thanks, Chad. Just put them there."

He dumped the files on the clean corner of her desk, then lingered, shifting from foot to foot, until Alex looked up from her computer screen again.

"I appreciate you bringing those up," Alex said again. "Is there something else you need?"

"Well, um, technically those are I.A. files, Captain, and, um, confidential."

"Yes," Alex said patiently. "I did ask the chief for permission to access them because they appeared to be related to the ongoing investigation on the attempted murder of Inspector St. Clair. You did talk to him?"

"Yeah, I did. I just wanted to make sure you knew that. It's… they're my responsibility, and I don't want the lieutenant to take my head off."

Alex smiled. "I promise you, Sergeant. I will protect you from the Inspector. You have my word."

"Yeah," he said again, rubbing his bald spot. "Okay, Captain. Thanks."

Alex smiled at him again, reassuringly, as he left. She looked at the pile of folders he had just delivered and sighed. She had no idea when she'd be able to go through them; after work was looking more and more likely. She stretched her arms, then picked up the phone to call CJ.

"How are you feeling?"

"Better," CJ answered. "Those pills really knock me out, though. I hardly heard you leave this morning."

"I tried to be quiet. It was hard." She dropped her voice and added, "I really wanted to kiss you awake. Several times."

"That is an impulse I will always approve of," CJ said happily. "How's the work day?"

"It's a mess," Alex answered, but didn't go into detail, since she didn't want CJ to feel guilty about the workload that had piled up while Alex was gone. "I have no idea what time I'll be done this evening, and I'm looking at a bunch of stuff I'm probably going to take home. Are Rod and Ana still scheduled to come over tonight?"

"Yes. Ana promised to bring me chicken molé, whatever that is."

Alex laughed. "How long have you been in Colorado again? We have got to get you up to speed on Mexican food. And Vivian is taking you to your doctor's appointment, right?"

"Yes, Mother. Stop worrying."

"Okay, all right." Alex sat back and said, more quietly, "I'm going to miss you tonight. Are you sure you don't want me to come over?"

"I do, but I don't. I'll take another pill tonight, earlier this time so I don't wake up, and I know you have a lot of work to catch up on. I'm planning on a nice quiet time this weekend. With you."

Alex smiled and said, "Define 'quiet.'"

"In bed."

"I'll clear my calendar. Call me if you need anything."

"I'm fine. I feel a nap coming on."

"Sweet dreams."

"Oh, they will be."

Alex worked, and went home, ate dinner, and then pulled out the files Chad McCarthy had given her. There was the I.A. file on John Simon, everything they'd gotten from CSPD on Robert Perrault, CJ's notes, and the transcripts of her interviews with Arthur Gammon and Elaine Ward. Alex read everything thoroughly, then went over everything again, making notes. By midnight, she had two new questions, a small one and a big one, that had no answers. She'd have to call Edelman in the morning.

It was too late to call CJ. Alex hoped fervently that she was sleeping soundly. She carefully put the files back together, put her notes on top, and went to bed.

"Well?" Vivian asked impatiently. "What did the doc say?"

"Let me get my seat belt buckled, for heaven's sake. He said I was fine. Heartbeat was fine, no signs of bleeding, blood work looked good. Apparently, the fact that I'm exhausted every ten minutes is normal at this point."

Vivian pulled out of the parking garage and accelerated onto Hampden Avenue on her way to the interstate. "Are you going to be back to normal, then?"

CJ laughed. "Well, eventually, anyway. He wants me to start walking, then build up my stamina."

Vivian shot her a sideways look with a smirk. "Bet you have a plan for that," she said.

CJ smiled and said, "I do, actually. She told me she loves me, Viv."

"Wow, the 'L' word," Vivian murmured. "It's the real deal, then?"

CJ answered slowly, "You know what the best thing is about a bad relationship? It teaches you what a good relationship is. Before, somewhere in the back of my mind, I always knew that something was wrong. This time, the back of my mind is telling me that everything is right."

"She's the one?"

"She's strong and honest, but she can be so gentle sometimes. She is the most intense person I have ever met, but she's tender, too."

Vivian drove in silence a moment, and then said, "I have to tell you, CJ, when I first met her, outside the emergency room, I thought she looked kind of, you know, average. But I must say... well, intense is the right word. She's unbelievably sexy, not her looks so much, just...herself."

CJ said, very lightly, "You're right, she is very sexy. And Viv, you may sleep with any woman on the planet who will have you. Except for Alex. Hands off, darlin'."

To her shock, Vivian suddenly seemed choked up.

"Oh, Viv," CJ began. "I was just kidding."

Vivian viciously wiped away a tear that threatened to escape. "Christ on a skateboard, I hate crying," she sniffed. "CJ, I thought you were gonna die. Alex was a complete basket case, and I wasn't much better. You are my very best friend in the whole world, so for the love of God, do me a favor. Next time, duck."

Alex got to the condo just before seven that evening, carrying the briefcase full of file folders. When she saw CJ in the doorway, she dropped the briefcase and circled her with both arms.

"Jesus, I missed you," she murmured, burying her face in CJ's neck.

CJ smiled into Alex's dark hair. "Me too, times three."

Alex kissed her firmly, and CJ broke away before she was pushed up against the wall.

"Darlin'," she gasped. "You did miss me."

Alex said, "You're really doing all right?"

"Clean bill of health. All I need is time to get my strength back. And ya'll will be pleased to know I specifically asked my physician about resumption of sexual activity."

"Did you? And how did that go?"

"He looked at me, cleared his throat, and said, 'As soon as you feel up to it. But don't overdo it.'"

Alex was nuzzling her. "What exactly does that mean?"

"I think it means no trapezes or dangling off the balcony."

Alex stopped for a moment and said, "How about bed? I mean, do you feel up for that?"

CJ made a low noise in her throat and said, "Yes, please. Would now be a good time?"

Alex put both hands on her face firmly and said, "Only if you're very sure you're okay."

"How about we go nice and slowly and see how it goes?"

Alex took her hand and led her down the hall.

Alex undressed for her, and CJ lay on the bed, watching happily.

"You're so lovely," she said.

Alex smiled and said, "Well, I'm glad you think so."

She lay down with CJ, caressing her, and said, "If anything doesn't feel right, tell me, promise?"

"I promise," CJ answered, pulling Alex on top of her. She felt feverish from wanting Alex, and arched against her joyfully.

"I want to feel your skin," Alex murmured in her ear, and began pulling at CJ's T-shirt.

A rush of cold came over her, and CJ said, "No. Alex, wait."

Alex froze. "What, sweetheart?"

CJ heard fear in her voice. "Alex," she began. "I…I'm still bandaged up."

Alex looked at her. "I know that." She slipped off, lying next to CJ. "You don't want me to see you," Alex said softly.

"I just…didn't want ya'll to be surprised. The surgeon said I could have some plastic surgery later. For the scar."

Alex looked full into her eyes. "CJ," she whispered, and CJ felt herself melting into her voice. "You are beautiful. Do you really think I'll care about a scar?"

CJ couldn't answer, love, desire, gratitude choking her throat.

Alex helped her slip the T-shirt off, and looked down at the bandage, carefully tracing it down with her fingertips between CJ's breasts.

Alex leaned down to kiss the very top of CJ's chest, and said, "If I see a scar, I'm going to remember how strong you were. And I'm going to remember just how much you love me."

She lay back and stroked CJ's skin. CJ lost herself, and found herself, in Alex's touch.

"Are you going to be all right at work today?" CJ asked the next morning, as she handed Alex a travel mug full of coffee.

Alex smiled, putting on the jacket from the suit she'd brought over the evening before, and said, "I've worked on less sleep before, don't worry. Besides," she leaned in for a final goodbye kiss, "it was so worth it."

CJ smiled back, then said, "Don't forget your briefcase. I don't even know why ya'll bothered to bring it over. Did you really think you were going to get any work done last night?"

"Nope. But I brought it over for you."

"For me? How thoughtful. Alex, what are you talking about?"

"I want you to read everything one more time, then look at my notes. I have a couple of ideas, but I want to see how they strike you. Do you feel up to that?"

"Of course, if you think it will help."

"It just might. Call me later?"

"All right. Would hourly be too often?"

Alex laughed and said, "Not for me, sweetheart."

Just before noon, CJ called Alex and said, "Do you have one minute?"

"For you, always. How are you? No ill effects from last night?"

"Ill effects?"

"You know, irregular heartbeat, pain, that sort of thing."

"Nothing like that. My chest is fine. My muscles are a bit stiff elsewhere. Would you like details?"

"Jesus, no," Alex answered emphatically. "Not at work. Did you read the files?"

"Yes. And I agree with your first point, although I'm not sure that it means much. Will you do two things?"

"Sure." Alex pulled a pen from the holder and grabbed a piece of paper.

"First, find out exactly where Robert Perrault worked. You're right, Alex. CSPD dropped the ball there."

"Glad you think so too. Want to let me in on your thinking?"

"Look at it this way. How do you find a hired killer, if that's what he was? You can't take out a newspaper classified or go on Craigslist, can you? It has to be someone you know, or someone that someone you know, knows."

"I agree. What's the second thing?"

"Forgive me."

"What?"

"I'm the reason, inadvertently, that Perrault showed up at your house and tried to kill you."

"I…what?"

"I know who the mastermind is."

CJ explained. Alex said, "Oh, my God. I think you're right."

"I think I'm right too. All you have to do is go get the evidence."

"Are you sure you're feeling up to this?" Police Chief Nathan Wylie asked.

CJ said, "I'm fine, Chief. The pain is mostly gone. I just tire easily. I'm still taking lots of naps."

When he'd called, asking to come to see her, she'd made fresh coffee. He set his cup down now and looked at her sharply. Everything about him was sharp: nose, chin, small, intense brown eyes.

"Are you on medication now?" he asked.

Uh-oh, CJ thought. This sounds like an official conversation.

"No," she answered. "Well, I took a couple of Tylenol this morning. I only take the prescription stuff at night."

He sat back in his chair, and CJ resisted the temptation to curl up on her end of the couch. She kept her feet on the floor and tried not to let her apprehension show. She'd known this was coming, she just hadn't expected it quite so soon.

"When I hired you," Wylie began without preamble, "it was because I thought your experience, both on patrol and as an investigator, would make you a good Internal Affairs head. You're making me seriously doubt my judgment."

CJ cleared her throat. She'd promised herself that, whatever happened, she wouldn't get defensive. You got what you wanted, she told herself. Alex is free and clear, now it's time to pay for that.

"I understand," she said.

That got her another sharp look. "Do you, Inspector? The last person in the department who gets to lie and cheat is the person in charge of investigating liars and cheaters."

The words stung, and she guessed he was using them deliberately, to provoke her reaction. She took a calming breath and replied, "Yes, sir. I would like to say at this point that neither Captain Ryan nor Deputy Chief Duncan had any idea that I wasn't telling them the whole truth."

"Lies of omission, was that it?" Wylie snapped.

What could she say? "Yes, sir, something like that."

He tapped his fingers against his knee. He must have had an

official meeting this morning, she thought, because he'd shown up at her door in his full dress blue uniform. "What the hell am I going to do with you, St. Clair?" he finally said. "First you sleep with my Investigations Captain, then you blatantly ignore the conflict of interest to continue working on an I.A. involving her. Really, what the hell were you thinking?"

Gently, she told herself. "If ya'll truly want to know, sir, I'll be happy to share my thought process with you."

"Did you actually have a thought process," he said, frowning, "or were you thinking with your hormones?"

CJ tried not to wince. "You may believe that I made the wrong decision, sir, and I'm prepared to accept any sanction you impose, but I did have a reason."

"What was it?" he snapped.

She made an effort to speak slowly. "I honestly believed Captain Ryan was being set up, framed for both the Perrault escape and Simon's murder. I thought that if I could establish her innocence on the I.A. corruption charge, the murder case against her would also be resolved, and we could concentrate on finding Simon's actual killer." She couldn't resist adding, "Which is, by the way, actually what happened."

"Don't be a results merchant with me, St. Clair," he said quickly. "That doesn't excuse your violation of the conflict of interest policy."

"It's not an excuse, sir," she responded quietly, "but it is a reason."

His finger tapping resumed.

"Hmph. Duncan speaks very highly of you, despite the fact that he's still pissed off about what you didn't tell him. And I am taking into consideration both the fact that your efforts did help resolve both cases, and that you paid a very high price for your involvement. Paul told me you almost died."

She sat still, waiting for whatever he was going to say next.

Wylie sighed and said, "I could have waited until you get back to work, but I didn't want this hanging over us. How long will it be before you're fit for duty, anyway?"

I still have a job, I guess, she thought happily. "Couple of months, my doctor tells me."

"Well, I'm putting an official reprimand in your file," he said briskly. "You're on probation for one year, Inspector. You screw up again, in any way, and you're gone, no further discussion. Clear?"

It was better than she could have hoped for. "I'm clear, sir."

"Good. Now get better," he ordered her. "We're going to need you back at work."

Two days later, Alex took Frank and Edelman with her to Colorado Springs. They met the Colorado Springs officers and went together out to the location.

Paul had worked out the details of the inter-jurisdictional cooperation. Alex's arrest warrant was for murder, conspiracy and attempted murder, and the Springs PD agreed to let Colfax be the arresting agency. Alex didn't know how many favors Paul or the chief had pulled in to work that out, but she did know just how much she ached to put handcuffs on the person who had almost gotten CJ killed.

They'd timed it to catch their suspect on the way into the office, and, for once, the planning paid off perfectly. They walked into the office sixty seconds behind him, and Alex asked one of the CSPD officers to wait outside.

The four of them went in together. As agreed, Alex did the talking.

"Arthur Gammon?" she asked.

He was seated behind his desk and he looked up at her. She could almost see him beginning to sweat.

"Yes? What? I'm very busy."

Alex said, "I have a warrant for your arrest, Mr. Gammon. Please stand and put your hands on the wall behind you."

She could feel Frank, Edelman and the CSPD detective behind her, all of them tense, watching him.

"Arrest?" He was really sweating. "For what?"

She didn't have to tell him, but she wanted to, very much. And she did.

"The murder of John Simon," she answered. "And the attempted murder of CJ St. Clair."

"I…what? I don't even know—"

"Stand up and put your hands on the wall behind you."

He pushed back from the desk and reached for his top desk drawer, jerking it open.

Alex had her Glock in her hand in a moment, and she saw Frank, Edelman and the CSPD detective draw down on him too.

"Don't move!" they shouted, almost together.

A terrible part of Alex actually wanted him to pull a gun from the drawer.

Go ahead and do it, you son of a bitch. I will fucking blow you away.

But he froze, and Alex thought she could catch the acrid smell of urine. Four cops pointing guns at you would do that, she supposed.

"I was just going to get my lawyer's number…" he babbled.

"Handcuff him," she ordered Frank. "And be sure to stay clear of my line of fire."

If possible, Arthur Gammon looked even more terrified.

When they got back to the police station, Alex left Frank to book Gammon, and went upstairs to brief Duncan. To her joyful astonishment, CJ was sitting in his office.

"Captain," CJ greeted her, eyes sparkling.

"Inspector," Alex returned the greeting. "I'm surprised to see you here."

"Just thought I'd drop by and make sure Deputy Chief Duncan hadn't given my office away in my absence."

Duncan grunted a laugh. "Yeah," he said. "Like I.A. inspectors are easy to find."

CJ laughed gingerly. "Ya'll are just saying nice things like that because I'm still on disability."

"It will be good to have you back," he said, tipping his big, square body back in his chair. "You agree, Captain?"

"Oh, I agree." Alex could scarcely keep her eyes off CJ.

"How did the arrest go?" CJ asked.

Alex described it, omitting her desire to fire on Gammon. She'd admit that to CJ, later, in private.

Duncan rubbed his head and said, "I understand this is the evidence you gathered: that Gammon's son worked for the same developers that employed Perrault, the phone records showing the phone calls between Perrault and Gammon, and the withdrawals from Gammon's account to pay off Simon and fund Perrault. What I don't know is how you finally figured out it was him."

"It was Inspector St. Clair who really broke it," Alex said.

"No, you're the one who asked the important question," CJ retorted.

"Oh, knock if off, you two," Duncan said irritably. "You sound like a mutual admiration society. Just tell me."

Alex sat back in her chair. "This whole damn thing was about Gammon's contract murder of his partner, Carl Ward," she began. "Gammon met Perrault because Perrault was doing day labor, landscaping, with Gammon's son. The land use consulting business Ward and Gammon owned was in trouble, but it wasn't a problem for Ward, who had plenty of money of his own. Gammon was going under, though, and the only way he could see out of his troubles was to kill Ward and collect the key man insurance they each had on each other."

"What put you on to him?" Duncan asked.

"The first thing that bothered me was a remark in the transcript of CJ's interview with Gammon," Alex explained. "CJ made a reference to 'Captain Alex Ryan,' and Gammon knew I was a woman—he referred to me as 'she.'"

"That's pretty thin," Duncan grumbled, rapping a thick finger on his desk.

"I agree, it was minor. But the better question was: how did Perrault get the job of killing Ward? He had to have some connection with one of the suspects. As CJ pointed out, you can hardly go around asking casual acquaintances for a referral for a good hit man."

"I actually thought it would be through Mitch Ward, the victim's son," CJ admitted. "But it turned out that Gammon's son was the connection. That's where he met Perrault, and that's how Gammon knew him."

"I see," Paul said. "So he gets his son's friend to kill Ward, and, when Perrault is arrested, Gammon tells Perrault to bribe Simon to let him go."

"Simon played along, but we think Simon tried to get more money out of Gammon," CJ said. "Of course, John didn't know Gammon, just Perrault, so when Perrault showed up to supposedly pay him off, Perrault killed Simon and tried, on Gammon's orders, to frame Alex. Simon had already laid the groundwork by telling Gammon he'd tried to divert suspicion from himself by implicating Alex in the escape."

"I get all of that," Duncan repeated, "but I still don't understand why Gammon ordered Perrault to kill Alex. They'd already framed her."

CJ cleared her throat and said, "That would be my fault."

"Excuse me?" Duncan demanded, his protective streak emerging on Alex's behalf. "Perhaps you'd like to explain that."

"During my interview with Gammon, I mentioned that the death of a police officer closes a pending internal affairs case," CJ continued. "I believe that Gammon thought that Alex's death would end any search for Simon's killer, and he could then get Perrault to vanish and get himself off the hook."

Duncan shook his head in amazement. "He sent Perrault over to shoot Alex just to cover his tracks?"

Alex nodded. "He gave Perrault the address, and he shot the woman he saw on the porch."

Alex was remembering, again, how close she'd come to losing CJ. CJ must have read her face because she reached over and took Alex's hand. Alex felt herself stiffen involuntarily and look at Duncan.

Duncan sighed. "Alex, you still haven't been over for dinner yet. How about you come over on Saturday? Perhaps Inspector St. Clair would like to come too."

Alex met his gaze and saw, if not acceptance, then perhaps a willingness to try. Beside her, CJ asked brightly, "Are we having tuna noodle casserole? I understand that's the house specialty, and I hear it's particularly good for recovering invalids."

Duncan snorted. "Get out of here, you two. I'll put in the request for casserole."

EPILOGUE

"My goodness," CJ exclaimed, looking out the passenger window. "How high are we, exactly?"

Alex glanced at the highway sign that said Telluride—2 miles and answered, "Around ten thousand feet or so. I realize you may not have been up at this altitude before, so be sure to wear sunscreen and drink lots of water."

"Have you seen my skin? I always wear sunscreen. And I'll have you know that we have mountains in Georgia. The Blue Ridge Mountains, thank you very much. I have, in fact, been to Brasstown Bald, the highest point in Georgia."

"Really?" Alex asked in amusement. "And how high would that be?"

"Almost five thousand feet above sea level."

"Wow. The highest point in Georgia, and it's not even as high as Denver, never mind Telluride."

"You're...you're a height snob."

"That's me. Undoubtedly why I picked you as a girlfriend."

"Ya'll are so funny. Are we staying in town, or do we have a remote cabin in the piney woods somewhere?"

"Neither," Alex answered, turning off the highway to follow a sign pointing to Mountain Village.

She followed the winding road up the mountain, passing the terminus of the ski lift, the gondolas swaying high above the grass. The road was lined with high-end hotels, beautiful mountain lodges and condos overlooking the town of Telluride below.

Alex pulled into the parking lot of Mountain Creek Lodge and said, "We're here."

CJ got out of the car, and Alex watched her carefully. CJ seemed fine most of the time, but Alex could still see her moving a little more slowly than she had before the shooting. CJ walked to edge of the lot and looked down the mountain.

"Alex, it's beautiful!" she exclaimed.

Alex opened the trunk and got out their suitcases. "You should see the view from the top of the gondola," she said. "It goes up over that mountain, and you can see the town of Telluride below you. It's really beautiful at night, with the white lights against the forest and the moon glowing."

CJ turned and grinned at her. "I had no idea you were such a romantic," she teased.

"You're a bad influence. Come on, let's check in."

Their unit had a view of the evergreen forest, a balcony that overlooked the ski slopes and a full kitchen. CJ exclaimed over it, and began unpacking the box of groceries they'd brought with them from Denver.

"We could have gone to the store when we got here, you know," CJ complained mildly.

"Food costs a fortune up here," Alex said. "You can see why—they have to haul it in by truck."

CJ dug the perishables out of the portable cooler and opened the refrigerator. "You know," she said, her voice still mild, "money is not really an issue."

Alex came over and leaned against the granite countertop next to her.

"I don't see any point in being a spendthrift just because you're rich," she complained.

"I don't see any point in not spending money for us to be more comfortable just because you don't want to take advantage of me," CJ retorted.

"Oh, I do want to take advantage of you," Alex responded softly, and CJ felt the now familiar pleasant tightening in her belly.

"In that case," CJ said brightly, "I should cook the steaks so we can eat first. I think I was promised a romantic moonlight ride on the gondola, and I have to keep my strength up."

"Wait a minute," Alex said, her face serious. "There's something I want to talk about first."

CJ turned to her and said, "You're not going to ruin our romantic getaway with something serious, are you?"

Alex said, "I actually do have something serious to say, CJ."

CJ felt flutters of both anticipation and anxiety. "All right, darlin'."

"CJ," Alex said gravely, "I don't want us to date anymore."

CJ felt her stomach drop. "You don't?" she said, trying to keep her voice light. "You brought me all the way up here to this beautiful place to break up with me?"

"For God's sake," Alex said in disgust. "I don't want to date you. I want to live with you."

CJ looked at her in happy surprise. "What is it with you and kitchens?" she asked. "You couldn't wait for the proper romantic moonlit night for this?"

Alex said gravely, "The last moonlit night I waited for ended with you in the hospital."

"Good point," CJ said.

Alex took CJ into her arms. "I can't wait," she said. "I almost lost you, we almost lost each other. It's too easy to let life slip away from us, and it's too easy to lose people you love. It took me half a lifetime to find you, CJ. I don't want to waste one more moonlit night."

CJ linked her hands behind Alex's back, fitting against her.

"Are you sure about this?" she asked. "I'm kind of a slob."

"I'm a little compulsive. It'll work perfectly."

CJ leaned down for the kiss.

"Yes," she whispered.

"Yes?"

"Yes."

"That," Alex murmured, "was the right answer."

Publications from
Bella Books, Inc.
Women. Books. Even Better Together.
P.O. Box 10543
Tallahassee, FL 32302
Phone: 800-729-4992
www.bellabooks.com

CALM BEFORE THE STORM by Peggy J. Herring. Colonel Marcel Robicheaux doesn't tell and so far no one official has asked, but the amorous pursuit by Jordan McGowen has her worried for both her career and her honor.
978-0-9677753-1-9

THE WILD ONE by Lyn Denison. Rachel Weston is busy keeping home and head together after the death of her husband. Her kids need her and what she doesn't need is the confusion that Quinn Farrelly creates in her body and heart.
978-0-9677753-4-0

LESSONS IN MURDER by Claire McNab. There's a corpse in the school with a neat hole in the head and a Black & Decker drill alongside. Which teacher should Inspector Carol Ashton suspect? Unfortunately, the alluring Sybil Quade is at the top of the list. First in this highly lauded series.
978-1-931513-65-4

WHEN AN ECHO RETURNS by Linda Kay Silva. The bayou where Echo Branson found her sanity has been swept clean by a hurricane—or at least they thought. Then an evil washed up by the storm comes looking for them all, one-by-one. Second in series.
978-1-59493-225-0

DEADLY INTERSECTIONS by Ann Roberts. Everyone is lying, including her own father and her girlfriend. Leaving matters to the professionals is supposed to be easier! Third in series with *PAID IN FULL* and *WHITE OFFERINGS*.
978-1-59493-224-3

SUBSTITUTE FOR LOVE by Karin Kallmaker. No substitutes, ever again! But then Holly's heart, body and soul are captured by Reyna... Reyna with no last name and a secret life that hides a terrible bargain, one written in family blood.
978-1-931513-62-3

MAKING UP FOR LOST TIME by Karin Kallmaker. Take one Next Home Network Star and add one Little White Lie to equal mayhem in little Mendocino and a recipe for sizzling romance. This lighthearted, steamy story is a feast for the senses in a kitchen that is way too hot.
978-1-931513-61-6

2ND FIDDLE by Kate Calloway. Cassidy James's first case left her with a broken heart. At least this new case is fighting the good fight, and she can throw all her passion and energy into it.
978-1-59493-200-7

HUNTING THE WITCH by Ellen Hart. The woman she loves — used to love — offers her help, and Jane Lawless finds it hard to say no. She needs TLC for recent injuries and who better than a doctor? But Julia's jittery demeanor awakens Jane's curiosity. And Jane has never been able to resist a mystery. #9 in series and Lammy-winner.
978-1-59493-206-9

FAÇADES by Alex Marcoux. Everything Anastasia ever wanted — she has it. Sidney is the woman who helped her get it. But keeping it will require a price — the unnamed passion that simmers between them.
978-1-59493-239-7